Speakeasy, Speak Love

Sharon G. Clark

Yellow Rose Books
by Regal Crest

Tennessee

ISBN 978-1-61929-334-2

First Printing 2017

9 8 7 6 5 4 3 2 1

Original cover design by AcornGraphics

Published by:

Regal Crest Enterprises
1042 Mount Lebanon Road
Maryville, TN 37804

Find us on the World Wide Web at
http://www.regalcrest.biz

Published in the United States of America

Acknowledgments

Thank you, Patty Schramm and Brenda Adcock, my fabulous editors; and, a special thank you to Cathy Bryerose for allowing the opportunities you provide me and my imagination.

Dedication

To my incredible son, Jeremy, for making me a grandma; and for always being there for your crazy mother.

In loving memory of John Minor Purcell, my TigerBro.

Chapter One

1921

FIONA CAVANAUGH SLOWED the Chevrolet truck, pulling close to the curb, shut the engine down and silencing the newest hit, "Second-Hand Rose", on the radio, and then watched the kids playing stickball in the street. Spring had officially started with a comfortable, warm day. This neighborhood was hers, and it didn't look too much different from her childhood though much had changed within her. She used to know most the boys and girls by name, which child belonged to whom, or at least recognized family connections by their facial features. It wasn't all that long ago she too participated in the same street games with her older brother Fionn. She didn't want to be a kid again, didn't miss the disadvantages that came with a childhood out on streets like these. Of course, returning to her childhood would have the advantage of still including her mother and brother, if she could go back in time. Maybe then, her dad would—

Fiona didn't finish the thought. Her father's abuse of them and his love of liquor wouldn't improve even had her mother and brother lived. The abuse spread out amongst them. She'd seen her Da getting worse, even back then. That's simply how Quinn Cavanaugh was, and would always be forever. No one could change the past. She had to move on to the present, think about her future. One thing was certain, though, and that being she couldn't pass herself off as a boy for much longer. Currently, it worked like a charm, as long as she kept a smudge of dirt here and there, bound her chest, wore baggy clothes, kept her hair short and mussed up; but she was smart enough to know time always caught up with lies, no matter how well intentioned the original untruth.

These gloomy thoughts weren't getting her anywhere, and Fiona needed to get back to work. Just as she shifted in her seat to start the truck, Fiona caught movement from the corner of her eye. Rushing toward the open driver's window was a disheveled Willie, a boy of fourteen. Willie lived in her old tenement building but didn't know her true gender, believing her to be her dead brother. As she turned, Willie pleaded breathlessly, "Finn, you gotta come. Junior's roughing up a young gal."

"Willie, I can't get between a—"

"No, Finn, you got it wrong. She's a stranger here."

Despite the urgency and genuine concern in his voice, Fiona hesitated long enough to smile down at him and wonder at his assessment. He was a kid, so how young was this "young" girl? She got out of the truck knowing she'd find out soon enough. Matching Willie's pace, she followed for half a block and into a littered alley.

True enough, Junior and two of his bullies were harassing a girl, and though young to be sure, she wasn't a kid. Lying on its side amidst the refuse, what appeared to be lunch and medical supplies spilled from a wicker basket. Picking up a two-foot piece of broken board from the ground, Fiona closed the distance. "Buzz off, boys," she said. One of the boys, Augustus Detweiler, Junior to most, was the middle child of eleven kids. She knew he'd recently turned eighteen because he never shut up about it. The only way he got his folks to remember him from the others was continually having cops knocking at their door for his current criminal activity. "Junior, don't give me a reason to wail on you."

All three turned in her direction. "This don't concern you, Finn," Junior said. "Just 'cause you got growed up, and working don't give you no rights more than me. I'm older, too. Remember? You got no claims on this one. I keep peace in the neighborhood, now."

Fiona rolled her eyes. "If you don't scram, you'll be pieces strewn all over the neighborhood." She took a step and slapped the board against her palm. "As Good Will Ambassadors, you fellas stink."

"Good what?" Junior asked.

"Exactly." Fiona shook her head. "Look at the stuff you're tossing around. You can see she's here to help someone who's sick. What if it's Wallace's kin kept from her nursing? You think he's gonna care you were keeping the peace?" Junior paled when hearing anyone from the Gustin Gang mentioned. She doubted this woman was in the same social circle—not that Fiona knew for certain—as Frank Wallace, but Junior and pals wouldn't know either. Fiona noticed one of the boys looked almost ready to lose his lunch. "Better hurry off before Sammy there pulls a Daniel Boone." Fiona snickered. "What kind of tough guy gets sick in front of a lady?" She recognized from the sour expression on Junior's face; he had realized he'd lost the intimidating edge.

"This ain't over between us, Finn," Junior snarled.

When the three rushed away, Willie immediately ran toward the woman, bending to return the dropped objects to the basket, mumbling when he had to leave the broken items. Fiona also moved closer, happy to note a more natural color than red returning to the woman's face, and grinned at her. "How much longer were you gonna keep a hold on your temper?"

Surprised green eyes met Fiona's. "Not much longer. Wish I had thought to bandy about a name or two." Giving Willie a brilliant smile, the woman took the basket he held out to her, his gaze set in an expression of puppy love. Then, she extended a hand toward Fiona. "Margaret. Margaret Graham. And you're Finn, right?"

"Finn Cavanaugh." Shaking the hand offered, Fiona nodded. "This here's Willie."

"I appreciate you, uh," Margaret frowned slightly, but her hesitation passed almost seamlessly, "gentlemen coming to my rescue. Guess that's what I get for releasing the cab so soon. I wanted to enjoy a bit of a walk. I worried losing my temper would only antagonize those hooligans further, and then I'd never get to my destination."

Fiona put her hands in her trouser pockets, surprised their quick physical contact had sent such heat coursing through her. She wondered if Margaret experienced the same reaction. "And where would that place need to be?"

Margaret glanced down the alley. "Just up the way, I think. Do you know Mrs. Donnelly?"

Breaking into a wide grin, Fiona playfully lapsed into an imitation of her mothers' brogue. "Quite a few of us Irish this part of town, Miss Graham, lots of clans. Can you be more specific?" She suspected whom Margaret referred to, but found pleasure from drawing out their encounter. No, this wasn't good, not good at all. This young woman was wreaking havoc on Fiona's pulse and her heartbeat—and they'd just met.

Blushing, Margaret tucked stray strands of dark brown hair behind her ear and stated, "Surname is all I know. We always referred to her as Nana. She tended my mother during her illness. I want to return the favor now I hear she's sick herself."

Willie perked up at this. "Mick's mom."

Punching him gently in the shoulder, Fiona said, "Officer Donnelly to you, runt. Be respectful." She gave her attention and a formal bow to Margaret. "If we may, Willie and I will escort you. You're right. She's just on the next street. When you've finished your visit, I'd be pleased if you allowed me to drive you home. I wouldn't want anything else to happen with Junior. Or having you think poorly of us down this way."

"That's appreciated, but not necessary," Margaret said. "I don't want to take you from anything important." Was Margaret seriously being polite, or did she doubt Fiona's claim to a vehicle?

"It would be my honor, Miss Graham. If you'd allow me," Fiona said, indicating the basket. Margaret handed it to Fiona, and they walked to the end of the alley and turned right. They went up two blocks and crossed the street.

Chapter Two

THE TENEMENT BUILDING housing Nana Donnelly was on the corner. Willie ran up the stairs ahead of them to make sure the way was cleared of more riffraff; and, to give warning to any of Nana's relatives who might not be expecting visitors, especially from strangers. People in this part of town treasured their privacy as the singular control most had in their possession.

As Fiona and Margaret started up the stairs, a voice called down. "Finn, are you down there?"

Fiona recognized the voice of Claire Donnelly, a childhood friend and the youngest daughter of the sick Mrs. Enid Donnelly. "Nana has a visitor, Claire."

"Yes, Willie told me," Claire said. "Please bring Miss Graham up."

Claire stood at the top of the stairs. When she and Margaret reached the top, Fiona leaned in and placed a quick kiss on Claire's forehead. "I'm sorry, Claire. I'd have come sooner if I had known Nana was ill."

She shook her head. "Like Ma would admit it, or let you find out. She even tells us she's just under the weather a'might." Claire turned to Margaret and extended a hand. "I'm Claire. Ma has told us of your mother. I'm sorry for your loss."

"Thank you." She pointed toward the basket. "It's not much, but I brought a few things for your mother, to assist with her convalescence," Margaret said. "I'll replace the lost stuff."

"Miss Graham had more to her offering, but Junior's up to his usual shenanigans," Finn said.

"Don't you be worrying yourself. She'll be pleased to have company other than family. Come in," Claire said, pointing to an open door at the end of the long hall where Willie leaned against the doorframe. As they went into the small apartment, Margaret flashed a smile at Willie. Claire pointed to the door at the back and the left. "Just go in. Ma's expecting you. Willie, wait in the hall, please. I need to speak with Finn."

Fiona handed the basket to Margaret. "I'll wait here to take you home." When Margaret entered the room and closed the door behind her, Fiona said, "You should have sent word."

With a shrug, Claire said, "I know things have been bad with your Da. It hasn't passed notice you don't come home when he's around. I didn't want to add to your burden, especially if I sent word by way of Mick."

"Yeah, would have been hard to explain that away. It's only — I thought maybe you were punishing me," Fiona said. She bowed her head, not daring to look into Claire's eyes. "I never intended to harm our friendship, Claire. I...I just—" Fiona knew the repercussions of her actions toward Claire could harm them in many ways, from incarceration in jail or commitment in a sanatorium.

With a sigh, Claire said in a whisper, "Please, Fiona, I don't want what happened to be an issue with us. I'm sorry if I'm still hurting you with it. It's all been such a shock, yes. First learning you're passing yourself off as a boy and not knowing where you are when you aren't at home, and then knowing our relationship changed in your heart and I can't fix it. I do love you, just not the way you want me to feel."

Fiona nodded. "Yeah, I get it." She did understand. Most would believe her a deviant and react violently. She may not have Claire's whole heart, but having her love was as important. "I desperately needed work, too, and by any means. What else was I supposed to do? Leave the responsibility to dear ole Da?"

"Well, no, definitely not, not him." Claire gave another strained shrug. "I worry about this charade you've set yourself. Where are you sleeping at night? Is it a safe place?"

"In the backroom of Old Man Chambers warehouse, or sometimes in the truck; both are safe enough, safer than Da's place, anyway."

Claire frowned. "You're gonna get hurt, honey, possibly killed if the wrong person finds out about you."

"I can take care of myself."

"Not everything can be controlled, particularly not men. Just don't cross the wrong one. And cross one you surely will if you run around playing Sir Galahad to every lost woman," Claire said, pointing to the door Margaret was behind.

"I have to —"

A loud bang from the front of the tenement and raised male voices had Willie running into the apartment. "Three of them and one's steaming mad."

Willie had just finished the announcement when a well-dressed man burst across the entrance; he had the build of one of Wallace's henchmen, his face flushed a bright red. "Where is she?" he asked, as two men followed him into the apartment. Obviously, this man believed an open front door invited bad manners.

Fiona moved protectively in front of Claire while tugging Willie's arm, so he stood behind her. "Keep your voice down. The woman of the house is ill. If you state your business, sir, we can help you."

The man darted forward, grabbed Fiona by the jacket's lapels, and jerked her closer. "I won't play games, boy. I want to see—"

"Eldon," Margaret said harshly from the bedroom entryway, softly closing the door behind her to shelter Nana from the heated conversation. "Put Finn down this instant." Fiona hadn't noticed any wedding ring. Mentally kicking herself for getting into the type of situation Claire had just warned her about was fully possible, evidently. Eldon complied and Fiona straightened her jacket. Margaret moved closer and put her hands on her hips in the same posture Fiona's Ma would use when prepared to chastise her. "What are you doing here?"

He looked Margaret over from head to foot, as if to assure her unharmed, before he answered. "Terry heard some boys were roughing you up, Babs. I came to take care of the matter personally."

"And Terry ran to you instead of dealing with the boys himself?" Margaret shook her head in disgust. "Where are your manners?" she asked him and turned toward the two men beside Eldon. "Wait outside. He'll be down in a moment. And close the door behind you." She gave Eldon a gentle push in the chest. Margaret nodded in Fiona's direction. "Finn took care of the bullies." She must have caught the crestfallen expression on Willie's face, because she added, "Willie helped run them off, too. Both deserve your thanks, not your harassment." Margaret turned toward Fiona and the others. "Finn Cavanaugh, Claire Donnelly, and Willie, this is my brother Eldon Graham, who still thinks I'm four years old. I apologize if Eldon frightened any of you."

Fiona held out her hand, instantly glad he wasn't a husband. Not that the distinction should matter, knothead, her inner voice said. This woman is out of your league. Not to mention the obvious issue: she's a woman and what her heart wanted just wasn't done if you were normal. "Pleased to meet you, Mr. Graham, Sir," Fiona said. Grudgingly, Eldon shook the hand offered. "I'd intended to escort your sister home after her visit. I would'na let her be in danger."

Eldon stared hard at Fiona. "I appreciate the consideration, kid, but I can take it from here." He turned to Margaret. "You shouldn't have come, at least not without telling me. You sure no one hurt you?"

"No, Eldon. As I said, Finn and Willie shooed them off before things got out of hand. They both escorted me to see Nana. She's been sick. I had to come and do something. She was so good to Mother, before—"

He grimaced. "Yeah, yeah. Don't go getting yourself worked up, Babs." Eldon reached into his inner suit jacket pocket and pulled out his wallet. "Your mom did well by us." He held out a few large denomination bills toward Claire. "Tell her thanks."

Claire's face flushed in embarrassment. She said, "That's not necessary, Mr. Graham. Ma received an adequate pension when released from her duties."

A loud *thwap* sounded in the room, and Eldon let out a low growl. "Stop it, Babs. Don't push me too far."

"How do you manage to run a business with your foot constantly occupying space in your mouth?" Margaret asked. Fiona recognized the fury in Eldon and wondered how much longer he'd let his sister get away with reprimanding him in front of strangers. "These are respectable people who deserve to be treated as such."

This action must be the breaking point, because Eldon shoved the money into his pants pocket, grabbed Margaret by the arm, and tugged her to the door. He yanked it open, and his men pivoted toward him. "We're leaving, take her to the car." Over his shoulder, he said, "Cavanaugh, follow me." He didn't wait to see if she complied.

Fiona squared her shoulders, gave Claire a reassuring smile, she hoped, told Willie to stay put and followed Eldon out of the tenement building. He remained silent until Margaret and his men sat in the car. "Going to school?"

"No."

"You willing to work?" he asked.

Fiona snorted and then nodded. "Already work for Mr. Chambers, delivering packages."

With a sigh, Eldon said, "Didn't mean to upset your girlfriend." He pulled the money he had offered Claire a moment ago. "Don't care how you do it, but see Nana gets this. She truly was good with my mother all the way up to the end. Margaret thinks the world of Nana."

"I'll see Nana gets it, sir." Fiona took the money.

"You didn't have to help my sister, but I'm grateful you did. I owe you."

Fiona gave a sniff. "We're jake."

Eldon shook his head and pulled out his wallet again. This time, he removed a business card, pulled a pen from a pocket, and jotted something on the blank side. "Come see me tomorrow, at the house, one o'clock. We have things to talk about. I want you to work for me if you're willing." He must have noted her hesitation to trust him. "Think of your future, kid. I can pay well for hard work."

Taking the card, Fiona stared at the address. She shook her head and squinted up at him. "What kinda work?"

"Lots of work, kid. I owe you. Plus, I could use a delivery boy," he glanced toward Margaret, presently watching them with curiosity, and a bit of worry in her expression. "Also, occasionally someone to look after her and drive her around, safely, so fools like Junior don't bother her. The pay would be better than Chambers can scrape together. Not that I doubt he's tried to do right by you. If you agree, I'll even compensate him for losing you without notice."

Fiona glanced in the window at Margaret's beautiful face. She impulsively winked, not thinking better of the action or curbing the impulse. Eldon didn't seem to notice, and Margaret blushed. Fiona would like to get to know her better, try to understand the strange emotions Margaret evoked all the way to Fiona's core with just a look. However, part of her heard Claire's warning, too. More money meant saving faster and getting out of this city sooner, uppermost in her reasons for agreeing. "I'll be there," she said.

With her agreement, Eldon smiled vaguely and got in the car. As the car drove down the street, Fiona wondered the extent of the trouble she just agreed to. She sighed loudly.

Chapter Three

"IF YOU THINK you just made a deal with the devil, you may have." Fiona heard the voice from directly behind her. She spun around to face Ian Donnelly looking down at her in grim seriousness. He must have been hiding in the shadows, but she didn't know for how long or what he'd overheard from her exchange with Eldon Graham.

"I'll be just fine, Ian." She gave him a sly smile, hoping to change the topic. "You're in uniform. Should I call you Mick?"

Ian shook his head and smirked, bending close to her ear. "Sure, if you want me calling you Fiona." He straightened, grinning at her gasp. "What gives, Finn? Why are you speaking to Graham?"

Fiona stuffed her hands in her pockets. "'Cause I need lots of work to get out of here, Ian. Besides, I didn't invite him here."

"I understand that," Ian said. He reached up and placed a hand on her shoulder. "We Donnellys are worried about you, honey. Graham is involved in a lot of nasty business. I don't want to see you hurt, and neither do Ma and Claire." She winced at the mention of Claire, and he seemed to notice. He slid his arm around her shoulders in a brotherly motion and pulled her close, dropping his voice. "The hurt from that matter will pass. You and Claire shouldn't let the guilt affect you, or the friendship you share."

"Claire shouldn't feel guilty at all," she said, harsher than she intended. "It was my doing, just me." She pulled away from him and plopped down on the tenement stairs, covering her face with her hands when he sat beside her. Luckily it was close to dinner time, and most folks were indoors, off the streets.

"My God, Ian, you shouldn't even know about what happened, let alone be so understanding. You should have kicked my ass. My Da would have, and he doesn't need an excuse."

He gave a gentle shove with his shoulder into hers. "I still can if it will make you feel better." Ian gave a quick bark of laughter when she winced. "It sickens me you're so upset and won't let the matter heal."

"I don't understand you, Ian. A pervert took liberties with your sister. Nana Donnelly's heart would break if she knew what I'd done. Why haven't you beaten me up, yet?" Fiona gave a smirk. "Hell, you're a policeman. You could've tossed me in jail, forgotten me, and been rid of me forever."

Ian cupped her chin in his palm and forced her face toward his. Fiona settled her gaze on the bridge of his nose. It seemed enough for him. "Though she didn't feel the same for you, I see how much you honestly love Claire. It was only a kiss." He tightened his grip a fraction. "If it had been more because she returned your love, I would have stood by you both, and protected you the best I could. As it is, you're torturing yourself worse than anything I could mete out. Give yourself a break. You deserve it."

"Thanks, Ian, I'll try," Fiona said when Ian stood. "You're a great guy."

"Yeah, I know." He smiled mischievously. "Seriously, Finn, watch yourself around Eldon Graham. Someone's going to take him out of business, and hard. Probably happen soon. He shouldn't trust his own men because of the stuff he's hip-deep in. Just can't say if it will be the justice system or an opponent who gets to Graham first. Don't be anywhere near him when it happens."

"Not intending to stick my nose anyplace it ought not to be."

"Don't mean it won't get shoved into something." He shrugged. "So you know, I got promoted to detective. I won't be in uniform next you see me, so should help keep your cover if you have need of me." Ian stood and started up the stairs, frowned, and then walked back down to stand directly in front of her. "Fiona, I don't know what happened to bring Graham here. I saw a girl—"

Fiona glanced up at him. "She came to see your mom."

He nodded solemnly. "Is she related to Graham?"

"His sister. Her name is Margaret."

"Mom says she's good people. Please be ever so careful, Fiona. He's a brother who won't be as understanding as me."

"No, Ian, you don't understand," she said. "Willie stopped me on my route because she was being harassed by Junior. I had to help her."

"I hope that's all."

Fiona stood. "Margaret just needed help, nothing more." However, as soon as the words were out of her mouth, Fiona knew them for a lie in her heart. From her physical touch with Margaret, Fiona's heart already wanted there to be more.

Chapter Four

WEARING HER SUNDAY best, though unremarkable to the people with money to buy store-bought clothes, Fiona stared at the imposing Queen Anne style residence of Eldon and Margaret Graham. Not only was it huge, but the house had so many windows there could never be a problem with receiving light. Privacy was probably out the window, too. Fiona snickered, catching her pun. At least two chimney's rose above the roof. Two rounded tower shapes were on either side of the front. A porch wrapped around the front and one side of the house. If the inside were anything like the outside, she was definitely out of place here.

Fiona expected she should use the servant's entrance, but believed Eldon Graham would have specifically stated that at their initial meeting. Was the unspoken rule supposed to be common knowledge? He was the type of man who would pre-think all details he intended and announce those points when necessary. Damn. The anticipation of earning money quicker, knowing anything Eldon Graham offered would surpass the pittance she had earned before now, may have had her acting too rashly.

Fiona turned away, ready to forget this whole idea. How could she possibly succeed if she couldn't figure which entrance to use? *I wonder if old man Chambers would give me my job back*—after a suitable amount of groveling, of course. At least Chambers would still let her sleep in the back room. She had just completed an about-face when Margaret's voice sounded from behind her.

"Never figured you for being chicken, Finn." Margaret's tone teased, and Fiona's heart beat more erratic than her nerves of just a moment ago.

"Kinda assumed I'd bitten off more than I could successfully chew," she admitted, not sure why she spoke honestly. With a shrug, Fiona asked, "Should I go to the back entrance?"

Margaret walked closer and locked an arm through hers. "Heavens, no. Eldon hates tardiness above most things, and you've managed to get here almost quarter-of-an-hour early. Let's not jinx it."

"Any other advice before I beard the lion in his den?" Fiona asked, puzzled to feel so relaxed around Margaret, as though friends for years. It obviously wasn't one-sided, either.

"He's always right, even when he isn't," Margaret said, giving a gentle shove of her shoulder into Fiona's arm. Margaret walked them through the front door into a wide foyer. She moved across the cream-colored marble floor and toward a closed door across from the staircase, and her voice grew quiet and serious. "Mostly, be careful of his mercurial temper." She knocked on the large mahogany door.

"Yeah," came from behind the door. Then it opened to reveal Eldon at a large dark wood desk. A bulky man of about five-foot-ten, thinning brown hair, mustache, and thick lips stood in the opening, still grasping the doorknob. "Good afternoon, Margaret."

"Hello, Jimmy," Margaret said as she pulled Fiona into the room and passed him on her way toward the front of Eldon's desk. Startled, Fiona almost forgot to remove her cap, which she pulled from her head and held tight in front of her.

After a quick glance at the grandfather clock on the right, Eldon stood and extended a hand to Fiona. "You're early, kid. I like that." He looked to where Margaret still held her arm. "I don't think Finn's gonna run, Babs, so you can let him go."

"You'd be surprised." She turned and looked directly at Fiona. "Have you had lunch?" Fiona shook her head. "Then come to the kitchen when you're done. I'll have a sandwich ready for you." She looked directly at Eldon. "Don't know if you have something planned for him already, but he needs to eat. He's too skinny." With that, Margaret gave a smile to Fiona and left.

As soon as Margaret crossed the threshold, Jimmy closed the door and positioned himself behind Eldon, crossed his arms and scowled at her. Eldon had retaken his seat once Margaret left and joined Jimmy in staring at her. Then, he leaned forward, put one elbow on the desk, his hand resting against his chin. "How old are you, kid?"

For a little less than two years, Fiona had been telling everyone she was almost sixteen, mostly to explain away not having facial hair, and decided it was about time to get older. She couldn't claim her real age of twenty-three, in fourteen days, because she looked like a teenager in male guise. "Gonna be seventeen in a couple weeks. Mr. Chambers didn't have no problem with me driving for him, so long as I didn't get caught by the cops. I ain't goin' to no school no more. Don't have a problem working hard, odd hours, I'm honest, and know how to mind my own potatoes. I hit on all six, Mr. Graham."

Eldon laughed hard and slapped the desk's top with the hand that had just cupped his face. "Take it easy kid. This isn't an interrogation. I was going to ask if I needed to talk to a parent before you start working for me." Fiona sneered. "I'll take that as a no. Okay, you're on your own, your own man. This is what I expect from you." He stood and put his hands in his pockets. "I have a couple restaurants in this town needing to be kept in supplies to feed the hungry citizens of our growing town. You'll mostly be delivering those supplies. Every now and again, you may need to deliver a package or run other errands for me with no questions asked. As my sister has plans for your stomach this afternoon, I want you to stop by Graham's Bit of Charm, on Chestnut Street, first thing in the morning. You do look like you could use a couple good meals. Margaret will need chauffeuring around every now and then. Jimmy would prefer to do it, but I need him with me for our business meetings."

Eldon went over the particulars and expectations for each establishment listed, and where to pick up the truck she'd use for these jobs. Also, she'd be solely responsible for keeping the truck in good running condition, any supplies to be put on his tab. At her nod of understanding, Eldon moved in front of her, leaned his backside on the desk, and crossed his arms over his chest. "You already know how important my kid sister is, so I probably don't need to remind you of what happens if she's harmed in any way. You do want to see your seventeenth birthday, don't you?"

"Yes, sir," Fiona said with a firm nod. "I'd never let anything happen to Miss Margaret."

"Good." Eldon moved back to his chair. "You do good by me, Finn, and there are chances for better jobs and more pay. I reward loyalty and hard work."

Fiona straightened her shoulders. "I won't let you down, Mr. Graham."

Eldon smiled wickedly. "You're the only one who'd suffer if you did." Fiona suspected he didn't use the word *suffer* lightly. He confirmed her assessment with his next words. "I punish with the same fervor as I reward. As for Margaret? Jimmy would kill you, painfully I might add, as he has his sights on my sister, Finn." As Eldon ignored the sharp intake of breath from Jimmy, Fiona decided she should ignore it too. "I haven't decided if I want to allow him the privilege. That would be granting quite the boon, to anyone."

"You don't have to worry, Mr. Graham." Fiona wondered at the underlying tension between Jimmy and Eldon. Was it because Eldon dangled Margaret on a string to keep Jimmy in line? Not a safe game to play, not with dangerous men, and both fit in that category. Fiona planned to stay as far away from it as humanly possible given her working conditions. She didn't want trouble.

Her plans were set in her mind, and she'd do whatever necessary to accomplish her goals and get out of this horrid town.

Seemingly satisfied with her answer, Eldon said, "Then start calling me Eldon. I hate the Mr. Graham stuff from people I like." Eldon handed her some money. "I expect you to wear a clean shirt and tie when on the clock. Make sure you pick some up before morning." He turned to Jimmy. "Show Finn to the kitchen, so Margaret can get some pounds on the kid. Oh, and Jimmy, try not to dawdle or drool over Margaret. We still have business reports to go over."

Jimmy started toward the door, and Fiona followed, noting Jimmy clenching and unclenching his fists as they went. He didn't even glance in her direction. Yup, trouble brewed between the two men. Not for the first time that day, Fiona wondered what she'd managed to get herself into this time.

Chapter Five

MARGARET SAT AT a table set close to a window niche in the kitchen, wondering how long Eldon would keep Finn in the office. For the millionth time, she straightened the silverware, adjusted the cloth napkin, and shifted the glass of milk. This time her hand paused. What if Finn didn't like milk or thought it baby stuff? Would he think her treating him as a kid? She frowned. Why had making an impression on a street kid, a male at that, become so important to her? Beyond, of course, appreciating he'd saved her from hoodlums, the comfort of their verbal interactions, and she couldn't forget the zinger she got from their first, innocently meant touch.

There was something she couldn't put her finger on concerning Finn that Margaret intended to understand. It was more than the fact Finn's dark brown hair, caramel colored eyes, and tanned skin made him so beautiful in his handsomeness. Or that those lips were so expressive, begging a kissing. There had been strength in the arm Margaret had latched on to when walking him to Eldon's office. However, what had grabbed Margaret's attention was the mix of compassion and loneliness she'd seen in Finn's gaze. The same aloneness coursed through her own blood. A solitary life awaited her and wasn't likely curable. Despite Eldon's wish for an advantageous marriage, Margaret had no interest in men.

Maybe what had drawn her to Finn was the need for a friendship with a comparable soul. Still, below it all lay the niggling feeling Finn was not as he appeared to be. In college, the more athletic, almost boyish women in her class drew Margaret's interest; so perhaps, Finn, young with a hint of feminine quality, simply reminded her of the very women she preferred to give her attention.

Footsteps sounded from the hall, and Margaret turned to see Jimmy enter the kitchen, with a subdued Finn right behind him. Her heart leaped at the sight of the young man clutching his Newsboy cap tight in a fist. "Finally," she said, as pleased at the sparkle lighting Finn's gaze meeting hers as she felt baffled by the pleasure she received from it. "I thought I'd have to bang down the door to rescue this poor kid. Please, Finn, come over here and eat." As Finn glided around Jimmy and did as told, Margaret said to Jimmy, "Thank you, Jimmy, you can go. I'm sure Eldon has better things for you to do than babysit us." She stood there until, with a grumble, Jimmy turned around and exited the kitchen.

Circling around, Margaret noticed Finn had moved to the table, but stood stiffly behind a chair. Smiling, she said, "Sit yourself down, Finn, or I'll cuff you upside your head."

"Yes, ma'am." Finn promptly moved back around the table and pulled out her chair. After she had sat, Finn returned to the other side, placed his cap on the chairs ear, and settled onto the seat.

"Go ahead, eat." Finn picked up the napkin and placed it across his lap before he bit into the sandwich. "You have very fine manners for a street kid. There's more to you, young Cavanaugh, than you let people know."

Margaret noted a half-second of fear flash across Finn's features before regaining his composure.

"Thank you, ma'am."

"You say ma'am to me one more time, Finn, and I will indeed cuff you. It's Margaret. Do you give your mother this much grief?" At the pained expression, Margaret said, "I'm sorry. Was it recent?"

Finn shook his head and took another bite, chewed thoughtfully and swallowed. Slowly, he took a drink of milk and wiped his mouth with the napkin. Such manners Finn had. Not even Jimmy ate so politely, and he was supposedly trying to impress her. "My mother and older brother were killed in a fire, four years ago." Finn's gaze fell to the milk glass as if it would drown the memories. "Would'a got me too, but I was...um..." Finn scrunched up his brow as if deciding how much to say to her. "I...uh...was playing in the streets, stuff I shouldn't have been doing. It was getting late, and I just didn't want to go home yet." With a halfhearted shrug, Finn said. "Kinda wanna stay outta trouble now, at least for a bit, 'til I get enough scratch to move west."

The way Finn glossed over the incident, Margaret knew Finn left as much of the story unsaid. From some of the conversations she'd overheard her father and his friends discuss years ago, Margaret knew the streets were not good for an adolescent. Things had become a bit more organized over the last thirty or forty years, but not any less brutal or deadly for children.

A lighthearted observation Margaret made of Finn was how decent his speech around her until he spoke of the past. Then it became slang-filled. "Do you think you would have been able to save them?" she asked. "Or would you have perished, too?"

"I dunno. The place was nothin' but tinder, so can't know if anyone, including me, would've been faster than those flames."

Margaret could tell from the slight twitch of his lips, the expression of emotions swimming in the golden brown eyes, Finn felt deep guilt, but whether from surviving because playing at the time or for not perishing with his family, she couldn't tell. "Well, I'm glad you're here, alive and well. If you weren't, goodness only knows what would have happened to me in that alley."

With a shrug, Finn said, "Willie would'a found someone else to help."

"Why do I doubt that?" Margaret smiled at Finn, who seemed to have trouble accepting compliments. One of the other things Margaret found fascinating was the little glint in the soft brown eyes when Finn used slang, and she wondered why it happened. She was just happy to know the meaning behind some of the slang words, thanks to college — words like scratch. "So what are you saving your money for, or shouldn't I ask?"

Another negligent shrug, this with only one shoulder. "Want to go west to live in the mountains, maybe get a job doing carpentry work."

"You like woodworking then?"

Finn beamed a brilliant smile. "Oh, yes, who wouldn't? The smell from cutting and working the wood is extraordinary. The feeling of accomplishment when you've finished a project and can stand back and see you've created something useful, something solid, even beautiful. You'd know in a minute if you'd done good or bad."

"Oh, Finn," Margaret said with a pleased smile. "Your enthusiasm is a striking thing. If you put as much heart into your carpentry work, I'm certain everything you create would be better than just good."

For a moment, Finn wouldn't meet her gaze, a deep red flush coloring his face. When Finn did look back to her, he asked softly, "What about you, Ma...Margaret, what would you need to be doing to make you happy?"

To be loved, cared for, and needed for me and not as a commodity, her inner voice responded. Yes, Margaret wanted someone to love her for herself; however, the possibility that person would be the gender she truly desired would be slim to impossible. She also knew Jimmy worked hard, daily, to get Eldon to agree to his bid for marriage with her. Since Jimmy had moved into the house, it was all but a matter of time. Margaret had resigned herself to the fact marriage would be her only future, but she wouldn't allow that man to be or be someone like Jimmy Bennett. These were things she couldn't tell Finn or anyone. She didn't think it would hurt to tell Finn a little of the truth. "I want to teach in a school, to be the teacher I went to college to be."

"Eldon doesn't want his sister demeaning herself?" Finn asked, his hand wrapping hers in a gentle blanket of warmth. The jolt it sent through her body surprised Margaret, as did the sense of safety flooding her.

Margaret knew she should pull her hand away, chastise Finn for taking liberties, but couldn't do it. Instead, she stared hard at Finn. "You can't be sixteen," she said firmly, "or even a boy. You're just too darn astute." Was that again a flash of fright in Finn's expression? What brought it on? She decided to deal with the questions later. The last thing Margaret wanted was to alienate the only person she seemed able to talk freely with, who made her feel safe talking about herself. "Yes, Eldon let me go to school because it made our mother happy, and I was out of his hair for a while. Now, I'm to learn my place, meaning marry and make him an uncle. The marriage arrangement would have to be lucrative to his business, somehow. Although I believe, a large part is to have me off his hands for good. Then our familial time can be relegated to holidays and special occasions."

"I think I'm glad for being a poor, unimportant kid, then," Finn said with a wry grin.

"Why's that?"

"Don't fit anyone's grand schemes. I could fall off the face of the world, no one would care." As though reluctantly, Finn released her hand and sat back in the chair.

"I seriously doubt that Finn," Margaret assured. She remembered the pleased excitement on Claire's face, the adoration on Willie's. Even Mrs. Donnelly's face had brightened at the mention of Finn on their visit yesterday. No, many would miss Finn Cavanaugh, herself included, and they'd just met. "I can't imagine anyone meeting you and not being positively changed by the experience in some way."

Finn seemed poised to dispute her comment when the click, click of heeled footsteps sounded outside the room. Clamping her teeth from uttering her frustration at the intrusion, and when Finn jumped to his feet, Margaret turned to see Lorraine swishing into the kitchen, a beautiful blonde blur in lavender taffeta nightclothes—and high heels. Margaret wondered if Lorraine, Eldon's live-in girlfriend, had internal radar alerting her when a fresh male was on the premises. "Good afternoon, Lorraine."

"Good—" Lorraine's perfectly manicured hand flew to her chest in feigned surprise. Margaret rolled her eyes at the other woman's repulsive maneuver to draw attention to her cleavage. "I didn't realize we had a guest, or I would have dressed. I just came down for some coffee," Lorraine said breathlessly. Somehow, Margaret suspected Lorraine did know about Finn and selected her outfit to best place a boy at a disadvantage.

"Well, you'll have to deal with the instant kind this late in the day." Margaret reluctantly stood, filled the kettle, and placed it on the stove. Lorraine still stood in the doorway as if uncertain what to do. Snorting, Margaret said, "Sit down, Lorraine."

Dutifully, Finn pulled out the chair he'd been using. When Lorraine glided over, gave a quick batting of her ice-blue eyes, Finn pushed the chair closer to the table and hurriedly picked up the dirty dishes and rushed them to the sink. "What a polite, and terribly handsome, young man you are," Lorraine crooned.

"Thank you, ma'am," Finn said quietly.

"No, thank you—" Lorraine raised a questioning eyebrow.

When Finn didn't take the bait, Margaret gave the introductions. "Finn Cavanaugh, Lorraine Mills," Margaret said, intentionally making introductions against etiquette by putting Finn first. She turned to Finn, "Eldon's girlfriend."

"Pleasure, ma'am," Finn said nodding. Finn raised one corner of his lips in a small grin, a strange underlying humor meant only for her to see, and once again, amazing Margaret by what appeared to be incredible understanding of human nature. "I really should be going, Miss Margaret. Thank you for lunch." Finn walked back to the table and reached behind Lorraine to grab his cap.

Quick as the snake she was, Lorraine grasped Finn's forearm. "Must you leave so soon? We've just met and haven't had a chance to chat."

Extricating himself smoothly from Lorraine's grasp, Finn said, "Yes, ma'am. I have things to do before starting work for Mr. Graham." Finn flipped the cap atop his head, gave a polite bow to Lorraine, and walked closer to Margaret. She watched with surprised absorption as Finn took her hand, gently placed a soft kiss on her knuckles, and said sweetly, "Until the pleasure of meeting again, Miss Margaret, good day."

Finn jauntily exited out the kitchen door leaving the room deathly quiet.

"Well, of all—" With a snort, Lorraine got up from the table and started for the main part of the house. "What about your coffee?" Margaret asked.

"Forget it," Lorraine snapped. "I'm going back to my room."

Margaret smiled wide at her departing back. "Thought as much." She expected Lorraine was incensed that a male occupied the room, even a boy of Finn's age, and she wasn't the center of his undivided attention. Gleefully glancing at the stove, Margaret mumbled at Lorraine's back, "That's why I never started the heat under the kettle."

Chapter Six

THE BACK DOOR to the restaurant had been propped open, making it easier for Fiona to unload the truck of the foodstuffs for the kitchen. She'd started on her third week of working for Eldon and, for the most part, the worst issues encountered were her tired and sore muscles. For that, she was grateful. However, after just short of a month, Fiona also realized there was more to Eldon's restaurant business than the public witnessed, more than probably legal.

Not that she cared overly. Fiona simply wanted to keep a low profile, build her savings, and run away to the mountains out west and start life with fresh memories. With some of the political changes breathed about, like the federal involvement in the institution of prohibition, she expected it would be more difficult to hide, let alone Eldon running his business. More law enforcement officers to impose the laws of prohibition, and more men willing to do whatever it took to be the top dog in a profitable business. As dangerous as life was now, it was about to get a lot worse.

Some days, however, being the proverbial fly on the wall, the person no one paid attention to, was easier said than done. "Hey, kid, got a kiss for us?" came a sultry voice behind Fiona. Lucky for her, Fiona wasn't garnering the negative attention of Eldon or Jimmy, but the notice of the women working Eldon's restaurants. Fiona placed the case of goods she carried on top of the others she'd brought in from the truck. She turned around with a smile, pulled her cap off her head, and bowed to the two women standing just outside the storeroom. "Now, ladies, do I look like a heel?" she asked teasingly.

"Maybe he's embarrassed to get caught kissing instead of working," said Molly, a tall skinny redhead.

The shorter, slightly rotund blonde woman, Dorcas, giggled. "How does a simple kiss make you a heel, Finn?" Fiona shook her head and walked between them to get out of the storeroom, nervous about being cornered. Dorcas latched on to Fiona's arm, forcing her to stop between them. With her other hand, Dorcas slowly ran her fingers through Fiona's already tousled hair. "You have kissed a girl before, haven't you Finn?"

Claire's image flashed in Fiona's head, and her face flamed.

"I'll take that as yes, Dorcas." Molly moved closer, so they sandwiched Fiona tightly in the middle. "Why won't you kiss us, Finn?" Molly asked, her lips softly brushing Fiona's ear. Goosebumps erupted in response.

"Why would it make you a heel?" Dorcas asked with an exaggerated pout.

Fiona shivered and nervously cleared her throat, her grip tightened on the cap twisted in her grip. She tried to think of an appropriate answer over the heavy hammering of her heartbeat. "Um, 'cause I can't kiss you at the same time, right? The first girl I kissed would think they were my favorite, breaking the heart of the other. I adore you both the same." Fiona gave a sad expression. "Don't make me choose, dolls. Give a fella a break, could'ya?"

"Wha'd'ya say, Moll's? Let the little cake-eater off the hook?"

"Aw, come on, I'm trying to be straight with you," Fiona whined playfully.

Molly pursed her lips in thought for a moment. "Okay, I'll give in if he agrees to give us a lift home."

Fiona sighed in relief. "It would be my pleasure." Dorcas and Molly each kissed a cheek, and she felt her face heat again. "Let me get the last crate off the truck." She smiled at each woman in turn and moved to the back door. Fiona stopped dead in her tracks seeing Margaret standing silently with a humorous expression on her face. "Miss Margaret," Fiona blurted the obvious.

"Morning, Finn," Margaret said quietly. "Am I interrupting?"

"No, ma—" Fiona didn't finish the intended address when Margaret quirked an eyebrow. "No. Did I miss an appointment driving you somewhere?"

Margaret shook her head. "Actually, no, I came—"

Before she finished her explanation, Jimmy plowed through the back door. "Did you find him?" he demanded of Margaret, before noticing Fiona. "Hey, runt, we need you to drive Margaret home. You can finish your deliveries afterward. Eldon and I have an unscheduled meeting. When you're done deliveries, come to the main office." Fiona resisted the urge to shudder at the violent glint in his eye and the sneer dancing on his lips. She knew her boss, and this goon was about to hurt someone—very badly, too, from Jimmy's excited reaction.

"I'm sorry, Finn. I know you had other work scheduled," Margaret said.

"Don't apologize to him," Jimmy said harshly. "He does as he's told. I'd better not hear he's been whining. You understand me?" Jimmy asked as he cuffed Fiona roughly on the back of her head. She winced but held her ground. Behind her, Fiona heard Molly and Dorcas gasp. She'd almost forgotten the other witnesses to this conversation.

Margaret insinuated herself between Fiona and Jimmy and swiftly slapped his forearm. "That was uncalled for." Margaret crossed her arms defensively, standing directly in front of Fiona. "You've brought me safely here, and Finn will safely take me home. I suggest you don't keep my brother waiting to conduct his meeting." Margaret snarled the last word. Fiona wondered if she knew the type of meetings her brother conducted.

With a grunt, Jimmy spun on his heel and stormed into the alley.

"Well, that was pleasant," Margaret said, turning to stare directly at Fiona. "Are you okay?" she asked. Margaret raised a hand toward her head, but Fiona managed to duck away from it, slapping her cap on her head. "Had worse," Fiona said, stuffing her hands in her pockets to hide their trembling. Margaret frowned at her, looking hurt by Fiona's avoidance. The look shot an unexpected pain through Fiona. What did the hurt expression mean? Fiona wondered. "Let me get that last crate, and I'll take you home, Miss Margaret."

Fiona did just that. She retrieved the last item from her truck, placed it in the storeroom, surprised to find three sets of eyes on her when she closed the door behind her. Two sets looked slightly uncomfortable, and one set determined. Margaret spoke first. "A promise is a promise, Finn. We'll take the ladies home before me, and then you can meet up with Eldon."

"As you wish, Miss—" Fiona noted the flash of frustration in Margaret's gaze. Swallowing audibly, Fiona simply said, "Okay."

It was a tight fit, but they all manage to squeeze into the cab of the truck, Margaret wedged closest to Fiona, because she would be the last out. Fiona had the driver window down, keeping one arm outside to give just a bit more space. Or so she tried to tell herself, ignoring the comforting warmth of Margaret's body and thigh pressed against hers, the soft curve of Margaret's left breast rubbing into Fiona's ribs with each breath she took. Torture, pure and simple torture the contact was, and the arm outside the truck helped ground her.

Fiona hoped her relief wasn't too obvious when she pulled up to the tenement the two women shared a room in. "Here you go, ladies," she said, pulling to the curb.

Dorcas exited first and rushed from the curb to the driver side door. She pulled Fiona's face through the open window and placed a loud wet kiss on her cheek. "You're a sweet kid, Finn."

"Yes, thank you, Finn," Molly said, batting her eyelashes

exaggeratedly as she closed the passenger door. Dorcas hurriedly joined Molly on the sidewalk.

Blowing an air kiss, Dorcas said, "We owe you."

"Have a great day," Fiona said, slowly pulling away. She knew her face was red, could feel the heat of embarrassment all over. Exacerbating the situation for her, Fiona realized Margaret hadn't made use of the extra room she now had on the seat, although she'd shifted, so they weren't so flush.

As Fiona carefully maneuvered the streets on the way to the Graham home, she wondered what went through Margaret's mind right now. The left corner of her mouth would lift subtly from time to time. Once again, Margaret broke the extended silence. "You truly are sweet. And the way you get all red in spite of the tan is so adorable. No wonder the women like you."

"Women don't—" She sighed deep and long. "I'm not adorable," Fiona said, groaning when her face heated for the hundredth time. I gotta learn to control this, she thought bitterly.

Margaret twisted, stared directly at her. Fiona saw Margaret in her peripheral and tried to block out the realization Margaret seemed more beautiful each time Fiona gazed at her. "You're a conundrum, Finn. I'll figure out your secret."

At this remark, Fiona felt the beads of sweat from fear pepper her forehead. Hoping to keep her tone light, she said, "Nah, I'm an open book. And a boring book, much like a school primer."

A warm hand touched Fiona's sleeve. "I don't want you uncomfortable around me, Finn. Please don't take this conversation negatively." Margaret took a deep breath. "What I mean to say is I enjoy our moments together. You make me feel comfortable—and able to be myself."

Fiona pulled in front of Margaret's home. She bit her bottom lip, not knowing how to respond. Was Margaret figuring out her secret? Was she letting her know she liked their time together?

As if reading her mind, Margaret closed the distance, pecked her on the cheek, warmer and gentler than Dorcas had, and said, "I don't know what you're hiding, Finn. Maybe I never will. Just let us enjoy our friendship, okay?" She nodded, and Margaret got out of the truck and walked into the house.

Fiona sat in the truck until Margaret closed the front door behind her. I'm so in trouble when it comes to her, Fiona groaned.

Chapter Seven

ALMOST RELUCTANTLY, FIONA made her way up to the second-floor office of Eldon's main restaurant, worried tremendously, not knowing why Eldon had directed her here. With Jimmy's involvement, it wouldn't be good. She checked in with Eldon's office assistant, Stan, only for him to direct her to the basement.

It wasn't smart to keep Eldon waiting, she knew, but the thought didn't make her feet move any faster to her destination. She'd delivered various foodstuffs to the main restaurant before, and Fiona remembered two storerooms and a large walk-in freezer at the far end of the basement. As she reached the bottom step, Fiona realized the freezer was to be her destination. Moaning and mumbling came from inside; the propped open door and the single light bulb suspended from the ceiling did little to brighten the area. Taking a deep breath, Fiona moved forward. Two of Eldon's bodyguards flanked either side of the door.

Fiona had just reached the threshold when Eldon turned in her direction. "Ah, Finn, welcome to the party."

"You needed me, sir?" she asked, hoping the tremor in her voice wasn't obvious.

Eldon leaned back against the doorjamb, luckily for her, thus blocking her view of those within. "This is taking longer than I anticipated, and thought you might want to see some Graham justice when a heel doesn't think through his actions." The wet sound of flesh pounding flesh punctuated the comment, as Eldon straightened and moved into the room.

Instinctively, her gaze traveled to the center, and nausea roiled. Terry, tied to a chair in the center of the room with plastic all around, face swollen and bruised, cuts coated with blood, his breathing shallow, and his moans barely audible. A grinning Jimmy hovered over Terry, absently rubbing the flesh of fingers surrounding by the brass knuckles he wore. Before she could stop herself, Fiona asked, "What'd Terry do?"

Walking to stand behind the chair, Eldon placed his hands on Terry's shoulders as if they were at some award dinner, and not watching the pulverizing of the man for some crime against Eldon. "I overlooked Terry's abandonment of Margaret weeks ago because your involvement in the matter turned out so well."

He squeezed Terry's shoulders, and the man winced. "You had no way of knowing Finn's involvement would have occurred, Terry, when you left her alone to get a message to me about the Detweiler boy. Margaret's safe, however, so I didn't reprimand you then." Eldon's gaze hardened, appearing manic in the dim lighting of the room. He stared directly at Finn. "However, it's come to my attention Terry here hasn't been entirely honest with his accountings of inventory at one of my restaurants."

From the way Eldon emphasized the last word, Fiona understood. Terry stole profits from the liquor sales of Eldon's speakeasies, possibly his legitimate profits too. Eldon shouldn't be surprised. He was a man breaking the law so shouldn't be shocked Terry, and maybe others, weren't loyal employees— Jimmy came to mind as a possible culprit. Greed is...well, greedy.

Eldon walked to stand opposite Jimmy. "One last chance, Terry, because I'm bored with this. Don't care why you did it. Tell me where my money is."

Tears fell rapidly from Terry's eyes, blending with the blood and making them indistinguishable. "I swear to you, Mr. Graham, I didn't take money from you. If I made a mistake with the books, I'll find it." Terry's breathing became more labored, desperation in his voice, even if barely above a murmur. "I used poor judgment with Miss Margaret, I admit it. But I swear to you I didn't—I wouldn't—steal from you. I swear on my life."

Shaking his head, Eldon tisked. "That's the problem, Terry. Your life does depend on your answer."

"But I didn't do it." Terry whimpered.

Fiona shifted uncomfortably in the doorway. To her, Terry sounded sincere. In his condition, she doubted it behooved him to lie any longer. Although, she suspected Terry wasn't going to make it out of this room alive, no matter what. Fiona prayed Eldon would dismiss her from the scene if that were to be the result. Please don't let me have to witness his death, she silently pleaded, feeling sick at the prospect. When she realized her movement caught Eldon's attention, Fiona stiffened and mumbled an apology.

"I want your opinion of the situation, Finn," Eldon said.

Her first instinct was to play stupid, but Eldon wouldn't tolerate such cowardice. As much as the situation disgusted her, Fiona didn't intend to piss Eldon off—ever. She needed this job for just a while longer. Margaret's image flashed in her mind's eye. She couldn't lose her growing friendship with Margaret just yet. Clearing her throat, Fiona shoved her hands deep into her pockets. She'd started the habit when noticing most of the rich men did it. Lately, it was the best way to hide her nervous trembling. "He sounds sincere. Is it possible to make the money up to you?" She shrugged. "What's to keep him from doing it again? If it's a mistake with the records, can't keep him from making the same mistake in the future. Were me, Terry's soles would be pounding the streets, not getting a chance to do it again."

"You're a smart kid, Finn. Gonna go places. You see the problem but, sorry to say, not the correct resolution." Eldon edged away from Terry's chair and gave a nod to Jimmy. He stopped in front of Finn, blocking her view of Terry. "Can't have him telling folks I'm soft. And I can't bet on the chance he might actually learn from this lesson." He shook his head. "If I flip a coin to determine the outcome, the deciding factor against Terry will be that he left my sister alone in an alley with thugs." Eldon paused, staring right at her. "Do it," he said, voice calm.

Fiona started at the thundering report of the gunshot in the confines of the freezer. She was glad Eldon blocked her from the view but didn't know why he still watched her. Why was it so important she be here, for this, for murder? Then a tightening in her gut as she realized the answer, Eldon's next words confirming her suspicions. "Sorry you had to see that, kid, but welcome to the family."

Oh, shit. Every instinct screamed to run as far away as she could. Fiona just stood there, not knowing what to do.

Jimmy sauntered over to them, a smirk on his face. "You look sick, runt." Jimmy made a motion to the two guards at the door, and they began the cleaning process, starting with releasing Terry from the chair. Jimmy chuckled. "Maybe you should get some fresh air. Looks like you're gonna be sick, and the guys have enough to clean up. Unless you can hit the plastic from here."

Eldon clapped a hand on her shoulder, and Fiona flinched. "Go on home, Finn, first time's always the roughest."

Fiona nodded sluggishly. First time? Eldon expects her presence for more lessons? Crap, hell, shit and damn. She was definitely going to be sick. As she trudged up the stairs, Fiona wondered just what in the hell she'd gotten into.

Moreover, how in the bloody hell was she going to get out of it?

Chapter Eight

IT WASN'T UNUSUAL, even after an urgent summons, for Fiona to cool her heels in the waiting room outside Eldon's office. She'd rather be doing something constructive. Not surprised though when the restaurant manager of her last stop of the day told her to drop his foodstuffs inside the door and get over to Mr. Graham's office immediately.

Immediately; yet Fiona still waited. Please, she silently prayed, don't make me watch another killing.

"It shouldn't be too much longer," said Stan, Eldon's office assistant. His expression showed genuine apology. She expected it wasn't the first time this had occurred. Seriously doubted it would be the last. Time's like this, as with Terry, Fiona wondered if she'd earn enough money to leave for the west—while she still breathed.

As if on cue, the main office door opened, and a man and woman exited. Eldon stood right behind them, holding the door nearly closed. "It's been a pleasure doing business with you," Eldon said. "Don't spend it all in one place." As the couple chuckled and left, Eldon turned his gaze on Fiona. "Just a moment more, Finn," Eldon said, disappearing behind the closing the door.

Fiona thought she spotted movement, wondered who else was in there, as she shifted uncomfortably for what would apparently be another long wait.

More minutes passed, and Jimmy came into the waiting area. He gave a sneer in her direction, before asking Stan, "He in?" Jimmy didn't wait for an answer, just burst into the room. From the corner of her vision, Fiona thought she saw a little girl leaning, unmoving, half on the top of Eldon's desk. Right before the door slammed shut, Fiona thought she heard Jimmy mumble, "Playtime."

Fear niggled at the edge of her conscious. No, it couldn't be. No, no, no. But Fiona knew exactly what was happening, what happened all the time to poor kids. She had to stop them. Fear became panic. If she burst into that room, Fiona could end up dead. It was none of her business. Keep your nose clean and your eyes down. That's one of the few lessons her father taught her; right after: I'm your father, take your licking quietly, or it'll be worse for you. So Fiona learned not to scream, no matter how bad it hurt. She learned to mind her own affairs. Like with Margaret? Yeah, but you know what's happening to—

"Hey, Finn, stop," Stan called after her.

Fiona couldn't stop, not and live with herself for doing nothing. She flung the door open. And pretended she didn't see Jimmy unfastening his pants, or Eldon casually sitting on the couch watching the empty eyes of a blonde-haired fourteen-year-old with her dress pulled up above her waist, and panties pulled down, bent over Eldon's desk. "Mr. Graham—"

"What the fuck, Finn?" Jimmy cursed loudly, but at least he'd yanked the girls dress down to cover her somewhat. Stan closed the door behind her.

She ignored Jimmy—and the girl, although that task so much harder to do—and directed her attention to Eldon. "I know you've got some business going on, but you also have me cooling my heels while money is wilting in the truck from deliveries I ain't making for you."

This time, Jimmy snickered. "Little pervert wants to watch." Said the black pot to the black kettle? she wanted to fling at him.

Eldon stood, walked to his desk as if a girl wasn't draped across like a discarded rag, and pulled a cigar from a box resting close to the girls' head. The girl never even flinched. "What do you see, Finn?" Eldon asked.

Squeezing her hands into tight fists, Fiona said, "I don't see nothin'."

"Nothing?"

"Nothing much." Fiona swallowed the bile rising in her throat. "Couple of men, entertaining company," she said. The words were thick sludge on her tongue. What have I become? Her inner voice answered. You're a survivalist. If they knew your secret, you'd be treated to the same—or worse.

Eldon nodded at her answer. In a voice, too calm for the circumstances, Eldon asked, "But you don't like it, do you?"

Fiona bit her lip, trying not to let her gaze flick toward the girl. "No, sir, I certainly do not. She's just a kid." She blinked rapidly to stop the building tears from spilling. "But, like I said, ain't my concern."

"I see." Eldon sat in his desk chair and slowly lit the cigar. "Since you mind your own, what did you call it, potatoes, you're blind right now, correct?" Fiona nodded, unable to speak. She knew if she opened her mouth, she'd spew. "Would it help you deal with this if I told you her parents just sold her to me?"

"Help, as make me feel better? No, makes it worse, sir," she said honestly. Fiona noticed Jimmy jerk the panties up and then grabbing the girl by the arm, her body unresponsive, tossed her onto the couch. When Jimmy plopped down beside the girl, Fiona had difficulty not moving to intervene, separate him from her. She squeezed her fists tighter, the blunt nails biting into her flesh. With the buzz of anger in her head, Fiona almost didn't realize Eldon was addressing her again. When Fiona focused on Eldon, his nod let her know he perceived her true sentiments on this matter.

"Bet you're sorry you burst in here, huh, runt?" Jimmy guffawed.

Fiona couldn't hate Jimmy more than she did right now. Glaring at him, she asked, "Did you—" She inhaled deeply. "Did you finish?"

"Nah, you kinda put the kibosh on the party. Didn't even get to start." Jimmy's tone held his honest disappointment.

The urge to slug Jimmy had her moving a step closer to him. Behind her, Eldon said, "Finn, stop." She did, twisting to glare at him. "I see you're upset, kid. Look, you know this is about business. Shit happens. But she's no use to me in this condition, as you see. Most of 'em whimper and cry, not become catatonic." Eldon dropped his cigar in the ashtray. "Take her to the house. I'll deal with this matter later." Deal with the matter, she thought with disdain. That's all this child was—a matter to deal with? Had Eldon any humanity in him? Fiona knew Jimmy didn't. Jimmy was scum, pure and simple.

"Take her to the kitchen entrance, though. Don't let Margaret know you're there. The housekeeper will take care of her. She sometimes handles my overnight visitors."

Was this a common occurrence for Eldon? At least, Fiona thought with a little relief, he wants to keep this from his sister. Maybe Margaret wasn't aware of this side of her brother's business. Fiona was glad of that. "Did the parents at least tell you her name?"

Eldon chuckled. "Won't knowing make dealing with her more personal for you? Keep your distance, Finn. It's for the best."

"Please, may I know her name?"

"Her name's Thelma."

This is the second instance where Eldon pulled her deeper into the dark drowning pool that was his business—and her life. "All right, Eldon. I'll get her to your house." Fiona, feet leaden in her dejection, went to the couch and bodily picked the slight form of Thelma up in her arms.

Chapter Nine

FIONA PARKED IN the rear of the house, close to the kitchen door. Jumping out of the car and moving to the passenger door, Fiona kept mumbling, "It's all right. It'll be all right." She knew it wouldn't be, not really. This particular atrocity wasn't erasable. So who was she trying to convince, herself or Thelma? Thelma stiffened involuntarily when Fiona reached a hand to her, and then just sat, unmoving.

Tears of helplessness and rage ran down Fiona's face. She reached into the truck and put an arm under Thelma's legs and another around her back, lifting her from the seat. Quickly, but gently, Fiona carried Thelma into the kitchen. "Hello, is anyone here?" she called, hoping Margaret wasn't home. How could she possibly explain this situation to her? "Hello? Please, I need help here."

Footsteps sounded from the back of a hall leading out of the kitchen. "Coming," came a voice before a young woman slid to a stop near the stove. "Finn?" Squinting in shock, the woman whispered, "Oh, my God, Fiona."

Staring back, Fiona recognized Brigid, a childhood friend who'd had an enormous crush on, which turned to an engagement to, her older brother, Fionn, the original Finn. She'd always been friendly and kind to Fiona. "Name's Finn these days. I...uh...I'm supposed to bring her here," she said, glancing quickly at the girl in her arms. "She's...she's been..." Fiona swallowed back more tears. "I didn't know what else to do but as I was told. They want her here to...to..." Fiona took a shaky breath, "to break her in before sending her to a brothel. I didn't want to obey, but—what else can I do?" The tears flowed again. "I'm babbling, sorry. Some boy I am, huh?" Fiona asked, "Can I rest her somewhere, please?"

"Yes, of course. This way," Brigid said.

Following Brigid down the hall where she'd just come from, Fiona came to a set of doors at the end, probably the household staff quarters. Brigid opened one of the doors and pulled back the quilt on the small, four-poster bed. She glanced around and noted an open door leading to a small bathroom, and another bedroom beyond. Gently, Fiona placed Thelma on top, as Brigid pulled off her shoes.

"My room." Brigid must have noticed her scrutiny. "Fiona,

why in the hell are you dressed like a boy?"

"Please, Brigid, keep your voice down," Fiona begged.

Changing to a loud whisper, Brigid said, "I thought you were your brother come back to life."

"I didn't know you'd be here. I'm supposed to turn her over to the housekeeper. Is that you?"

"No, she left a little while ago. I stay on full time for whatever needs to be done. My room is attached to this one by way of the washroom." Fiona scowled. Brigid must have noticed. "No, Fio...Finn. Daddy still works at City Hall, and even Jimmy wouldn't dare risk his wrath. I'm safe." Fiona couldn't do anything other than take her word, even if she doubted Mr. Connor's job would protect Brigid for long.

"I wouldn't bring you the pain with Finn's reminder on purpose," Fiona said. "Things got bad with Da, and I just couldn't be a servant in someone's house. I had to do something, and all Finn's clothes were there for the using. As soon as I make enough, I'm going west."

Squinting an examination, Brigid stared at her face, looking for fresh bruises, Fiona guessed. Then Brigid asked, "Your father still beating you, blaming you for his own mistakes and failures?"

"When he finds me, yeah, but I can take it better than before." Fiona smirked. "Mostly, I just stay out of his way. He's usually too canned to notice what day it is, let alone whether he's seen me recently."

"Hope he drinks himself into a hole and never comes out. Just don't want him taking you to the grave with him. You shouldn't have to get better at taking a beating, Fiona. That's not right." Brigid tenderly pulled the bedding back over Thelma. She gazed at Fiona with a sad expression. "You work for the Grahams now?"

Taking a step back, Fiona looked down at Thelma, so small and helpless, currently staring up at the ceiling with vacant eyes. "I'm doing odd driving jobs as a delivery boy named Finn. I didn't know about this or what was happening, Brigid. I just watched that man and woman leave his office. I waited for him to call me in for some emergency job change. When Jimmy went into the office— Well, I don't know, something wasn't right, so I busted in, claimed being worried about the stuff in the truck. I didn't stop them—" Fiona took a deep breath. "Eldon told me to bring her here to the house. She's intended for a brothel I suspect from overhearing Jimmy's conversations with the other guys. But I never guessed little girls were involved."

"You broke in on them? They could have killed you." Fiona nodded dejectedly. Brigid came over to Fiona and wrapped her in a hug. "Fiona—"

"It's Finn, please. Have they brought girls here before?"

"Not in this state and never this young. Jimmy's involved, so it isn't entirely surprising. The few others seemed fine, almost accepting," Brigid said.

"Accepting of what?" she asked.

"I figured they owed Mr. Graham money and had to work if off through indenture," Brigid said. "They told me they'd only spend the night, before going to work at the businesses." Brigid gave a sneer. "I assumed the restaurants."

Fiona bit her bottom lip. "I can't leave her here. This is wrong."

"We can only do what we're told. If we go against Mr. Graham, we're dead. So now I ask, how do you think it'll go for you when they find out you're a woman?" Brigid indicated the bed with a toss of her head. "You'll get that and worse for trying to pull one over on them."

She'd already come to the same conclusion earlier. "I have to do something," Fiona whispered hoarsely. "I...somehow I have to help her. I can't let them—anyone—do that to her again."

"They won't." Fiona spun around to see Margaret standing in the doorway. She entered the room, walked to the bed, and sat down at the foot, her gaze never leaving the girl. "Do we know her name?"

"She hasn't spoken, yet, but El—" Fiona felt herself panic inside, wondering how much Margaret overheard. "Her name is Thelma."

Margaret nodded. "Finn, I need you to go get our doctor." She gave Fiona the address. "His name is Dr. Matthews. Tell him I sent you and he'll come. Explain as much or as little as makes you comfortable telling him." She must have felt Fiona's hesitation. Margaret turned to look directly at Fiona. "It's okay, Finn. Right now, we have to help Thelma. Together." She gave a weak smile. "Brigid will keep me company until you return."

With one last glance at each of them, Fiona went to get the doctor.

SO MANY EMOTIONS swirled inside Margaret. She couldn't believe what she'd overheard, yet deep down she always suspected some of the atrocities linked to her brother, some she'd hoped weren't true. Yes, she'd overheard Finn and Brigid. All of it. Finn was a woman, not a boy with feminine attributes. The flood of relief nearly had her trembling with excitement. And, she heard Eldon was almost as despicable as Jimmy in the lack of morals category. Margaret couldn't think of many redeeming qualities of the horrid man, which was one of the reasons she kept rebuffing Jimmy. Granted, it wasn't the most important reason. Living a lie is one thing to contend with in life. Living a lie with someone you despise is entirely another.

However, she never expected or suspected Eldon to do something like this.

"Brigid." Brigid stood just behind her, wringing her hands. "It's truly all right." Margaret stood. "We need to clean Thelma up, and make her as comfortable as we can before the doctor gets here."

"Miss Margaret?"

"You get some soap and water, maybe a nightdress. I'll get her undressed."

Brigid touched Margaret's arm lightly. "How much—"

Margaret shook her head firmly and said, "That's not important right now. We have to get her ready for when the doctor arrives."

"It *is* important," Brigid said. "Mr. Graham—"

"Mr. Graham what?"

While Brigid gave a dreadful squeak of alarm, Margaret turned toward her brother, but not before noting Thelma's body going rigid. "Mr. Graham will probably be angry, I'm sure is what she's worried about, Eldon."

Eldon appeared confused. "Why are you here, Babs?"

Margaret noted he never asked about Thelma's condition and avoided looking directly at her. "Why are you?" She should have considered that if she were able to approach quietly, then anyone else could as well. Not that she expected it of Eldon in his own house.

Shifting uncomfortably, Eldon said, "I, uh, I came looking for someone to make me a sandwich, but I can wait. Um, where's Finn?"

"I sent him to get the doctor."

"What for?" Eldon asked too sharply.

Margaret glared at him. "In case you hadn't noticed, a strange child is in this house, and she isn't well." He bit his lower lip, a sure sign of him formulating the pros and cons of his next remark. For Thelma's sake, and before Fiona came back with the doctor, Margaret had to get him to leave. Since Eldon prepared a lie, she'd beat him to one. "Finn said," she noted Eldon stiffen, "the girl was wandering around, lost and acting, what he called, funny. Fearful for the child's safety, he brought her here. That's all we know since the girl hasn't spoken at all."

"Why not take it to the hospital?" Eldon asked. Margaret

wanted to slap him for pretending Fiona had the option available to her. Not that she suspected the hospital would be any use to an abandoned child if the excuse were legitimate.

"Finn's still a kid, Eldon. Probably didn't think everything through in his panic."

"I see," Eldon said, beginning to back out of the room. "Don't worry about lunch." He started down the hall, turned quickly and said, "Have Finn come see me when you're through with him running your errands." Margaret nodded. Certain Eldon walked far enough away, Margaret closed the bedroom door on any more unwanted visitors and inquiring ears.

When Margaret returned her attention to Brigid, she detected the trembling of her body. "Please, Brigid, relax," Margaret whispered. "I would never do anything to harm Finn. Her secret is safe with me. She should be safe from Eldon's retribution if that's what he intended. I guess he gave specific orders to her, none of which included my knowledge of this matter."

While they awaited the doctors' arrival, Margaret and Brigid tended to Thelma, trying to make the silent girl more comfortable, at least.

It wasn't too long before a tentative knock came at the door, and Brigid opened it to Dr. Matthews and an anxious Fiona, who hovered in the doorway. "I'll just wait out back," Fiona said, worriedly glancing at the bed.

"Just a moment, please, Finn." Margaret turned to address the doctor. "Anything the child needs, please see to it. Brigid will take any direction required of you. If you need anything else not available in your bag or the house, I'll send Finn for it. If she needs to go to the hospital, we'll take care of that, too." Grasping Fiona by the elbow, Margaret left the room and closed the door behind them. "We need to talk," Margaret said firmly. She could feel Fiona tense beneath her grip.

If the situation wasn't as tense and wrong as it was, Margaret would be grinning from ear to ear at the knowledge she wasn't losing her mind. She wasn't falling for a mere boy, but a young woman. One more innocent in nature than a street child from an abusive home should be. Again, her heart did a flip. Maybe she was more aware of the darker side of life than Margaret believed of her. Fiona was softened by her compassion, not necessarily weakened by it.

Once outside, Margaret noticed dusk had fallen. Practically dragging Fiona toward the back yard, Margaret kept walking until she reached a stand of trees at the back, which worked as a property divider. It also had a stone bench behind the oldest and thickest tree, one she often used to relax and think. Margaret knew no one watching from any of the windows would be able to see them, and with night falling, it would be more impossible. She lightly pressed Fiona onto the bench.

"Damn, Finn, you should have told me," Margaret said. She decided it probably best to help maintain the charade by using Fiona's alias. No sense in making the charade more precarious by a slip of pronoun that could be overheard.

Fiona blinked in bewilderment. "About what my boss did? How I didn't do anything to help, even knowing what happened to Thelma?" Apparently, guilt riddled Fiona.

Margaret suspected Fiona understood exactly to what she referred. However, what caught her attention was the way she worded the question. "Why didn't you call him my brother, or speak of him by name?" Turning away, Fiona shrugged. Then, Margaret understood. Placing a hand on Fiona's thigh, she said, "Thank you, for trying to temper words to protect me. You have to be the sweetest person I know. And I'm glad you're not an Ethel." Fiona gave a grunt to her reference for an effeminate male. "Please, Finn, look at me," she said, placing a hand under Fiona's chin and turning her head until they faced. Margaret noticed fresh tears in Fiona's eyes. The compassion and guilt she saw in the light brown eyes were nearly her undoing. Glimpsing the gravity of Fiona's emotions, Margaret felt a pull on her own. She shivered at the intensity of her attraction to this simple, yet complex, woman.

"I should get you back into the house," Fiona whispered, mistaking her physical reaction as from cold. Neither moved. Did she feel the same warmth of attraction, the same comfort in their physical contact? Margaret hoped so. Since the moment in the alley, Margaret hadn't been able to get Finn out of her head, her body heating at the mental images of her memory, of the subsequent fantasies. Fantasies exciting and nauseating her simultaneously, truth be known.

"In a moment, please." Margaret felt she could drown in the honey-gold depths of Fiona's eyes; get lost in the incredible swirl of emotions there. Before she could think better of the action, Margaret lightly caressed Fiona's cheek, then leaned forward and kissed her expressive, full lips. The contact was as if a flash fire had consumed her. One of them moaned, though Margaret couldn't tell whom. She wanted more, and deepened the kiss; suddenly feeling starved and craving a taste of every morsel she could get.

Fiona pulled away, breathing heavily. Now, her expression showed remorse, shame. "I'm sorry. I shouldn't have done that."

Attempting to get her own breath under control, Margaret

gave a soft laugh. "Shouldn't have turned my insides to mush giving me the best kiss of my life?" She intended to make Fiona feel better with a quick peck on the lips. The feelings invoked by Fiona's returned kiss were like being zapped by electricity.

"I shouldn't have kissed you at all," Fiona said, barely above a whisper.

"Finn, I kissed you. You've nothing for which to be sorry. And honestly, if I had known you weren't a boy before today, I'd have done it sooner."

Frowning, Fiona shook her head. "But you're a girl, and I'm a girl."

Margaret waggled her eyebrows. "That kiss was from no girl I ever knew."

"I know it's not right, not normal." Her voice lowered to a whisper. "We could be sent to jail." She paused. "Or worse."

Clasping Fiona's hands in her own, Margaret stared her right in the eyes. "Finn, honey, that kiss was the most 'right' thing to happen to me in a very long time. It may not be acceptable to some people, but the kiss wasn't wrong in any way. And only we know." A horrible thought occurred to Margaret, more frightening than the threat of jail or the sanatorium. Just because she was attracted to Fiona, didn't mean she returned the feelings, even if she dressed as a boy. With an awkward smile, Margaret added, "The only thing not right was my taking advantage of you. Guess it must be a Graham thing. I'm sorry. I hope you'll forgive my behavior. I just—"

Placing a trembling finger to Margaret's lips, Fiona said, "I'm sorry if I'm a knucklehead. The last time I kissed—" Fiona exhaled a long breath. Margaret decided to leave the story for another time so didn't encourage Fiona to finish the thought. "Right or wrong, I've wanted to kiss you since I saw you in the alley. Thank you. And, for the future, don't ever categorize yourself with your brother. You're nothing like him." Standing, Fiona gazed down at her nervously. "This isn't safe. Eldon or Jimmy, anyone could find us. I won't see you hurt. Right now, I need to be ready to take the doctor home." Her brow furrowed. "Or maybe the hospital."

"Yes, you're right. I'm glad one of us is thinking logically." Margaret rose and linked her arm through Fiona's. "We'll finish this discussion later. Let's go get an update on Thelma." As they slowly walked back to the house, Margaret shared what she had told Eldon about the conversation Finn allegedly told her about Thelma's presence. "After you return Dr. Matthews home, you'll need to come back here and report to Eldon in his office."

"Earlier, how'd you know I was at the house? Or what

possessed you to go to the servant quarters?" Fiona asked quietly.

"Because, since you started working for Eldon, I watch for you. I'm pining away for a mere boy, which confused me no end." Margaret shrugged. "Yes, I know, pretty childish."

"I think it's cute." Fiona promptly flushed bright red at the admission. Oh, Fiona got more adorable with every moment. Margaret knew she had to keep an eye on this one.

Margaret stopped. "Gosh, I never asked you. How old are you really?"

Fiona gave such a dazzling smile, Margaret thought she'd melt into a huge puddle of something warm and icky. "Well, Finn is about seventeen. Fiona, however, is twenty-three today."

"It's your birthday? Why didn't you say anything?"

"Because it's not important."

They started walking again. "I need to give you a gift."

When the arm Margaret held quivered, she glanced up to find Fiona chuckling. "I thought you just did, under the tree."

Chapter Ten

IF FIONA HAD been a couple minutes faster, she might have been gone before Eldon made another immediate-presence-required request. She squeezed her eyes shut, silently praying this invitation didn't involve watching a man killed or another rape of a child. This time, her arrival didn't have her cooling her heels forever either, as Stan stood up as soon as she arrived, opened Eldon's office door, and announced her.

"Ah, Finn, come in, kid, and have a seat," Eldon said.

"Everything okay, sir?" Fiona asked. She hated much of what Eldon did, but Fiona wasn't ready to give up the money—or Margaret.

"You're a smart kid, Finn."

"Thank you." Fiona frowned. Was a "but" coming? The other shoe ready to drop? Compliments from Eldon usually ended badly for the recipient of the praise. "I miss something, and you're calling me on it?"

Eldon shook his head. "What do you know of my business?"

Like that wasn't a loaded question. Fiona could play stupid and lose her job for being an idiot; or, could tell him the truth and know too much to continue breathing regularly. She figured playing dumb would be least likely to ingratiate herself with Eldon Graham. "See you got some mighty fine restaurants and nightclubs, but don't see the blind tigers. See you own a couple tenements and hotels, but didn't notice if they were panel houses and brothels."

Fiona suspected one of the panel houses was where Eldon intended to send Thelma. She was young and small, so would be perfect for hiding in the panels to pick the pockets of those otherwise occupied with the prostitutes. Much as it disgusted her, Fiona knew some men liked kids—boys and girls. She'd bring a high price, kids always did. Eventually, Thelma would get too big, and she'd be the one occupying the men. "I see you are important and an upstanding businessman, but don't hear a word when folks call you mobster. Sir." Fiona added the last for good measure. Politeness sometimes came in handy when the alternative was getting what Terry got—dead.

"You have a lot of spunk, Finn. I like that."

"And I thank you, again, Eldon," she said, hoping her voice

didn't betray how nervous she was getting. "There a point to this chat?"

"Again, you're very astute." Eldon stood and peered out the window. "There are folks who'd be concerned with all you can't see. I, on the other hand, am grateful for your poor eyesight. Need people I can trust, kid, and so far you fit the bill." He turned and regarded her for a moment. "I'd like to add to your duties, such as run a few errands I only want us—as in you and me—to know about. I'll amply compensate you for these tasks, of course. There's no need for us to involve Jimmy and mention any of these extra duties. Think you can do that?"

Fiona pursed her lips as if considering. "So you're asking me to run some errands." Eldon nodded. "This is between you and me, and Jimmy can go hang himself?"

Eldon chuckled. "Ah, I think we understand each other perfectly. Can you keep Jimmy out of these particular transactions, no matter if he becomes persistent?"

"You and me are jake, boss. I don't owe Jimmy nothin'. Plus, I get persistent from my old man. I can take it." He stared at her for so long Fiona thought she'd overstepped her attitude against Jimmy. Jimmy was Eldon's business partner after all.

"Yes, I'm betting you can, Finn." Eldon returned to his desk.

Fiona, assuming herself dismissed, shoved her hands into her trouser pockets, and headed for the door. Since she was about to do a big favor for Eldon, and he seemed a bit at odds with Jimmy, Fiona turned back to him and asked, "Um, Eldon." He glanced up at her. "I know you don't owe me anything, but, well, can I ask a boon here?"

Eldon frowned. "What is it, Finn?"

Fiona swallowed hard to clear the lump of fear lodged there, hoping she wasn't about to lose all the ground she'd apparently gained with Eldon. What she really wanted to do was to loosen the tie currently strangling her with her unease. But she needed to do this, as options weren't too plentiful on some matters. This matter was very important to her. "It's about Thelma, sir. Miss Margaret has taken a liking to her, and the kid's become kinda like a mission for her—and for me since Miss Margaret believes the line I gave her. I couldn't have her mad at her own brother, could I?"

Fiona decided to lay all blame at Jimmy's feet. Maybe that would make his decision easier. Bringing up Eldon's own participation would be suicidal for her and Thelma. "Well, could you keep Jimmy away from her, let her stay at the house? I'll pay for any extras she needs. Just don't wanna see her hurt, ya know? Thelma ain't got nobody but us, and she's just such—" A helpless child, Fiona wanted to scream at him. You and her parents have brutally ripped innocence from her.

"Yes, I know." Eldon walked back to the window, this time giving her his back. "I'd rather Margaret never find out the truth, where the child is concerned, or about the brothels. All right, Finn?"

"She won't hear anything from me." Guess it's okay if Margaret knows about the gin joints, Fiona deduced.

"That's good." Eldon turned to face Fiona, his expression cold, deadly. "Neither Jimmy nor I will touch her as long as Thelma keeps her mouth shut. Otherwise, all bets are off, Finn. Understand?"

Fiona recognized the moral issues she broke, making the decision for Thelma, but she couldn't let Eldon or Jimmy near her. Eldon could make the kid—and her—disappear in a heartbeat and painfully. At least Fiona, with Margaret's help, could better keep Thelma safe until other options opened. "Yeah, I understand."

"Good. See Stan on your way out," Eldon said. "Let's get our new arrangement started."

Fiona bent her head in acknowledgment and left, closing the door behind her. I might as well become a pig farmer, she thought bitterly, with all the shit I keep walking through.

Chapter Eleven

FIONA'S AWKWARD GRIP on the three oblong dress boxes was slipping as she made her way to the clubs' dressing room at the far end of the basement speakeasy under *The Fisher's Net*. The club itself was referred to as *Fishing Favors*. Luck was with her. The door was slightly ajar, and a thrust of her hip into the door nudged it open.

"Finn," Molly said, darting forward and removing the top box. "How are you?" Her question punctuated with a kiss to Fiona's left cheek.

"I have new costumes," Fiona said, hoping her blush would be mistaken for the flush of exertion.

"Ever the hero, Finn," Dorcas said kissing Fiona's right cheek.

Movement from the end of the row of make-up stations turned Fiona's gaze. The club's main headliner, Fatima, sat shaking her beautifully coiffed red-brown head. Fatima stood at six-foot, had an athletic frame, and long thin fingers and a smattering of freckles. "This is why I'm glad to be a man during the day," Fatima said. Fatima could sing the blues like no other in amazing and sultry tones. Too many times Fiona had nearly cried, along with a captivated audience, while listening to her sing. Of course, their first meeting a couple weeks earlier had been a bit of a surprise.

Delivering the weekly boxes of costumes from the dressmaker, Fiona caught a handsome man in the process of unbuckling his trouser belt, standing at Fatima's station.

"You should stop right there and leave," Fiona announced in her firmest voice.

"And miss further chances in shocking you?" the man said, and then pursed his lips in a mock pout.

Shock her he did. Fiona recognized Fatima's voice coming from the male lips. "I don't understand."

He stepped forward and extended his hand. "Frank Galloway, a mortician by day, and Fatima, the club singer extraordinaire by night." He flashed a genuine smile. "Can't be too shocked, Finn, since you know all about disguises."

Still, it was hard not to be surprised. Fiona knew his last statement should worry her, but decided to table it for now. After all, Frank probably didn't want his secret revealed to too many, either. "Guess what confuses me is how that amazing voice comes out of you, and how you can become so gorgeous."

Frank laughed. "Oh, the girls are right. You are wonderfully adorable."

Fiona and Fatima had spent many a night, since then, in relaxed conversations and teasing Dorcas and Molly about their performances every chance they found.

"So Finn," Molly said, dropping her box on the station behind her. Fiona dropped the other two on top, stepped back, and pulled her Newsboy from her head, stuffing the cap in her pocket. "The Undertaker is having one of her to-die-for parties tonight. Come with us. It's in a safe location," she added in a whisper. "We can be who we are without recrimination and retaliation."

"The Undertaker?" Fiona asked. She shivered at the image the name brought. And she again felt the jolt of fear. Others saw through her male disguise. Had she over-played her hand for too long?

"My sister Siobhan," Fatima said, pursing blood red lips. "Her transformation makes mine look like a six-year-old playing dress-up in mommy's closet." She turned to Dorcas and Molly. "Be careful not to insult Finn, either. Just because she dresses as a male to survive this city doesn't mean she's of a like mind as you two." Fiona thought she caught a slight tremor in Fatima's voice. She realized they shared her fears of detection in that area. It confirmed Fiona's disguise hadn't fooled them.

Dorcas flushed and her expression one of horror. "We never meant to insult you with our assumptions."

"Shit. Please don't let our mistake make you think less of us," Molly said, tears building in her eyes. "Are you gonna turn us in?"

Three frightened faces waited for her reply. Fiona shook her head vehemently. "No, of course not, you're my friends. But I have to ask—"

From the hall came the loud clang of a metal bucket hitting the floor. They all turned toward the partially open door where Margaret had a fist raised to knock on the door, her gaze diverted down the hall toward the noise.

"Miss Margaret," Fiona said, breaking the stunned silence.

Looking embarrassed, Margaret said, "I'm sorry I interrupted, Finn. I can wait for you in Eldon's office upstairs."

"Was I supposed to take you somewhere?" Fiona asked. Had someone forgotten to let her know there was a change in her day's duties?

"No, Finn, you're fine. I was with Eldon today, and Jimmy called him with a problem." She shrugged. "So he asked me to wait around. I'm sorry to interrupt. I heard your voice, and wanted to see a friendly face."

"You're fine." Fiona waved her inside, even as she stepped toward her and placed a hand to her elbow, feeling the sappy grin plastered on her face. She gently kicked the door closed. "Come meet my friends," she said. It had been a long time since Fiona had been able to say that about anyone besides Claire and Ian, and it felt incredible.

MARGARET STARED UNCOMFORTABLY at the four people focused on her. She assumed the dropped bucket was a cue from someone to alert them of her presence. Margaret heard part of the conversation and become curious; choosing to announce herself because she missed Fiona and wanted to spend every minute she could with her. She nearly regretted her actions because of the stares from the other three in the room. That is until Fiona looked at her with such joy written on her own face.

"You remember Dorcas and Molly," Fiona said, pointing at each one respectively. "This," Fiona said, stopping in front of the gorgeous woman, "is Fatima. Her singing voice will bring tears to your eyes."

Fatima smirked at Finn before extending her hand to Margaret. "In a good way, I hope you meant."

Fiona blushed. "You know I did."

Margaret shook her hand, noting the telltale gentling of the grip in return. "It's a pleasure. I'm sorry for interrupting. Please continue with whatever you were discussing." They grew quiet as if no one dared talk first, or continue with the original topic. Margaret wanted to say it was okay, but she'd be alerting them she'd heard more than they believed.

Apparently sensing the crux of the matter, Fiona said, "She knows about me too. I trust her unquestionably." Margaret could almost hear the tension lessen from them, like static leaving. She literally held their lives in her hands. No matter what she said, Margaret was the unknown factor who could turn on them. Fiona's word alleviated their hesitation.

Dorcas overtly glanced from Margaret to Fiona. To no one in particular, she said, "That answers one question. Finn is like us."

"I beg to differ," Fatima announced, draping herself over the nearest chair. "You can't use 'us' as we don't know about Miss Graham." She pointed one finely manicured hand at her own chest. "I happen to like women." Her face scrunched in consternation. "Okay, not the point I was going for." It wasn't until then Margaret recognized what Fatima admitted. With effort, Margaret hid her astonishment.

Molly gave Fatima a kindly slap on her shoulder. "Good thing we understood you. Men are safe from Fatima's siren spell." Her gaze targeted Fiona, and she took one of Fiona's hands in hers. Margaret felt a stab of jealousy at their physical contact. It's not as if Fiona belongs solely to you, Margaret chided herself. "The party starts at midnight. Come with us. We can leave from here after the show."

Fiona shook her head. "Maybe another time, ladies, if future invitations are opened to me."

Margaret sensed Fiona's distress. Her posture suggested she was beaten. "What's wrong, Finn?" she asked, keeping her male name. It made the chance for mistakes easier.

Fiona yanked her cap from her pocket and plunked it on her head, a delaying tactic Fiona used to extend her thinking time. Shaking her head, Fiona said, "What gives me away? I had it down for so long."

Dorcas said, "Oh, Finn. Most aren't gonna notice without really looking."

"Which most people just don't do," Molly added. "For me, it was the softness of your cheek when we teased you that day delivering supplies. A teenaged boy's skin should be getting course, as peach fuzz gives way to whiskers."

Margaret felt Fatima's gaze on her, studying. Her own reason for knowing Fiona's secret was because of eavesdropping, but she didn't believe she should share that tidbit. After what felt like an eternity beneath the Fatima mental microscope, she released Margaret. Fatima stood with sensuous fluidity. Margaret was in awe. She wished herself half as graceful. Fatima pulled Fiona into a tight hug, and the stab of jealousy reasserted itself—and she needn't with Fatima. She realized Fatima whispered something to Fiona. After a moment they separated. Fatima patted a non-existent lock of hair back into place.

"Well ladies, as fun as this is, I'm going to work the crowd before my first set." Fatima walked to the door blowing air kisses. "Tah, tah, ladies." She opened the door and shook her head. "Watch yourself, Finn, these women are dangerous." A pause. "And inexhaustible."

Margaret decided she truly liked Fatima. She also wondered—and worried—what Fatima shared with Fiona that couldn't be shared with the rest of the room.

Chapter Twelve

MARGARET ENJOYED FATIMA'S performance from the back of the *The Fisher's Net* restaurant. Drinks appeared to be flowing freely in the guise of tea, she assumed in the case of a raid, but even the inebriated stopped to listen to Fatima. Margaret stood quietly in the doorway leading to the office, kitchen, and dressing room. Margaret's awe of Fatima increased after her performance. All too soon, Fatima finished her set to resounding applause as she exited the stage, replaced by scantily clad dancing girls, which included Molly and Dorcas.

As Margaret watched the dancer's exposing silken white expanses of their legs, she couldn't help but wonder about Fiona's legs, imagining them bared under low lighting. Her focus on Fiona was more intense since her moments of jealousy earlier, in the dressing room. Viewing the scantily clad woman had her mind wanting to know what all of Fiona looked like under her male guise. Speculation must work like a magnet. Margaret had barely completed the thought when Fiona stopped behind her. Since learning the truth of her gender, Margaret couldn't seem to get intimate fantasies of Fiona out of her head. The longer Fiona worked for Eldon, Margaret managed to wheedle moments, a lunch here, an errand there, to spend with her. On the rarer occasions, Margaret and Fiona managed a few discreet touches and kisses. Luck was with Margaret, and Eldon had been accommodating for the most part.

"What'a'ya thinking, I wonder," Fiona whispered close to Margaret's ear, "staring through the door's crack?" Her husky tones had the power to ignite Margaret's insides in ways she never believed possible — before Fiona.

Margaret felt a firm hand rest upon her hip, moving slowly up her waist, grazing alongside the swell of the breast before grasping the doorframe. Margaret smiled to herself. Their stolen moments appeared to have emboldened Fiona. Her own voice was a breathy whisper when she replied, "Possibilities."

"Care to expound?" Fiona asked, her other hand gently perched on Margaret's outside hip. The warmth of Fiona's breath against her neck sent a shiver through Margaret. She gave a short chuckle, and ready to reply when Fiona's body heat suddenly disappeared, accompanied by a noticeable and sharp intake of breath.

When Margaret turned around, Eldon stood over Fiona as she

massaged the back of her head where it slammed into the wall, before sliding to the floor. "Watch your hands, boy," Eldon snarled.

"Sorry, sir," Fiona apologized, slowly getting to her feet, after retrieving her Newsboy from where it had fallen during the assault.

Eldon spun to stare at her, "And you, Babs. You wouldn't be all flushed and flustered if you'd quit peeking at the entertainment."

Margaret didn't dispute his misunderstanding of what had caused her face to heat. Instead, she said, "You're right of course. Finn said the same thing when he tried to pull me from the door – right before you attacked him." Margaret closed the door all the way. She moved closer to Eldon, noting he did not intend to apologize for his actions. "Are we ready to go home? Should I get a taxi?"

He shook his head. "I've got some unplanned business that will take me a little while longer." Eldon kissed the top of her head. "I've got to do it, it's important." Tossing his chin, and then his keys, in Fiona's direction, he said, "Finn, take Babs home. Stay at the house until I get there. Use my car, not the truck."

Her face turning red, Fiona stared at her feet as she shuffled from one to the other. "That's not a good idea, Boss. What if I scratch it?"

Reaching over, Eldon grabbed Fiona's tie and tugged until she swayed, pressed flush against him. He lowered his head until their forehead's touched. Because she was mere inches away, Margaret heard his whispered threat. "You scratch my car, I slap you around. If you lose merchandise from one of my trucks, I bloody you. Let someone hurt Babs, and I kill you. We understand how my priorities work?"

"Yes, sir."

Eldon pulled a white handkerchief from his suit pocket and handed it to Fiona. "Damn it, kid. You manage to keep your clothes clean. What is it about managing the habits of soap and water that alludes you?"

"I'll do better, sir," Fiona said, taking the handkerchief from him and swiping it ineffectually at her cheek.

"Good kid," he said, gently pushing her back and tousling her hair. "Now get Babs home. Stay with her, so she's safe. Don't leave even if Jimmy tells you it's all right. You go when I tell you to leave." As Eldon walked away, Margaret heard him mumble, "Jimmy with my sister is at the top of my 'don't trust' list." Margaret wondered if Eldon would finally reject Jimmy's proposal.

OUTSIDE, THE NIGHT air was cool, and the stars shone brightly. Reaching the car, Fiona gallantly opened and closed the door for her. Margaret was glad the evening had turned out this way, and she had a few moments alone, hopefully without possible interruption, with Fiona. "How's your head?" she asked.

"Full a' rocks," Fiona said. "I shouldn't have taken liberties, so I deserved it. Think Eldon's gonna make me pay for holes my hard head put on his wall?"

Despite herself, Margaret laughed at Fiona's feigned expression of horror at the question. "Really, Fiona, are you all right? He tossed you pretty hard."

"Yeah, I'm fine." Fiona flashed one of her disarming smiles. "Are you offering to kiss my boo-boo, Miss Graham, if I say I'm not okay?" Margaret adored this playful side of Fiona, which could heat her blood in an instant.

"If all you're offering is to be kissed, I'll take it. You didn't take any liberties, you know. I enjoy your touch. Even in passing." Margaret scooted closer to Fiona on the car's seat. Another positive of their time together being Fiona seemed more relaxed with her innuendo, and often returned repartee as good as she got. "I know we might have Eldon's people following, but can we take a longer way home?"

"Might not just be Eldon's men, Margaret," Fiona said seriously. "Don't trust Jimmy not to have someone following you too. And worse, I wouldn't put it past other—" She paused and frowned.

"Businessmen?" Margaret supplied with a quirked eyebrow.

Fiona laughed, and immediately Margaret's insides warmed at the sound. "Yeah, businessmen. Okay, sure, I'd like to extend this ride. Just so you know, if I think we're being followed, I gotta take you directly home, so you'll be safe."

Margaret placed a hand on Fiona's thigh. "I understand." And she did. Jimmy's interest bordered on obsessive and Margaret wished the topic one she could bring up with Eldon. Because of this, Eldon put more care into her safety, causing her to fear if it would only push Jimmy to do something rash.

Tonight was a great night for driving. This night made special because Margaret actually liked the company she was in. Fiona was silent except for the occasional note of the surrounding points she thought Margaret might find of interest. Driving by the Bay, Margaret, amazed by the city lights reflecting off the water, likened the sight to floating stardust. Startled by the realization had her wondering why she should be amazed. She'd seen this view plenty of times with Eldon and her parents. Glancing at Fiona, Margaret realized sharing this with Fiona is what made it so wonderful, vowing to always keep this time in her mental memory book.

An odd but familiar noise broke into her thoughts. Margaret glanced at Fiona's quickly reddening face and understood the cause. "Finn, did you eat today?"

"Um, think I had an apple before work. Been a busy day."

"Take me straight home," Margaret said, her tone terser than intended.

"Are you mad at me? 'Cause I'm hungry?" Fiona asked. Her expression showed alarm, however, not enough to cause her to disobey the command.

"Fiona, we were at the nightclub and could have had dinner together there. Heck, we could have stopped any number of places for food."

"No, we couldn't have, Margaret," Fiona said, weariness in her tone.

"If it's about money—"

"That's not it, not exactly." Fiona nearly snarled the words.

"I'm sorry, Fiona. I didn't mean to offend you. Honest." Margaret took a deep breath to regroup her thoughts and words. "I worry about you because you work for my brother and are around Jimmy. Worry about women who want to wheedle kisses and favors." Women who can touch you so freely, where I can't, she thought. "It isn't safe for a man, let alone a woman pretending to be a boy."

"I can handle myself." Fiona stiffened and pointed her chin toward the car's window. "We're here." She stopped Eldon's car on the drive beside the kitchen, light still burned inside, and Fiona turned off the ignition. They sat in silence for what seemed an eternity to Margaret, neither opening their doors.

Margaret knew she'd offended Fiona, no matter it was unintended. "Fiona, look at me," she said, cupping Fiona's cheek and gently turning Fiona's until they faced each other. Fiona did raise her gaze to meet Margaret's. "I didn't mean to be insulting about money. I know you don't want to be indebted to anyone, and can earn your own way. But, it's the only reason I see for you not wanting to be seen with me. Do I embarrass you?"

Fiona snorted. "For a college gal, you can be dense. I'd be proud to be seen with you, to spend time with you. But you see me, Fiona, who's pleased as punch by your attention. Everyone else will see a dirty waif you took pity on. And charming as the thought is in response to your compassion, those same people won't want that boy eating in the same room as them. Doing your Christian duty is one thing to your peers; however, they don't want to watch it playing out in front of them."

Bam. She hit that nail on the head. "My God, you're right," Margaret said. Knowing Fiona's gender, Margaret could easily see beyond the façade. She thought of Fiona as a friend — someday hopefully more — so much so Margaret forgot she was supposed to see a filthy street urchin. That gaffe could be dangerous for Fiona if Margaret ever slipped up. "I'm sorry, Fiona. Someday, this will be moot. Until then, I realize I need to be more careful, for your sake."

"And for your own sake, Margaret, as I don't think Eldon or Jimmy would be even a little amused if they found out you knew the truth and kept it from them. They wouldn't be too happy with the obvious evidence of you crushing on a mere young slum rat." Fiona's voice cracked when she said, "I don't think I could bear it if anything bad happened to you."

Margaret, too, would be devastated if anything happened to Fiona, especially if it were from her own carelessness. Fiona's stomach growled again, and Margaret laughed. After a brief hesitation, Fiona joined her. "We don't have to worry about Eldon, Jimmy, or even Lorraine coming home for a while yet. Today's Mrs. Baumann's cooking day, so the larder will be bursting with goodies. Come on," Margaret said, tugging Fiona out through the passenger door and into the comforting warmth of the kitchen, her favorite room in the whole house. "Sit there," she said, pointing to the tall stool at the marble island between the stove and Frigidaire. Fiona promptly sat after hooking her cap on the chair's ear.

"Who's in my kitchen?" boomed a voice from down the servant quarters hall.

Margaret smiled, and hollered back, "The biggest snack raider in this whole household. This time, I brought help."

Mrs. Baumann was a husky and buxom six-foot woman, with grey-blonde hair whose appearance portrayed cruel, but Margaret knew her to have the gentlest heart. Entering close behind were Brigid and Thelma. Thelma rushed forward and grasped Fiona in a tight bear hug the second she caught sight of Fiona, which Fiona immediately returned with enthusiasm. Thelma, who shared she was nearly fifteen, still barely spoke, but always asked after Fiona during her extended absences. "Well, I hope the back door is secured," Mrs. Baumann boomed. She pointed to Fiona. "This boy's sure to blow away with even a gentle wind. Doesn't anyone feed you?" she asked of Fiona.

"They try, Ma'am, but I'm kinda hard to wrangle," Fiona said. She pulled out the chair beside her and settled a blushing Thelma into it. Margaret wondered if Fiona was aware of the adoration Thelma felt for her. Fiona's tummy growled again, and

Margaret enjoyed the giggle Thelma gave. It was slow going, but the young girl showed signs of healing little by little physically, and emotionally. "I appear to have successfully avoided the lasso today as well."

With a grunt, Mrs. Baumann flung the icebox door open, pulled a fried chicken leg free, and waved it under Fiona's nose. "Gnaw on this until I rustle up something more substantial for you." Returning to the icebox, she pulled out eggs, milk, and other items, placing them on the counter.

"Oh, Finn, you're about to get the most incredible, melt-in-your-mouth, omelet in the entire world," Margaret said enthusiastically.

"This is a special occasion, Maggie dear. We're all having omelets and getting acquainted. You get to assist," Mrs. Baumann said, handing her the whisk. Then, she flashed a scowl at Fiona, who held the chicken leg as if it were foreign to her. "Do I have to force that down your throat?" Fiona shook her head and bit into the meat with exaggerated gusto, which made Thelma giggle again.

Before long, multiple omelets were cooked and consumed, laughter and conversation shared, Brigid and Margaret helping with the clean up when everyone had their fill of food. Fiona and Thelma sat quietly at the counter. As she finished drying and returning the last of the dishes, Margaret heard their whispered conversation, watching their interaction with interest.

Fiona asked, "Are you doing well, Thelma?" Thelma scrunched her face. "What's wrong?"

"Don't like my name."

Nodding, Fiona said, "You have a new life, could have a new name. Gimme a minute to think of something, okay? Is Miss Margaret teaching you your lessons?" Thelma nodded. "You're good for her?" Another nod. "Anything you need you'll tell me, right? I'm gonna take care of you from now on." This last remark brought such a beaming grin, and Fiona responded in kind. Margaret smiled too as she realized Fiona was a natural at putting people at ease. "That's it," Fiona said. "I'm calling you Sunny 'cause your smile is bright and warm."

Brigid and Mrs. Baumann stood leaning on the island counter. Margaret returned to her seat beside Fiona, and said, "Finn's right, honey, Sunny suits you."

Tears in her eyes, Thelma flung her arms around Fiona's shoulders and cried. Fiona rubbed little circles across Thelma's back. "Hush, honey, there's no need for crying."

Brigid saved them from further emotions. Placing her hands on Thelma's shoulders, she said, "It's late, Sunny, we need to get you to bed. Good night, everyone." Thelma let Brigid lead her away.

"That should be my cue, also." Mrs. Baumann straightened and gave Margaret a hug. "I'll see you next week, Maggie. If you need anything, you get hold of me." She flicked a glance in Fiona's direction. "But I think you're in pretty good hands."

"Do we need to drive you home?" Fiona asked.

"No, thank you, Finn. My son will be along any moment."

"Thank you, Mrs. Baumann, for a wonderful meal," Fiona said. "It was appreciated."

"Oh, dear Finn," Mrs. Baumann said with a quick caress to Fiona's cheek. "Not as appreciated as meeting you and Thelma." Just then, a knock sounded on the kitchen door. "See, my ride has arrived."

After Mrs. Baumann had left, Margaret took Fiona's hand and led her through the house and up to the second floor. To the left of the landing, Margaret opened the door to her room. "This is mine," she said to Fiona. She pointed to a padded armchair at the end of the hall. "Bring that over, and you can relax out here." Fiona released her hand and brought the chair just to the left of the doorway. Margaret considered inviting Fiona into her room, but couldn't take chances of discovery, either awake or innocently asleep, by Eldon. As it was, Margaret knew she'd sleep better knowing Fiona was near. On the other hand, it could have the opposite effect and with Fiona so near keep her sleepless.

Margaret moved close to Fiona, taking her hand again. "What you're doing for Thelma—"

"Sunny," Fiona corrected. "She's earned herself a new beginning."

"Yes, she has. But that's not all you're doing for her, is it?" Fiona stared at her, confused. "Eldon thought I'd be as amused as he by your offer to feed, clothe, and pay for her boarding."

"And keep Jimmy away from her." Fiona gnashed her teeth. "I'm glad I can provide entertainment for the Graham household, Margaret."

Margaret placed a finger to Fiona's lips. "Hush. I wasn't laughing at you. I know Sunny's safety and protection are important to you. I hope you know how important it is to me, too."

"Is Eldon gonna back down on our deal?"

"I don't know what deal you have, and can only pray you're careful about whatever it is on your side of the bargain. Brigid and I don't leave Sunny alone, so she's safe from Jimmy. Same goes for Mrs. Baumann, when she's here."

"I mean to keep her safe."

"I believe you, but you need to understand something. If this is only about some attempt to assuage any misguided guilt you feel, you aren't doing either of you any favors. I know guilt is a small factor behind your actions, and you truly want this safety net for Sunny." Margaret pressed herself against Fiona, wrapping one palm on the back of Fiona's neck. The tingling rush of warmth consumed her. If she didn't say her goodnights and put a closed door between them, Margaret was going to do something they could both regret later. "Your compassion is one of the things I adore about you."

Margaret pulled Fiona's head closer and jammed her lips against Fiona's. When the kiss deepened, and she felt the familiar wetness between her legs, Margaret regrettably dragged her lips from Fiona's and sighed. "One day, Fiona, I'm going to take full advantage of you." Having said that, Margaret entered her bedroom and softly closed the door between them. Shaking, Margaret leaned against the hard wood, trying to get her breathing under control. How was it possible for Fiona to get her wet with just a kiss?

From the hall, as Fiona also leaned against the door, she heard Fiona's husky whisper, which Margaret expected would cause her to remain awake most the night. "One day I'll let you."

Chapter Thirteen

FIONA DOZED IN the chair outside Margaret's room. A beat of heels on the marble floor of the entryway, which could only be Lorraine, startled her awake. She sat up and rubbed her tired muscles strained from the awkward sleeping position. She prepared for the inevitable confrontation. Lorraine had an issue with Finn since the morning in the kitchen when Finn ignored Lorraine's flirting. Fiona didn't mind the distance between them. Maybe her lack of bowing and groveling at Lorraine's feet held more an effect than should be normal. Fiona doubted many males dismissed Lorraine to pay attention to Margaret. The situation probably irked Lorraine in the worst possible way. She leaned forward, elbows on knees, waiting for Lorraine to top the stairs. Lorraine vainly tried to hide her inebriation.

When their eyes met, Lorraine smirked. "Babysitting?" She sidled over toward the chair, swung a hip to the side and nearly toppled over, before barely steadying herself.

Ignoring the question, Fiona stood, wanting to be on her feet for any possible confrontation. The smell of alcohol was strong, and she wondered how Lorraine had managed to get home in one piece. With more speed than Fiona believed a drunkard could muster, Lorraine reached out and cupped the back of Fiona's head, jerking on Fiona until their bodies were flush. "How about you let a grown woman teach you about being a man?"

Reacting automatically, Fiona pushed Lorraine an extended arm's length away. "Don't need anyone to teach me anything, and especially not coming from you." Fiona took a step backward, which only resulted in pinning herself against the wall. She knew the situation could turn ugly, probably would, and didn't want any ruckus to wake Margaret. Grasping Lorraine's elbow with more force than necessary, Fiona practically dragged the woman to the closed bedroom doors off on the right. "Which one is yours, Lorraine?"

"Knew you couldn't resist," Lorraine slurred. She walked to the last door on the right at the end of the hall, then spun around and clutched at Fiona's tie. "There's a fire in you, Finn. I see it in your eyes. You'd treat a woman right. Is your daddy the one to teach you that?"

Fiona jerked her tie from Lorraine's hand. No way could

Quinn Cavanaugh teach her something he had no concept of himself. "If I had been remotely interested, Lorraine, you just killed the moment by bringing up that bastard."

"Yeah, some daddies aren't good at proper lessons." A flash of pain, quickly hidden again, sparked in Lorraine's eyes. "Come on kid. A gal gets lonely having to entertain herself at night." Lorraine gave an exaggerated pout of her red lips. "If you're worried about miss goody-two-shoes, I promise not to tell and ruin your reputation. It's obvious you're sweet on her. I can be, and have been, discreet."

"Discretion isn't necessary, I'm not interested." Fiona found herself mildly curious about the issue from the past Lorraine referred to, but didn't wish to address the matter. It might result in encouraging her. "As for liking Miss Margaret, yes, I do. But it's not like that."

"Of course not." Lorraine snickered.

"Please, Lorraine," Fiona said, "you should get some sleep. I'm sure Eldon will be home any moment now." As if the name conjured an appearance, Fiona heard the front door open, and then slam shut. "There you go, Eldon's home. Now I can get to my home before work starts."

Only Eldon wasn't the one who walked up to the second-floor landing, glaring nastily at them. Jimmy? Fiona knew—expected—Eldon's second in command to spend a lot of time at the house, but didn't expect to see him in the house this late. Was that why Eldon had told her to stay until he got home? Did Eldon suspect and worry for Margaret's personal safety?

"What the hell's going on?" Jimmy asked in an overloud voice. If Fiona didn't know better, she'd think Jimmy had caught his wife with another man. An odd reaction since Lorraine was Eldon's girlfriend.

"Nothing, Jimmy," Lorraine said. Her voice trembled in nervousness, and the unexpected emotion puzzled Fiona.

"Really?" Jimmy's hand shot out and held Fiona's chin in a painful grip. "Then why's the brat covered in your lipstick?"

Before she could consider the repercussions of her response, Fiona balled up a fist and punched Jimmy just below the armpit. He tugged away and raised his other arm to smack her.

"Don't do it, Jimmy," Margaret said from behind Fiona. Jimmy paused, as if considering the request, then dropped his arm to his side. He's still trying holding out hope for Margaret's good impression, Fiona thought. "You can see Lorraine's drunk, though sloppily done, giving Finn a belated birthday kiss. I'm sure no harm was intended by either of them."

Fiona wondered how much Margaret had truly witnessed.

Despite the evidence, would Margaret believe nothing had happened?

Lorraine's confused expression showing her surprise at Margaret's defense of her. "The kid helped, like a true gentleman, by escorting a lady to her door."

"Yeah, what a kid." He released his hold on her, pushing Fiona roughly into Margaret. "The ladies are safe now, so scram."

Fiona shook her head. "No can do. Eldon's my boss. I only take orders from him, and his last order's to stick around until he got home." She crossed her arms over her chest. "Which he ain't yet."

His gaze flicked toward Margaret, then to Lorraine. Jimmy's jaw clenched tightly, and Fiona heard the quick grind of his teeth. She suspected he would have said—and done—more if Margaret hadn't been there. Instead, he roughly grabbed Lorraine by the back of her neck and pushed her into her room.

Fiona may not get along with Lorraine, but Jimmy's temper needed a release. She'd seen that same look in her father's eyes too many times. Fiona wouldn't let him take his anger out on Lorraine. Fiona stepped one foot forward, but Lorraine caught her eye. There was resignation to her fate in Lorraine's ice-blue gaze. Even with Jimmy's tight hold, Lorraine minutely managed to shake her head. Fiona read the message: don't interfere. Fiona fisted her hands, realizing she and Lorraine might be more alike than she originally believed.

"Leave it, Finn," Margaret whispered in her ear, a hand to her back.

Breathing so deeply her nostrils flared, Fiona turned her attention to Margaret, attempting to control herself at the same time. The door to Lorraine's room slammed shut. "You should get back to bed, Miss Margaret." At Margaret's door, Fiona said, "Thank you for your intervention."

"You're welcome, Finn." She swiped a thumb across Fiona's cheek. Lipstick darkened the pad when she pulled her thumb away.

"Margaret—"

"Shush." Margaret placed a finger to Fiona's lips. "I heard it all, not that you owe me an explanation."

Fiona closed the distance between them and said into Margaret's ear, "I wouldn't hurt you in that way." She pulled back a little and shot a gaze at Lorraine's door. Whispering, she said, "I don't like Lorraine's tactics, but I might have a better understanding of her reasons."

Margaret nodded sadly. "But you can't save everyone, Finn. I'm afraid for you. Afraid, one day, the object of one of your crusades will turn on you." Goodness, Margaret sounded like Ian and Claire.

Fiona felt the concern radiating from Margaret, her heart buoyed by it. She couldn't let Margaret go to bed with this as the last words spoken. Fiona didn't know what to say without it sounding condescending or discounting of Margaret's feelings. Leaning into Margaret as she turned the knob and opened her door, Fiona nipped at Margaret's earlobe, rewarded by Margaret's shiver. "Sweet dreams."

Without a word, Margaret entered her bedroom and closed the door. Fiona grinned and shook her head. "Temporary cease-fire."

MARGARET OPENED HER bedroom door, and was propelled forward by a heavy weight as a large hand clamped on her upper arm. Damn, she thought, I'd let my guard down and not paid attention to my surroundings. She tried to spin toward Jimmy, but he forced her flush against the wall, his hot breath against her ear. "Are you avoiding me? Hardly see you since that night with Finn sitting for you." Jimmy ran his thick hand up and down the left side of Margaret's body, from shoulder to thigh. "Deny me all you want, Babs, but I know you want this. You'll be mine one way or another."

"You haven't been given permission to call me by my brother's nickname." Margaret tried to back away and only managed to push herself against the wall. She had no way to get away from Jimmy and his unwanted advances. Correcting him would only antagonize him further. "I don't want anything from you, Jimmy, and I don't know why you can't understand that," Margaret said. She prayed her voice didn't give away how frightened and helpless she felt at this moment.

Roughly, he grasped her left breast and elicited a pain filled whimper from her before she could stop the sound's escape. He squeezed harder, ran his thumb across the nipple through her blouse, and then pinched the nipple hard. "You say one thing, but your body speaks another," Jimmy said hotly, latching onto the lobe of her ear and pressing himself flush against her.

"No, Jimmy, you don't seem to understand, I don't want you." She tried ineffectually to push against him, to shove him away. Suddenly Margaret heard a low snarl. Before she knew it, Jimmy had moved a slight degree away from her, and then Fiona's voice sounded behind him.

"Miss Margaret told you she ain't interested."

Margaret hadn't heard the door open. Had Jimmy closed it

when he pushed her inside?

With speed belying his size, Jimmy swung around and roughly grabbed Fiona by the throat. He spun her around and slammed Fiona into the wall beside Margaret. "I don't need the peanut gallery telling me what to do, you little runt. I'm tired of your interference."

"Careful, Jimmy, he's just a kid," Margaret said.

"I don't care, right now he's in my business, and deserves whatever punishment he gets. And I have every intention of giving it to him—if he doesn't back down." Jimmy leaned in closer until his face was scant centimeters from Fiona's nose. "As a matter of fact, let me make you a bargain, runt. How 'bout I make sure that you come on our honeymoon." He gave a sneer in Margaret's direction. "I'll make sure you get to watch every little thing I do to her while you're strapped to a chair in plain view." Jimmy chuckled as if this idea was the most humorous thing he'd ever said. "And when I'm done, and Babs is satiated, I'll toss you out the nearest door." Jimmy gave one final squeeze to Fiona's neck, the red coloring of her flesh quickly turning purple from lack of oxygen. He stalked out of the room.

Panic for Fiona's well-being filled her. Margaret grabbed her, pulling Fiona into her arms while Fiona gasped for breath. "Are you okay?"

"Yeah I'm fine," Fiona wheezed. "Someday that sonofabitch—"

"Let's hope you're far away," Margaret told her, "before that type of situation occurs." She shook her head sadly. "Not that I don't appreciate your intervention, but what the hell are you thinking?"

Angering Jimmy was akin to repeatedly poking the devil in the nose. They'd never be safe until they put as much distance between them and Jimmy Bennett. Margaret wondered, would Fiona want me to follow her to the mountains? Does she ever see us together, in the future?

Fiona gazed at Margaret steadily. "I won't let him hurt you, I promise."

Margaret carefully caressed Fiona's cheek. "It's not me I'm worried about."

Chapter Fourteen

MARGARET HOPED TO maintain more of Eldon's attention, but he seemed intent on the paperwork in front of him, absently spinning a pencil in his forefinger and thumb. His distraction annoyed her, but could work in her favor. The episode with Jimmy earlier that morning scared her more than she would admit aloud. Fiona's reaction—what she might do in retaliation on Margaret's behalf—terrified her even more. "You know you can get anyone to make Finn's deliveries. How many people do you trust to look after my well-being as you do with Finn? At least you know Finn's trustworthy enough not to make unwanted advances."

Eldon snorted. "With you as the temptation, Babs, it won't last too much longer. The boy's growing up, after all."

"He looks up to you," Margaret said, rolling her eyes. The lie would stroke Eldon's ego, again maybe working in her favor. "If he were standing under mistletoe, had your permission, I still doubt I could get a kiss on the cheek from Finn." Okay, closer to the truth, much to Margaret's chagrin. So far, she had initiated their kisses. Although, she remembered the nip at her earlobe and Margaret's body reacted with a clenching in parts of her body getting harder to ignore. "Please, Eldon. I'm only asking for a little while."

"What is it you intend to do?" Eldon asked. "I won't have you gallivanting around the city. Your safety is important to me."

"All the more reason I want Finn by my side. His street smarts have him seeing trouble ahead of time."

Eldon gave a loud guffaw. "What is it you think the kid is going to do?" He sat back tossing the pencil onto the desk. "He's not all that sturdy. Wind would blow him down, and it wouldn't have to be very strong."

"Finn's a lot scrappier than you give him credit for," Margaret said. She didn't doubt Fiona could hold her own in a fair fight. She just hoped she'd never have to find out. Her brother was paying attention now, which proved he would consider her request. "There are just some things I want to do downtown, for the less fortunate, and for the church. Mother would've wanted me to help those who couldn't help themselves and would be doing it herself if she were still here. As you don't see fit to allow me to teach, I have to do something with my time."

"Yes, you should be considering matrimony. You know Jimmy's still interested," Eldon said.

Margaret felt the blood drain from her face. "Eldon, I'm not sure—"

"I get it, Babs. Truly I do," Eldon said wearily. "If not Jimmy you need to start considering someone, any respectable man will do. Say the word and make it happen."

"But I'm not interested in anyone," Margaret said.

Eldon sighed, picked up his pencil, and returned his attention to his paperwork. "You can have Finn for the next week. Use the time wisely, Babs, because, at the end of that period, you either show me another suitor worthy of your hand, or I tell Jimmy he has my permission to marry you." He raised his hand to forestall her reply, realizing her ready to argue. "Two weeks Margaret. That's final."

AS HAD BECOME her habit, Fiona took lunch in the kitchen. Today, to her surprise, Jimmy was at the table. Mrs. Baumann noticed her entrance and indicated Fiona sit next to her and not the table. She patted the tall chair beside her. "So how is your day going, young Finn?" Mrs. Baumann asked.

"Aw, it's going just fine." Fiona settled into the chair, took a sip from the glass of the milk alongside her sandwich.

"We have another busy schedule," Margaret said. "It's amazing, Mrs. Baumann, how one young man accomplishes as much as he does." Fiona caught her quick shrug. "I don't know how I would've survived without his assistance." They were on their third day of Margaret's self-imposed errands.

Jimmy snorted and patted Margaret on the thigh. Fiona wanted to whack the hand away, crush the bones to dust. She wouldn't mind slapping the smug expression off his face either. "I'd be more than happy to take you on your errands," Jimmy said. "I'm sure anything the boy can do, I can manage." Jimmy tossed a glare in Fiona's direction. "And probably a lot better too. I know how to wash my face."

Margaret stood from the table, effectively removing Jimmy's hand without making it obvious, and stood by the sink just behind her. Jimmy stood too and came to stand beside the counter mere inches from Fiona. "You needn't participate in such menial labor, Jimmy. Nor can I take you from my brother's side, where you're needed most."

Fiona gave a broad smile, and then instantly regretted it. Jimmy's glare turned into a red-hazed fury. There was no way she and Jimmy were ever going to find mutual ground. They were enemies, plain and simple. She knew it since their first meeting. Fiona did worry how far Jimmy would go in his obsession with Margaret, especially after the incident of a few days ago.

"Enjoy it now," Jimmy whispered harshly, leaning too close to her. "Before long, she'll be my wife. You won't have the same access to her as you have now. Nor the same privileges in this house." With that said, as was becoming his habit, Jimmy stormed off.

Margaret came to her side with concern written on her features. "What did he say?"

Despite a cold rush of dread, Fiona smiled and said, "Nothing we haven't heard before." Fiona shrugged, hoping it appeared a carefree gesture. "He really should consider getting someone to write him some better threats."

Mrs. Baumann lightly cuffed the back of Fiona's head. "Watch yourself young one. He's one wicked individual you do not want to cross."

"I understand," Fiona said. "He's dangerous. The problem is everyone's a target," Fiona said. "Not just me."

"The least you could do to help the matter," Mrs. Baumann said, "is quit finding ways to piss him off."

Fiona crossed her arms over her chest. "And where's the fun there? These are modern times, where everyone lives dangerously."

Margaret shook her head sadly. "That's the part which frightens me, Finn. The whole point is to live."

Pushing the plate of sandwiches closer to Finn, Mrs. Baumann said, "And you're walking a mighty fine line, you little hooligan."

Chapter Fifteen

AS THEY FINISHED a fun day of shopping—not that Fiona considered shopping fun—with Margaret, Brigid, and Sunny, she could tell Sunny was tiring. Fiona, relegated to the position of a packhorse, found it a newly favorite task because of the way Margaret grinned at her each time she added to the burden. Fiona couldn't believe how much comfort Margaret's presence brought her. Fiona had friends in the Donnelly's and enjoyed Claire's friendship. She wouldn't consider those friendships a wasted effort. However now, with Margaret, she felt different things inside her head and body, things she wasn't able to explain or understand. The three kisses they'd shared kept Fiona awake at night with conflicting feelings of joy and fear. She and Margaret needed to talk, but Fiona was afraid the reaction wouldn't shift in her favor.

They were almost to the car, one of the concessions Eldon made to ensure Margaret's comfort as well as her safety, and they all benefited from it.

Then the very thing to scare Fiona happened.

Scant seconds elapsed for Fiona to notice Detweiler in the crowd and realized they wouldn't make it to the car in time. Without alarming her companions, Fiona said, "Hurry, into the alley." Though it wasn't her intention, she could see the alarm on their features. They didn't argue, rather hurried to do her bidding. That's when Fiona recognized one of Detweiler's lackeys, from their original meeting with Margaret, racing toward them. She doubted his intent a friendly one. Someone from the crowd of pedestrians seemed to recognize the Detweiler's man and his intent, the yelling of "gun" by several voices, and the sidewalk burst into pandemonium. A flash of blue and a police officer tossed the gunman to the ground, but not before he'd pointed the barrel at Fiona.

Fiona managed to get the girls down an alley, glancing about to find the best means of protection. She felt an instant of relief, but didn't intend to rely on it. No one was following. She recognized the area. They were close to Old Man Chamber's garage. Fiona steered her companions in that direction. She had just made it to the end of the alley when Fiona felt the burning pain in her shoulder followed by the report of a gun. She stumbled, but quickly righted herself. Fiona hustled the girls into the open bay of the garage.

"Hey what the—" Chambers rushed forward. "Shit Finn, what's going on?" He appeared to recognize the fear on the three faces in front of him. "Come, come over this way," he ordered, ushering them to Fiona's room. Once inside, he slammed the door behind them, and said, "Stay here. I'll get rid of them."

Ear pressed to the door, Fiona listened. She heard Detweiler's voice inquiring about their whereabouts. Then, the old man exclaimed in surprise, "They went out the back." The racing footsteps as Detweiler and crew rushed to find them.

In her other ear, Fiona heard Margaret's distressed whisper. "You've been shot."

Fiona attempted a careless shrug, only to wince at the responding pain. She glanced around the small room. Brigid and Sunny stood holding the packages from their daily purchases tightly in trembling arms. "I've got to get you all back to safety. I don't want Eldon worrying when he hears of this."

"Not until you get some medical attention," Margaret said through gritted teeth.

Fiona snorted. "If I don't get you back to Eldon, I'm going to need more medical attention than I do at this moment."

"Fine," Margaret said. She turned toward Brigid. "Can you drive the car?" she asked. Brigid gave a slow nod. "See, Brigid can take the car back and let my brother know what happened."

Shaking her head, Fiona said, "No. It's my job to make sure you're all safe. All of you. Then I'll—"

"And how safe are we going to be, if you're not conscious so you can protect us?" Margaret stepped back, her hands on her hips in defiance. "Fine. We'll do it your way. Brigid can drive us all back to the house. From there I'll take you to a doctor—or send for him."

"We don't even know if it is safe to go back to the car yet," Fiona said. "I know it's not the nicest place for you ladies, but here's safe." She looked around the room and found a couple of old rags, as clean as they came in a garage, wadded one into a square, and moved to place it against the wound.

Margaret, reading her intention, grabbed the rag away from her. "Dammit, Finn, if you're going to be this stubborn, at least let me help." Fiona didn't have to see the anger on Margaret's face because she felt it in pressing of the cloth a bit rougher than probably intended against her wound. Fiona flinched. Contritely, Margaret hissed, "Sorry."

Feeling a bit lightheaded, pain making it difficult to think, Fiona took a deep breath hoping to stave off unconsciousness. She had to get Margaret to safety, had to make sure Brigid and Sunny were safe also. "Okay ladies," Fiona said with more strength than she felt. "Let's see if it's safe for us all. I'll go get the car."

Old Man Chambers had his hand raised to knock on the door when Fiona opened it. "They're gone." He glanced to Fiona and from his widening eyes saw the blood. "Why don't you give me the keys and I'll get your car."

Fiona shook her head. "It may not be safe. I wouldn't want you hurt."

"The same works in reverse, Finn." He shook his head. "Been 'round long enough, I'll know what to look for. I won't let anybody follow me." He glanced at the women behind Fiona. "Once that's done, what are your plans?"

Fiona paused in answering. She'd always trusted the old man, he'd done right by her, but her pool of trusted people grew smaller. Her options were limited, and she had to get the three to the security of the Graham house. "Gotta get these ladies home."

"And I can take her to a doctor," Margaret snapped.

"I'm not sure it's safe," Fiona said. "Besides, I'm sure Mrs. Baumann or Brigid can take care of this little scratch at the house."

"So now you know what's best for me?" Margaret asked. "Have you now risen to the station equal with my brother? I'm not capable of making my own decisions?"

"That's not what I meant," Fiona said. Seeing the look in Margaret's eyes, Fiona knew she would not win this battle. As she attempted to make another suggestion, Margaret stopped her with a raised palm.

"You could compromise." Fiona and Margaret turned to the old man. He blushed at their intense attention. "I can drive the young ladies home," he said to Fiona. "And since she's so adamant," he said pointing at Margaret, "she can get you to the doctor. I got a truck you could use. You can get it back to me when you can."

Margaret glared at her for a long moment before agreeing. "All right then. As long as Brigid looks after Sunny, and lets my brother know what's transpired down here."

"I'm sure he'd feel better if you told him directly," Fiona said.

"Since we don't know if they intended to shoot you or me originally, then I think it best we remain together. I know a place we can go."

"But what about—"

Margaret glared at Fiona. "As long as Eldon knows I'm safe, and with you, he'll be less worried. If it makes you feel any better, I'll write him a note."

Fiona shook her head. "I don't know why you're so difficult."

Margaret shrugged negligently. "Because I can be."

"And that's not scary for me?" Fiona said. "I'm not sure what's more frightening. What Eldon will do if anything happens to me and I can't protect you? Or, could it be what you'll do if I don't agree with you?"

"For the time being, I suggest you don't try to find out the answer."

Since Margaret agreed with the plan, Chambers went to get their car, after Fiona gave its location. On his return, the packages, Sunny, and Brigid were settled into the car and he drove away. Fiona sat behind the wheel, after another quick argument with Margaret, and followed in the borrowed truck, watching to see if anyone paid too much attention to Eldon's car or trailed them. After a few blocks, when it appeared they weren't followed, Fiona turned her head to Margaret. "They seem safe."

"Good," Margaret said, nodding. "Drive to Dr. Matthews' house. We'll be safe there."

"Safe from thugs," Fiona whispered. "Who's gonna protect me from you?"

The wicked gleam in Margaret's gaze gave Fiona a surprising tingle in her body, as Margaret said, "Suck it up, handsome. You're the one who lives for danger, every day I may add."

Fiona laughed while simultaneously blushing from the compliment. "Here I thought I could rely on you to be my safety zone."

"I'm the only form of dangerous you can positively live through," Margaret said.

"Then I'll let you harm me in a thousand ways." As soon as she spoke the words, Fiona wished to take them back. She had meant them, with all her heart, but she'd never intended to be so open about her feeling for Margaret.

At least not yet.

The double entendre of her words contributed mental images, which made concentration on driving difficult. Margaret's type of danger may be more than she could handle—and Fiona did not intend to avoid the prospect.

Chapter Sixteen

ANY OTHER TIME she and Fiona drove around, the scenery would lure Margaret into soothing daydreams of possibilities. This drive was different. She didn't see the magnificent homes surrounded by tree lined streets and yards, or the beauty of the approaching sunset. Instead, she noticed the paling skin and odd winces as Fiona slowly bled beside her. Margaret could tell it was a chore for Fiona to remain focused, maybe even conscious. "Pull over Fiona. You're ready to pass out. How can you expect to keep me alive?"

"I can make it, we're almost there," Fiona said. "Besides, I'm the driver here," she added.

"I'm serious," Margaret said. She appreciated Fiona's attempts to dismiss her concerns, but Margaret wouldn't allow it. No matter their short association, Fiona meant too much to her already. Was she the only one who felt it, this attraction between them? "Please, let me drive. I know you're trying to be stoic, but you're scaring me, unintentionally of course." Fiona balked for only a moment, and Margaret assumed Fiona finally realized her correct. Once the truck stopped, Margaret rushed to exit the passenger side and enter the driver's side, where she nudged Fiona across the seat with her hand. "Now we can get there in one piece."

Fiona had it right earlier, the ride wasn't far. They reached the suburbs where houses were larger and extravagant, unlike most of those in the inner city, unlike Margaret's own. Dr. Matthews lived here for as long as the Graham family had known him. When her parents were alive, the family used to visit Edward's home often, their relationship more than doctor slash patient, since before Margaret's mother became ill and her father had died. Growing up, Edward Matthews was as close to an uncle as she had. Which is why she felt a need to put Fiona's life in his hands. If anyone could—and would—keep Fiona's secret, he would. She hoped.

Margaret pulled the truck up to the house and turned the engine off. Twisting toward Fiona, she said, "Slide back over here and let me help you out."

"I can do it on my own," Fiona said, an edge of frustration in her tone.

Margaret nodded solemnly. "I know you can, honey, but

please let me help you." Fiona complied, grudgingly from her mumbling, and together they made their way to the front door. She rang the bell with the hand not clasped around Fiona's waist. Margaret prayed Dr. Edward Matthews wasn't at the hospital, unsure how much longer Fiona could move under her own power. When the door opened, a thin and greying older man stood there. "Hey Peter, is Edward at home?"

Peter gave a cry of delight. "Margaret, it's so good to see you. In fact, Edward has just returned home. We're getting ready for supper. Why don't you both come in," he said. His glance took in Fiona's bleeding shoulder, and he shifted to stand beside Fiona to support her left side. "Oh, my. Appears his office hours aren't over yet."

"I'm sorry to do this," Margaret said. "You know I wouldn't be here if it weren't an emergency."

"No, my dear, I know you wouldn't." Peter closed the door behind them and started walking down the hallway toward the back of the home. "Follow me, and I'll get you settled before I go find Edward."

Margaret and Peter ushered Fiona into a sterile white room outfitted like a hospital exam room. "If I didn't need his help as I do, I'd be surprised he has this room in his home."

"You'd be surprised how often this room gets used. Not that we mind," Peter said. "Keeps Edward on his toes and not getting lazy as he..." He paused, gave Margaret a wink, and helped Fiona onto the examination table. "As he matures."

"Matures?" she repeated. "Is that how one refers to aging after hitting sixty?"

Peter pressed a hand to his chest and shook his head solemnly. "I, the ever considerate spouse, wouldn't dare use the word 'old' to his face, not with his temperament. Would you?"

"No, I suppose not." Anyone who truly understood Edward knew he was sensitive about his advancing age.

"Exactly," Peter said. "Must maintain the peace, after all, I need live with the outcome of his ranting." He shifted his attention to Fiona. "How are you holding up... uh..."

"Finn," Fiona said. Her quietening tone suggested her weakening.

"All right, Finn. I'll be right back." Peter left the room to get Dr. Matthews.

Margaret moved to remove Fiona's jacket. She started to unbutton Fiona's shirt, but a surprisingly firm grip stilled her hand. Fiona shook her head. Margaret stared at her gravely. "He's going to figure it out as soon as he starts treating your wound."

Fiona lowered her head. "I'd just as soon the shock comes later than sooner, give the poor man an opportunity to prepare himself." She raised Margaret's hand in hers, brought it to her lips, and placed a gentle kiss on the knuckles. "Thank you, for wanting what's best for me and helping."

"I do want what's best for you," Margaret said softly. "Just know I wouldn't have brought you here if I didn't think we could trust him. And you can, Fiona, trust Edward."

"And Peter too?" Fiona asked. Margaret smiled, privy to information Fiona was not. The playful side of her anticipated the shock Fiona would surely feel when she learned of it also. Margaret considered sharing, but Edward had arrived during her deliberation.

"What have we here?" Edward asked as he entered the examination room. Peter didn't enter any further than the doorway. Margaret adored both men, but Edward was her favorite. He wasn't a tall man, standing just a couple inches taller than her five-foot-five height, about fifty years old, pudgy, but not heavy, and wore wire-framed glasses. He had thick dark hair slicked neatly back from his face, and a matching mustache above full pale lips, which were currently pursed in thought.

"I'm sorry to interrupt your evening Edward, but I've need for your assistance and your secrecy."

"You're the boy who found the injured girl?" Fiona nodded. Edward moved fully into the room and stood alongside Fiona while visually examining her from head to foot. "Everything seems to be in order, with the exception of some bleeding. Knife wound?"

"No sir," Fiona replied. "Seems my shoulder got in the way of a flying bullet."

"Ah, nasty business that. You might want to avoid dangerous and speeding objects in the future," Edward said, a teasing smile playing across his lips under a bushy mustache.

Fiona returned his smile, albeit weakly. "Would have avoided it this time, had I known it was coming. Good thing I wasn't in my glad rags."

"Yes, indeed. Not sure the shirt will make it, young man. Let's get the shirt off and see what we have to work with."

Margaret winced. "Oh, about that, you see Finn here isn't exactly a young man."

"Not exactly an old one either," Edward said. He teased, and Margaret realized he'd already figured out the situation.

"That's not exactly what I mean." Margaret gave a quick glance to Peter. Returning her gaze to Edward, she said, "You see, it's—"

Fiona gave a sigh, her body trembling and then swaying slightly. "I'm female."

Dr. Matthews raised one eyebrow slightly. "Changes very little with the situation, but I can see where you might be uncomfortable with Peter here."

"Actually sir," Fiona said quietly, "throws me with either of you in the know. Do what you must." Margaret met the clouding gaze of Fiona and gave her a nod. "Margaret trusts you, and so will I."

Edward gave a gentle squeeze to Fiona's knee. "Very well, Finn, is it?"

"Finn in this guise," Margaret explained. "Fiona Cavanaugh by birth."

"Let's fix this up so you can rest," Edward said.

Given the go-ahead, Peter entered the room and moved to a cabinet against the far wall, and said, "Or so you can pass out. I would have by now. You'll stay overnight, of course." Peter pulled out items from the drawers, placing them on a rolling instrument stand. Margaret unbuttoned Fiona's shirt.

When Peter returned to the examination table, Edward gave him a tender smile. Next, he asked, "Would you be so kind as to bring me hot water and towels?" Peter nodded and left. "Let's see what we have here," he said moving closer to Fiona.

Margaret finished removing the shirt, tugged the Henley undershirt over her head, wincing when Fiona hissed in pain. She gasped in surprise at the tight bindings around Fiona's chest. The exposed flesh was soft to her touch and pale. Margaret marveled at how slender and yet feminine Fiona's body was under her baggy clothing. She pulled her hand away and balled it into a fist to curb the impulse to explore her flesh further. This wasn't the time for that curiosity or exploration.

Another weak smile and Fiona said, "Not exactly necessary given my lack of attributes, but can't take chances." Margaret raised a hand to caress Fiona's cheek, simultaneously touched by Fiona's admission and upset Fiona felt herself lacking before Margaret. She worried Fiona might be unaware they weren't alone, speaking of something so personal in front of others, in her pained state.

"Well, it works wonders for your privacy with Peter and me." Edward gave Margaret a barely discernable shrug, and whispered near her ear, "She appears to be focusing on you in order to remain conscious, which works in my favor."

Margaret flinched each time Edward poked and prodded the damaged area from the bullet wound and eliciting a groan or wince from Fiona's lips. The examination seemed to take forever, but she doubted more than a moment passed.

Peter returned with the basin of water, washcloth, and towels, before retreating into the doorway once again. "I'll wait outside until you need me, Edward." At Edward's nod, Peter stepped into the hall and closed the door.

"Okay, Finn, let's get this cleaned and see what we're working with."

As he washed away the blood, Margaret watched the revealing of torn and ripped flesh. Her stomach felt queasy seeing the harm done in order to protect her. "Is she going to be okay?" Margaret asked.

Dr. Matthews must've seen her current condition wasn't much better than Fiona's. He tilted his chin in the direction of the chair. "Sit down before you fall down, dear." He returned his attention to Fiona's wound, but grinned playfully. "You'll see everything from there, and can make it back over here should you feel I'm harming your friend."

From her chair, Margaret shook her head. "It's not that I'd think your—"

Dr. Matthews guffawed. "I understand." He glanced from Fiona to Margaret. "You care deeply?" Margaret nodded knowing what he asked. "Then I shall take exceptional care."

For the next few minutes, Edward tended to Fiona's wound, mumbling as he worked. Finally he took a step back from his suturing, and reaching for the gauze and tape, said, "That should do for now. You'll need to keep it dry, and to change the dressing in the morning." He turned to Margaret. "Now, however, I strongly suggest you join Peter and me for supper. There's plenty. Food will help with the healing process, and make it easier to stomach the medicine I'll give her for the pain."

"No, no medicine," Fiona said quickly. "I have to stay sharp, in case someone tries to harm Miss Margaret again."

Edward placed a hand gently on her non-injured shoulder. "It's not like you're going anywhere tonight, young lady. I have a small cottage in the back of the house, enclosed in a treed area. Few know it's there, so you'll be safe. Tonight you'll need a healing rest. We'll reassess the injury in the morning."

If Fiona's fears weren't so clear on her face, Margaret would've chuckled at her obstinacy. Fiona's gaze bore into Edward's skull as Margaret glanced between them. It took several moments, in which Edward crossed his arms challengingly over his chest, before Fiona finally said, "We'll do it your way unless I see a reason to do otherwise."

"As you wish," Edward said. Margaret could tell when he turned away he was trying to hide a smile. He turned his attention to her. "Quite the protector you have here." Margaret nodded. "I hope there's not an occasion for this to happen again."

"I would agree," Margaret said. Seeing Fiona hurt had been and still was difficult, even as she understood Fiona would be okay.

"Come, join Peter and me for dinner. It's been a while since we've entertained such charming women." Margaret got up from the chair and helped Edward assist Fiona from the table. He quirked an eyebrow in Margaret's direction, and asked, "I assume Peter can be himself?"

Margaret nodded. "Entirely himself."

Edward tenderly pat Margaret's cheek. She noted the confused expression on Fiona's face. Teasingly, she said to Fiona, "Not to worry, honey, you'll understand soon enough."

Chapter Seventeen

DINNER AND CONVERSATION with Edward and Peter turned out to be the happiest experience for Fiona since time spent with her family and the Donnelly's. Before, that is, her father got so angry and almost constantly drunk after her mother and brother died. Edward proved to be humorous and a great conversationalist. Peter, with all his sense of humor and flamboyance when he entertained, wore his heart on his sleeve, staring at Edward with such adoration and love. She wondered if anyone would ever look at her that way. Hoped it could be Margaret.

Much as Fiona wanted to enjoy every moment, especially since she could be herself and not the Finn persona, the shooting and the medication were taking a toll on her. Fiona tried not to yawn. She clenched her teeth hoping to stifle the rude action. If Fiona didn't rest soon, she'd fall asleep in her dessert.

Margaret must have recognized her predicament. "As pleasurable as this evening is, gentlemen," Margaret said, pushing her chair from the table. "Fiona needs her rest."

Peter jumped to his feet. "I'll walk you out to the cottage. Check to make certain you have what you need for the night."

"Let me know if there's any problem with the wound," Edward said.

Margaret gave Edward a kiss on the cheek, but Fiona settled for shaking his hand and voicing her thanks. "I'm at your service if you ever have need of it, Finn."

"Appreciated, truly, but hope it's for friendship and not your medical services," Fiona said.

"As do I. Good night, you two." Edward turned and cleared off the table.

Peter took Margaret by the hand and led her into the hallway. They made their way to the back door, picking up Fiona's undershirt from the hall table, where Peter had placed it earlier after washing. Outside, at the back of the house, he walked across an immaculate lawn, toward a small structure barely recognizable in the darkness and through the surrounding trees. As they got closer, Finn could see the structure was a small but lovely cottage. "Here we are," Peter said. He pulled out a key and unlocked the front door.

Fiona and Margaret followed Peter inside as he turned on a light and hung Fiona's undershirt on a coat rack secured to the hall wall. The room consisted of a small kitchenette on the left-hand side, a couch, a rocking chair, small fireplace, and against the back wall a full-size bed, and a closed door two feet to the right. Fiona took a step to investigate when Peter said, "Bathroom." Only two windows gave view to the outside; one on the left behind the table, and one on the right, beside the fireplace, both covered in thick dark cloth curtains. "To keep the outside light out," Peter said. "And keep the inside light from getting out." Peter smiled and gave a half shrug. "In the off chance someone happens by, they won't know occupants are inside.

Margaret cupped his hands in hers and gave him a quick peck on the cheek. "Thank you, Peter, for all you and Edward are doing for us. We are indebted to you."

"Nonsense my dear," Peter said. "There is no debt where the family is concerned. And you're as much our kin as any blood relation."

Fiona stepped forward and extended a hand. "Truly Peter, you're going above and beyond. Anything you need, which is in my power to provide, just ask me."

Peter handed Margaret the key. "Just bring it up to the house when you're ready to leave in the morning. I'll provide breakfast before you return home. The bathroom is fully stocked," he said. "All the supplies you'll need are in the cabinet for nightly ablutions, and seeing to Finn's wounds." With a quick glance around the room, Peter left.

The door closed and locked behind him, Margaret turned toward her. "Okay sweetheart, time to get you to bed." The image popping into Fiona's head of Margaret lying beside her in repose brought Fiona's face to a burning blush. Margaret chuckled. "Why my dearest heart, you're positively blushing," Margaret said. "Rather fetching on you, I must say."

"I'm sure it has a lot to do with exhaustion and having a bullet removed. What else could it possibly be?" Fiona asked, making her way to the room's bed. She turned staring at Margaret. "If you have no objection, I really would like to get some rest."

Margaret walked over and gently nudged her onto the mattress. She bent and began removing Fiona's boots. "I'm sorry Fiona, I shouldn't have teased." Dropping the last boot in her hand, Margaret stood and gently caressed Fiona's cheek. Fiona's eyes closed in delight from the feeling. "I meant no harm. I truly do find it beautiful when you blush."

Fiona shook her head. "It's something I'm working on controlling. As you can see, I have yet to master this reaction."

Margaret unbuttoned Fiona's shirt gently, careful as not to cause further injury to her wound presumably. Margaret tossed it onto the floor. She stared at Fiona's bindings. Fiona'd worn it so long, being without made her feel compromised, disconcerted as if all her secrets were as exposed.

"Is this as uncomfortable as it looks?" Margaret asked.

Fiona nodded. She wouldn't speak for fear of alerting Margaret of the roiling emotions zipping through her body, causing heat and wetness in areas she shouldn't be thinking of, and inciting Fiona's heart to beat faster. Margaret stared into her eyes for a long moment before she asked, "May I remove it?"

Again, she nodded. Awkwardly, Fiona turned her head, not only due to embarrassment, but also due to not wanting to witness the revulsion and disgust Margaret might display at her boyish frame. She heard Margaret take a deep breath. "Oh, Fiona, you're beautiful."

It took every ounce of Fiona's willpower not to turn her head. Fiona felt tender fingertips skim across the skin just below her breasts. She squeezed her eyes shut and bit her lower lip hard in an attempt not to face Margaret, not to sigh or moan at the ripples of goosebumps cascading across her flesh.

"Margaret, honey—"

Margaret placed a finger to Fiona's lips to halt further words. "No need to sweet-talk me," she said. Margaret wiggled her eyebrows. "Not that I don't like it because I do. Immensely." She reached for the top of the duvet and pulled it down, revealing the blankets and sheets beneath. "Come on, scoot up here." Fiona did. "Okay, take your pants off." Fiona shot her a flabbergasted look. Margaret met her gaze with the wicked gleam. "I could do it for you if you'd like?"

"No, I've got it." Fiona quickly removed her trousers and dropped them to the floor. "Happy?" she asked, glaring at Margaret. She yanked the covers up to her chin, wincing at the jolt of pain the hasty action caused her wound.

Fiona's gaze followed Margaret as she crossed the room and turned off the lights. In the darkness, Fiona heard the rustle of clothes as Margaret undressed. A few moments later, Fiona felt the mattress shift as Margaret climbed in bed beside her. She stiffened, not sure what Margaret expected of her.

"Relax, Fiona," Margaret said softly, her breath warm against Fiona's ear. "Let me hold you?"

"Um, yeah if you'd like." Fiona felt awkward, and immature like her every day persona. She shifted closer and felt Margaret's arm reach around her as she pulled Fiona's head onto her shoulder, Fiona's body half on top of Margaret.

"I won't hurt you," Margaret said. Fiona felt the kiss placed on the top of her head. "I want to fall asleep with you in my arms.

That's all." Fiona let her body release tension, only to stiffen again when she felt Margaret's soft chuckle. Was she laughing at her? Margaret must've felt her begin to pull away because her arm tightened around Fiona. "No, stay, I'm sorry. I'm not laughing at you. Honest." The curtain on the windows did their job, keeping the room in darkness. Margaret didn't appear to have the same handicap, her aim unhindered. Her hand caressed Fiona's cheek, her thumb tracing Fiona's lower lip. "I know I shouldn't be surprised, but the boy shorts were just too cute."

Fiona moved the hand resting on Margaret's stomach and tentatively glided it in a small circle. Even though the thin silk of what Fiona assumed to be the material of her camisole, the tender, soft flesh that was Margaret felt wonderful. Fiona inhaled the flower scent indicative of Margaret. She extended the circumference of the circle, and her fingers lightly grazed the underside of Margaret's breast. She jerked the hand away and pulled her fingers into a fist.

A warm hand covered hers. "It's all right. You don't have to be embarrassed or afraid."

"I'm not." As soon as the words left her mouth, she realized Margaret knew them for the lie they were. Fiona was embarrassed, having gone further than a kiss. Not that she wasn't enjoying it because she had—extremely. What made her afraid was that the feeling she had for Margaret might not be returned, might be transitory. She didn't want this—whatever it was or could be—to end.

"Fiona?"

"Yeah?"

"Are you okay?"

"Mm-hmm." She wasn't certain that was a lie.

"Tell me, are they comfy?"

It took a moment for Fiona to realize to what Margaret referred. When she did, Fiona rolled onto her back and stared in the direction of the ceiling. The silliness of the situation hit her, and she laughed. "Actually, they are quite comfortable. Can you imagine if I didn't wear them? If someone was to unexpectedly find girl's undergarments in my boy's laundry?"

MARGARET SMILED DOWN at Fiona's sleepy expression as her eyes sluggishly opened. Her hand rested on the bone between Fiona's breasts, and it took every ounce of restraint not to caress those small firm mounds. "I thought you were beautiful before, but now it's a toss-up."

"Toss-up for what?" Fiona asked. She tried to sit up, but

Margaret held her down with a subtle amount of pressure on her chest.

"Are you more handsome nearly naked and embarrassed, or just waking up from sleep?"

"Now you're just being silly," Fiona said. She turned her face away, but not before the blush reddened her cheeks. Her embarrassment was also evident in the flush spreading across the rest of Fiona's exposed flesh.

"I'm not actually, but I suppose you've never learned to accept a compliment." Margaret did give in to the impulse to explore Fiona's breast. Leaning down, Margaret gently sucked a nipple into her mouth, flicking the tip of her tongue until it peaked. Fiona gasped, arched into her mouth, while the rest of her body stiffened. "Mm, ambrosia."

"Margaret?"

Margaret released the nipple and raised her head to place her mouth over Fiona's in a slow kiss, deepening the kiss and relaxing her body on top of Fiona. Even through her camisole, Margaret could feel the heat suffusing Fiona's skin, felt the contrast of the soft pale skin covering muscles from all the lifting from her deliveries. Her own body responded with a warmth between her legs. Fiona made her so hot. She pulled away when Fiona's breathing became rapid. "Your kisses send a fire through my blood. I adore the magic of your lips." She sat up and tucked her legs under her, as she stared down on a now squirming Fiona. "Much as I wish we could spend a lifetime here, like this, I suppose that's impossible." Margaret sighed. "There are pleasures I'd like to share with you, Fiona, but you're healing, and your health is important to me."

Fiona pushed herself into a sitting position and leaned her head against the headboard. Her hands trembled as she tugged the sheet until it covered her nakedness. "May I ask—" She inhaled a deep breath. "It's not that I'm ungrateful of your attentions, but why me?"

Had anyone but Fiona posed the question, Margaret would be offended and angry. This was Fiona, however, with all her insecurities and lack of experience. She wasn't fishing for compliments; Margaret doubted she'd know how. Gazing deep into the honey-gold eyes, Margaret could see her honest confusion. "I won't promise forever, but I hope that's where we're heading. Your heart is kind and caring. You hide it from being too obvious, but I can see you've an unfathomable love for Sunny, not just in protecting her. That, in itself, has helped heal Sunny and allowed her to return step-by-step to this world, in her head and heart as well as her body. And if you can share even half that affection with me, I'll be the luckiest woman." Margaret reached for the hand not clutching the sheet, and held it in her own. "You're easy to look at, you treat me like I'm special to you, and when we're together, I feel you're focused on me with heart and mind." She squeezed the hand in hers. "The road ahead will be difficult, but I'm willing to do what it takes to keep you."

Margaret started to worry she'd offended her when Fiona stared expressionlessly in her direction. After a long moment, Fiona leaned forward and gave a quick kiss to her lips, and then climbed out of bed. She picked up the material for binding her chest and paused, probably realizing the wound would make the action difficult. Margaret jumped from the bed and stood behind Fiona, wrapping her arms around Fiona's waist, her head resting on Fiona's back. "I'll help you dress in a minute, Fiona. Tell me what's wrong."

Fiona's body stiffened. "Nothing's wrong." It wasn't by much, but Fiona relaxed her body just a smidgeon. If she was trying to deflect Margaret's concern, it wasn't going to work.

"Oh, honey, there is. You've emotionally distanced yourself from me." She clutched Fiona's waist a little tighter, turned her head, and placed a kiss between Fiona's shoulder blades. "Please don't hide secrets from me."

Lowering her head, Fiona groaned, her posture sagging in defeat. When she finally spoke, Fiona's voice was barely above a whisper. "I don't know why I feel the way I do for you. These feelings scare me. But, here's the truth." Fiona looked over her shoulder at Margaret. "In a perfect world, I'd want forever, but the world is cruel, Margaret. So is Boston." She turned away again. "As soon as I can put enough money together, Sunny and I are leaving for the west. I would consider it a dream come true if you'd join me, too. I'd do my best to take care of you, give you what you need. I can't promise it will be easy, not like Eldon can provide for you. In fact, life will be hard, I'm certain. But I'd never hurt you like Jimmy will, like maybe even another man would."

Margaret ran a hand across Fiona's bare shoulder and down her arm. She grinned at the goosebumps that erupted. She took a step back after releasing Fiona's waist and retrieved the clean gauze roll she'd taken from Edward. "Arms away from your sides," she said, standing in front of Fiona. She began the task of binding the beautiful breasts in front of her. Lordy, what a shame to hide them, she thought. "Yes, I want to leave with you and Sunny, Fiona, but we'll have to carefully plan our departure to disguise any trail three lone females will make." Margaret tucked the end into the layers of gauze. When they went to the main house for breakfast, Margaret would need to get some tape to secure her handiwork better. "In the meantime, we need to conduct our lives much as we are now."

Fiona nodded. "I understand."

She didn't want to bring up the next topic, but Fiona would find out soon enough, and Margaret not telling her could cause more hurt feelings than the subject matter. "I need to tell you about a deal I've had to make with Eldon just to have more time with you."

"What kind of deal?" Fiona asked.

"Eldon has given me two weeks to find an appropriate suitor, or he'll accept Jimmy's proposal." Fiona's body tensed again, but she remained silent—if you didn't count the gnashing of her teeth. Margaret let the information sink in before she dropped the other shoe, and took the time to retrieve the cleaned undershirt and the button shirt.

As she re-dressed Fiona, taking care to put as little strain on the injured shoulder as she could, Margaret gave a glance into Fiona's wooden gaze. "In order to comply with Eldon's demands and make an effort, I'll be going out more, starting with Janice Hartwell's party in a couple of days." Because of the deal with Eldon, the situation would be hardest on Fiona. Finn would be required to conduct business as Eldon's driver, and as her driver to these festivities. Margaret would have to be more creative in finding time to be alone with Fiona.

Fiona bit her bottom lip. "Boy or girl, I don't fit into your world, Margaret. We don't come from the same culture and status." Fiona placed her hands on Margaret's shoulders. "I understand your need to appease your brother. Like it or not, any chance to stay clear of Jimmy is a good move. Can't say I'll like seeing you with someone else, but I understand the need." She dropped her hands to her sides. Margaret saw a flash of pain in the caramel depths of Fiona's eyes before she masked the emotion. "I just hope the charade isn't a lengthy one." With that said, Fiona turned and pulled her trousers on.

Margaret took her cue to get dressed, realizing this discussion was over. She had to agree with Fiona in wanting this farce to be a short one. Since when had her life become so complicated?

Chapter Eighteen

FIONA COULDN'T CALM the anxious beating of her heart. Her nervousness must be evident because Margaret reached over and squeezed her thigh in a gesture of reassurance. "It'll be all right," Margaret said. Fiona felt the tremor in Margaret's hand, realizing she too feared the outcome of confronting Eldon.

"We will know for certain all too soon," Fiona said, noting Eldon with arms crossed standing before the front door. She slowed the truck in front of the house.

The vehicle hadn't come to a complete stop before Eldon yanked the passenger door open and pulled Margaret into his arms. "Dammit, Babs, I've been worried sick." Placing the truck in gear, shifting the engine off, Fiona got out and stood a few feet from brother and sister.

"You should have suspected where I'd take Finn to get patched up quietly. We couldn't have been safer."

Eldon slammed his hand against the truck's hood. Margaret and Fiona startled. "You would have been safer here. I don't know what the hell you were thinking," he said, his voice growing louder. "There were places—"

Fiona couldn't stand Eldon berating Margaret any longer. "The decision was mine, Mr. Graham," she said edging closer to Margaret. If Eldon decided to aim the next blow at Margaret, Fiona wanted to be in place to take the slug. "I didn't know if I could get Miss Margaret to a safe location before you got word where to find us. I took a chance Detweiler, and whoever sent him, didn't know about the doc."

"No way was I going to let Finn bring me somewhere, even for my alleged safety, while he's bleeding and hurt after taking a bullet meant for me without some means of helping him."

"It could have been Finn's bullet. You don't know for sure," Eldon growled.

"Neither do you." Margaret scowled at Eldon. Fiona worried an argument might result, relieved with Margaret's next words. "Can we finish this discussion inside? Or are you fine sharing this conversation with the neighbors?"

Eldon remained silent for a long time. "Fine. Let's finish this in my office. How's the wound, by the way, Finn?"

Fiona didn't fool herself into believing he cared more than superficially. She wasn't going to slit her own throat being rude now, either. "Got no beef with the Doc's skills. I'm jake, but Junior won't be after I give 'im a sockdolager in 'is kisser."

"Put that on hold, kid. We have a lot to discuss."

Fiona felt nauseous with fear of the unknown. She knew the danger visited upon Margaret put Finn in a precarious position, teetering on being hero or villain in Eldon's eyes. Fiona hoped for the former.

MARGARET AND FIONA followed Eldon into his office. Margaret wanted to complain, seeing Jimmy sitting on the room's couch reading the paper, wanted to have him thrown out, but decided not to push Eldon's temper too far since she was already on thin ice with him. Instead, she walked to the two chairs in front of Eldon's desk and sat in the left one, farthest from Jimmy.

"Take a seat, Finn," Eldon ordered, pointing to the chair beside Margaret. She knew the position placed Fiona at a disadvantage, any possibility of a quick escape severely hindered. Margaret hoped that response wouldn't be necessary. Eldon steepled his fingers under his chin, then sighed wearily. "You performed remarkably in your responsibility to keep my sister safe. I'm in your debt for that, Finn. However, God forbid this situation reoccur, you're first priority is to get Margaret to me. I will always be her best protection. Understand?" Fiona nodded. "That being said, I owe you more than you can know."

"As do I," Margaret said. She directed her gaze to Eldon. "Granted this incident has put you behind with business, but Dr. Matthews recommended Finn rest his shoulder, as well as himself for a couple of days."

Eldon dropped his hands to the desk. "This gives you a chance to work on the deal, Babs. Any headway in that matter we discussed?" The crux of Eldon's long-term plans, marry her off. Margaret hoped the attack and the fact he'd given her two weeks and only a couple of days had transpired, would postpone his request. Maybe cancel the matter altogether. Seems I've misjudged Eldon's familial patience, she thought dismally.

"What deal?" Jimmy asked, jumping from the couch. He glared from Eldon to her as he stood at the side of the desk, shifting his weight from one foot to the other.

Eldon glowered at him. "It's a family matter Jimmy and not your concern."

Margaret would have smiled at Jimmy's rebuke, but expected it would only infuriate him more. Instead, she ignored him and stared back at Eldon. "Yes," she said. No emotion accompanied the word. "I've decided to accept Janice Hartwell's invitation to her party at the end of the week."

"Good, good," Eldon said. Margaret could almost see relief flash in his eyes, and in the relaxing of his shoulders. She felt a little respite of her own, hazarding the hope Eldon was second-guessing his initial championing of Jimmy. Eldon returned Jimmy's continued glare. "Sit down or busy yourself elsewhere. I won't have you hovering, damn it." A long moment of hesitation, but Jimmy complied, dropping dejectedly onto the couch like a pouting child. "Now," Eldon said, focusing on Fiona. "You've proved yourself trustworthy, Finn. Not to mention you're invaluable to me as a driver, and protector of Graham valuables—personally and financially. I'd like you to be more accessible to me." Eldon leaned back in his chair. "I'd like to offer you a room in the servant quarters."

"Excuse me, sir?" Fiona sputtered.

Margaret brightened. She and Fiona would be under the same roof, seeing each other every day. Just as quickly, her emotions deflated for the same reasons. How hard would it be to feign an uncaring attitude with Fiona present every day? "Wonderful," she said with a nod. "Finn will be better able to heal with constant supervision."

From behind her, Margaret heard Jimmy snort rudely. "We can keep an eye on the little shit," he said in a whisper.

Ignoring his comment, Margaret asked, "Can he go there now? Finn should be resting, Eldon."

Eldon gave her a look she couldn't decipher. It made her uncomfortable and worried about missing something. Was Eldon noticing some of her true emotions in her responses? Feelings she thought hidden. "You know your importance to me, Babs. So, for keeping you safe, and probably taking a bullet on your behalf, you must agree Finn needs to be rewarded."

"And a room in the house is the best reward, sir," Fiona said. "Thank you."

"No, boarding you here at the house is more for me than your benefit, kid." Eldon glanced at Margaret, then Fiona, and stopped on Jimmy as he continued. "You've been concerned enough about the girl you...found, going so far as to pay her boarding and such. So, I give...ah, I give—" Eldon seemed too uncertain to continue.

"Thelma?" Margaret supplied. She was afraid where this was going.

"Yes, of course, Thelma. I give her to you, Finn, as a reward for Bab's safety."

Behind them, Jimmy mumbled, "Fuck."

Fiona rose slowly to her feet, her face flushed. Margaret noted the barely perceptible trembling in her body, hoped Jimmy and Eldon didn't. "Sunny is not a possession to be passed around. She's a human being. She's also just a kid."

"And she's only a couple years younger than you, Finn." Eldon shifted in his chair and leaned his arms on the desk. His focus turned to Margaret. "I suspect you believe there's more to the story Finn originally gave you. The truth is her parents sold her to me. Thelma is indentured."

"That's barbaric, Eldon," Margaret said, standing.

"Be that as it may, dear sister, Thelma is my property. If Finn doesn't agree to my gifting of her, I will find other duties for her." Jimmy guffawed, causing Margaret to shudder. "Jimmy, go get her so she can learn her new duties under this roof."

"Gladly," Jimmy said, all too eager.

"Don't touch her, Jimmy. She's formally off limits to you," Eldon said, his tone serious. Mumbling something unintelligible, Jimmy left.

Margaret, and surely Fiona, was stunned by this turn of events. This wasn't the Middle Ages where marketing in slavery was an established occurrence. Yet, if she and Fiona didn't take this situation as a positive, Thelma would be the one to suffer the most. She only hoped Fiona would see it that way—eventually.

FIONA FELT SICK. How could Eldon treat a human, a beautiful child, as if she were an item for bartering? As quickly as the rage surfaced, Fiona accepted this course could make protecting Sunny easier. Eldon had warned Jimmy off if she agreed to this. If she explained this to Sunny, would she understand?

Before she could debate the pros and cons of the situation, a smirking Jimmy needlessly nudged Sunny into the room and beside Eldon. He walked behind Eldon's chair and stood like a guard. Fiona knew he didn't like Eldon's proposal, but she hoped Jimmy wouldn't cause trouble, at least on this matter.

"Thelma," Eldon said, directing his gaze at her. "You're aware of the deal your parents made with me, correct?" Sunny paled and gave a barely discernable nod. Tilting his head in her direction, he asked, "Are you aware Finn has requested to be your guardian? Has, in fact, been paying me to let you stay in my home, clothed and fed?" Sunny turned a surprised gaze on her, and Fiona shrugged. Returning her attention on Eldon, Fiona watched as Sunny shook her head. "Well," Eldon said. He stood and placed his hands on Sunny's shoulders. Sunny flinched noticeably. Fiona resisted the urge to rush to Sunny's defense and forcibly remove his hands from her. "You no longer belong to me. For saving Miss Margaret, I have turned my ownership of you over to Finn. He's moving into your room with you."

Margaret shuddered beside her. "Eldon—"

Sunny gawked at Eldon, then at her. In a mere whisper, Sunny asked, "Truly?"

Fiona gave a nod. "Yes, Sunny. I'm responsible for you now." Sunny darted away from Eldon, and launched herself into Fiona, clutching at her waist.

"I'll be your property," Sunny said, her words muffled into Fiona's shoulder.

"You're my ward, Sunny, not my property." Fiona hurt that Sunny would willing accept Eldon's terms. What kind of life had her parents given her? "I'm gonna take care of you."

Jimmy's verbal interruption tainted any positive mood inspired by the moment. "Fuck you regularly, he means, aye, runt?"

Fiona wanted to launch herself at Jimmy and pummel him. Instead, she tightened her grip on Sunny, startled by Sunny's whimper. Loosening her grip, Fiona took a deep breath to get her anger under control. If nothing else, Eldon's proposal would reinforce her gender charade.

Margaret must have sensed her mood, as she gently placed a hand on her injured shouldered, and said to Eldon, "Now this matter is settled. Sunny and I will get Finn settled in, fed, and resting. Doctor's orders, remember?"

Watching his sister more closely than the moment warranted, Eldon finally said, "Fine. We'll talk more later, Babs."

Not wanting to prolong this any longer than necessary, Fiona allowed Margaret to lead her and Sunny from the room and into the kitchen. Once there, Margaret pointed toward the table. "Sit down, Finn. I'm going to feed you, then get you settled into your room."

Sunny took the seat on Fiona's right, and whispered in her ear, "I sleep in Brigid's room 'cause it's safer than being alone. She has a spare bed." Fiona nodded. "I'll still stay with her, okay?"

She wasn't sure why, but Margaret's tone seemed distressed. "Miss Margaret?" Fiona didn't believe Margaret was upset with her. This entire awkward situation was never under her control. However, something Eldon said or had done in his office concerned Margaret deeply. Fiona suspected it wouldn't bode well for any of them. She'd let the matter wait.

"Not now, Finn. Eat and then rest." She glanced toward the kitchen entrance. "We'll talk later," Margaret said, her tone barely audible.

Fiona nodded, then reached over and gave Sunny a one-armed hug, hoping to relay her happiness. Right now, Fiona would revel in the knowledge that Eldon had released Sunny into her custody. Later, she would mull over all the possible implications.

Chapter Nineteen

FIONA PUSHED OPEN the door to the apartment she'd shared with her father—until she ran from herself, him, and his violence. She glanced around and wrinkled her nose in disgust. Strewn about the room were dirty clothes and empty booze bottles. On a table in the designated kitchen area in front of the apartment's only window, unclean plates and utensils, some with food caked to them, covered the top. She wasn't surprised the contents of the table—and the table itself under the weight—wobbled from damage done when her father, Quinn, had launched her onto it with a wicked right cross. The smell of sweat and old food accosted her, and she fought the urge not to gag. If Eldon providing her room in his home had no other positive outcome, Fiona appreciated never having to come back to this hovel.

She shook her head and went to the far corner of the room with the radiator attached to the wall. Fiona knelt on the mattress tossed on the floor. When the former apartment had burned down with her mother and brother still inside, she and her father had moved here. Even though she was the one to pay the rent, as the senior adult her father had taken the only bedroom. Fiona pulled back the corner of mattress closest to the wall until she revealed the loose floorboard beneath. She pried it open, pulled out the handkerchief with her precious savings and keepsakes, shoved her treasure into her pants pocket, and stood. Fiona didn't need to look inside the kerchief. She knew what lay within. A picture of the family at happier times, a cigar tube holding the money she'd squirreled away, and a gold chain with a single teardrop pearl once belonging to her mother. Unimportant to most, these simple items meant the world to her.

Fiona needed to leave before father got back. She'd made certain, before she'd come upstairs, to pay the next two month's rent for her father. This would be the last time. No matter what happened with Eldon Graham, or Margaret, she would need to leave this horrid city soon. She replaced the board, recovered it with the corner of the mattress, standing and stomping lightly to assure no evidence of tampering remained. Hand inches above the doorknob for her escape from the room, the door roughly pushed open, and her father stood in the doorway.

"What the hell are you doing here?" he demanded. Quinn

stormed two steps toward her, grabbed her by the throat, and squeezed so Fiona couldn't gasp air. "Where the hell've you been?" Quinn raked a gaze of disgust from her head to her feet. "What the fuck is this? How dare you embarrass me dressing like this?" He shoved her away from him so hard she barely stayed on her feet.

"Just let me go, Da. I came for my things, and I'll never come back." Fiona gauged the distance around him and to the door. He must have caught her gaze because he kicked a foot out behind him and the door slammed closed.

Quinn's brown eyes blazed with fury, darkening them to black orbs. It was odd for Fiona to stare at an older, male version of herself with so much hate. "How dare you come back, taunting me with visions of my son?" Fiona would have rolled her eyes if she didn't suspect it would anger him more. "You'll pay for this disrespect." He lunged at her, but Fiona managed to twist and sidestep him, her attention focused on the exit.

Fiona, again with the doorknob in hand to pull the door open, felt an object connect painfully with her left temple. Quinn, she realized, had thrown a bottle at her. Luckily, it didn't break. The blow thrust her face forcefully into the wood. Before she could reorient herself, Quinn's hand grasped her back collar and jerked her backward, slammed a kick into the bend of her knee, effectively dropping her to the hard floor. Pivoting to the right, extending a hand in front of her on the floor to gain a modicum of balance, Fiona was rewarded with a kick to her abdomen hard enough to raise her inches off the floor, before a second kick that landed in her solar plexus. Quinn gripped her shirt in his fist with his left hand and elevated Fiona just enough to slam his right fist into her face, once, twice. She could feel the warm blood dripping from various gashes on her face, feel the edges of darkness envelop her.

"What the—" Quinn's voice growled his dissatisfaction of being interrupted from his fun.

"You sonofabitch, I should kill you for this. You disgust me." Fiona recognizing Ian's voice from somewhere in the room and took the opportunity to stand on unsteady legs. Her balance slow to return, she moved to lean on the wall beside the open door.

"I disgust you?" Quinn asked in a disbelieving tone. "The stupid bitch is dressed like a boy, but you're not sickened with that, are you? Did your family encourage this pathetic behavior?"

"No, none of us did." Ian turned an assessing gaze in her direction, just as Claire burst into the room scanning the scene and settling her attention on her. Claire pressed herself to Fiona's side, allowing her a chance to use Claire for support. Fiona now in the hands of Claire, Ian sneered in Quinn's direction. "Fault Fiona her means to an end in silence Quinn as none of the Donnelly clan will join you in that endeavor. She's paid your rent and keeps you fed, or would if you didn't drink her money away. Fiona's why you're not out on the streets." Fiona didn't know what Ian was trying to do because Quinn wouldn't hear anything he didn't want to hear. Anything positive involving his daughter would fall into that category.

In her ear, Claire whispered, "Are you okay?" Fiona nodded, immediately sorry when her head throbbed at the movement. "Let me clean you up at our place."

"No, she's gonna stay here." Quinn shouted. "It's about time she quit shirking her duties around here." He glowered in her direction. "You'll clothe yourself appropriately, and set your ass to cleaning this place up. It's about time you quit these repulsive shenanigans and get yourself a husband. Starting now." He barely took a step in her direction when Ian stopped him with a sharp blow to Quinn's chest. "Dammit, Mick, I've got a right to discipline my own daughter."

"Your brutality is not discipline." Grabbing him by the collar, Ian jerked upward, so Quinn's feet barely touched the floor, and then shoved hard. Quinn tottered backward clumsily until he collapsed onto the mattress. Without taking his scrutiny from Quinn, Ian asked, "Do you have all your belongings, Fiona?"

"Yeah."

"Good. Please take Claire home for me?" Fiona would smile at his allowing her to preserve some dignity, but she feared her injuries would make the action too gruesome for Claire. With Claire's assistance, Fiona left her father's apartment for the last time. She wanted to do it standing straight, but her stomach muscles protested. Behind her, Fiona heard Ian's comment, "If Fiona wouldn't be angry, I'd get her money, which she just handed over to the landlord. Stay away from her, Quinn. I find you anywhere near her, I'll kill you."

Claire opened the door to the Donnelly apartment and helped Fiona to a chair. Once seated, Claire said, "Stay here. I'll get some hot water and cloth to clean you up." Fiona nodded obediently. She leaned her head to rest against the chair back and closed her eyes. She heard Ian's stomping gait, a sure sign of his agitation, as he entered the room and closed the door. He didn't say anything and hadn't moved. Fiona's eyes flew open in surprise when Claire returned and said, "Fred, bring the side table over here." Who in the hell is Fred? Her gaze went to the couch and saw a young man, tall from the looks of it, with a mop of thick, curly blond hair on his head, large hands and feet, and about as gangly as her. Freckles heavily splattered across his nose and cheeks. She suspected it his normal physique, being at least mid-twenties and well past any growing spurts. Fred watched every move Claire made as if her actions were the most enjoyable spectacle to witness. His adoration of her friend was obvious.

Ian answered her unspoken question. "Fred Morton. Fred is my partner on the police force." He pushed himself away from the door and sat at the opposite end of the couch, and across from her location. "Had some things to talk to you about, Finn. Gotta say, this wasn't the condition I'd hoped to find you in."

Fiona gave Fred a quick assessment and decided to trust him if Ian trusted him. "Not happy with this myself, Mick." Claire, washing the blood away, hit a particularly tender area on her face. Fiona flinched. "I'd intended to be in and out before he returned. Damned Irish luck of mine, anyway." Her face was swelling, if the tightness was any indication, and prevented Fiona from flashing a smirk in his direction. "How's Nana?"

Claire slapped her shoulder, mindful of her tender flesh. "Don't change the subject. She's visiting neighbors down the street." Fiona glanced up at Claire, not surprised to see the concern in her friends' eyes, but sorry she'd been the reason nonetheless. "Almost done," Claire said, putting a plaster on the worst of the cuts. Claire kissed Fiona's forehead to announce the completion of her task, something Claire had done since they were children. Fiona gave Claire an appreciative smile.

She returned her attention to Ian. "Level with me, Mick, gimme the goods." From the worried expression on his face, Ian had news for Finn, not Fiona.

Ian smirked at her, shaking his head. "If you weren't already in a sorry condition, I'd smack you myself for that smart-alecky mouth of yours." He leaned forward and rested his elbows on his knees. "Don't want to put you on the spot, Fiona, because I know what your final goal is with this..." he pointed a finger in her direction, waggling it to indicate her disguise. "...this charade. Yes, before you ask. Fred knows and is okay with your disguise, at least as much as I am kiddo. I gotta ask, are you sure you're not in too deep?"

She thought of seeing Terry murdered, and of Sunny's rape. Fiona couldn't look at him when she explained, "Honestly Mick, I'm in way deeper than I intended. I know of and have seen stuff that makes me one of your bad guys, Detective. Case of the wrong places at the wrong times, you know?" She inhaled a deep breath, and then met his gaze. "I'm not just looking out for myself anymore."

"Graham's sister?"

Fiona gave a small shrug. "Her, too, I guess. No, I need to protect Sunny until we can leave the city." Claire sat between Fred and Ian having done what she could for Fiona. She gave Ian an abridged version of what happened in Eldon's office, and how Thelma's parents had sold her outright. "Sunny was bought to work for a panel house. Now I'm trying to protect her from Jimmy Bennett."

Fred perked up. "Bennett? Is that—"

"Yeah, it is." Ian shook his head. "Listen, Fiona. Word on the street is Jimmy's running his own deals, deals to take over Graham's business. What he intends to do with Graham and family isn't known to us, yet." He rubbed a hand across his jaw. "Bennett's working with, and been seen with, a rival boss, and even a couple of out-of-towner's."

"He's slimy enough to be a double-crosser," she acknowledged.

"Let me be honest here, Fiona. I don't care what happens to any of them, not even Graham's sister." The heat of rage burned across her face, and Ian raised a hand to forestall any reply. "I realize you care for her, Fiona. And, for this Sunny kid. But there are a couple new wrinkles in this whole blanket of crime."

"Being?"

"The feds are making their intentions to take down bootleggers and speakeasies known, no matter what it takes. It is common knowledge finks are coming out the woodwork everywhere, turning anyone, including family, in for the deal."

"You said 'wrinkles', plural."

Ian stood, walked over to her, and placed a hand on her shoulder. "Second wrinkle, Junior's working with Bennett. His sole purpose, at Bennett's request, is get rid of you. Permanently."

"Didn't know Jimmy set him the task, but I knew about Junior. Well, there was a chance he'd been aiming for Margaret. I have a scar on my shoulder, courtesy of Junior and his goons." She directed a weak smile at Claire, who'd gasped at the statement. "Look at me, Claire." Claire did, meeting Fiona's gaze with a watery one. "I'm fine, and got worse from Quinn than I took from Junior."

"How long can that last?" Claire asked. "There has to be a safer way for you to earn enough to leave."

Fiona rose from her chair, grunting softly at the initial spasm of pain from her bruised body. She flashed a wry smile. "It's an age thing."

Ian snorted. "Sure, then I'm blessed with eternal youth."

Slowly, allowing her body to adjust, Fiona knelt in front of

Claire, taking her friend's hands in her own. "It's a dangerous world, Claire, and I can't make promises when so much is out of my control. I will promise what I can, and that is to be aware of my surroundings and avoid as much trouble as possible."

Claire nodded, her bottom lip clenched between her teeth. She released her captured lip and asked, "Will you come say good-bye before you go?"

Fiona cupped Claire's cheek. "I wouldn't disregard our friendship by not saying farewell." At Claire's nod, Fiona slowly stood and turned to Ian. "Damn, think I could use a nap." Ian snickered. "If I ever learn enough to help you, Mick, I'll find a way to get the information to you."

"Be safe, that's the important thing. You're family." He pointed a finger in Fred's direction. "The ugly guy here is trustworthy, too. If you can't get hold of me, find Fred." Ian rolled his eyes dramatically. "Plus he's trying to earn brownie points to date Claire."

"Good to know," Fiona said, hoping the spasm of jealousy of what could never be, wasn't apparent in her expression. She started toward the door. "Gotta go. Give my best to Nana. Maybe our next get-together will be on a happier note."

"Watch your back and stay away from Quinn," Ian said.

"Quinn who?" she said. Fiona snickered and left the Donnelly apartment, already working on how she was going to explain her newest injuries to Margaret. So much for her first day off.

Chapter Twenty

AS HAD BECOME the norm, Margaret found Fiona with Sunny in the kitchen. This wasn't a Mrs. Bauman cooking day, so only the two of them were there, sitting at the table, Fiona listening while a soft-spoken Sunny read aloud to her. The teenager, still skittish around others, came alive when near Fiona, even going so far as to smile warmly at her. Had Margaret been a jealous person, Sunny's demeanor would have caused those feelings in her, but it hadn't. The adoration Sunny exhibited was more a young sibling emulating an older one. The change in Sunny was short of miraculous, especially when she believed her and Fiona alone.

Margaret also enjoyed watching Fiona. Her tenderness with Sunny and others, her relaxed teasing, the way she put everyone's well-being before her own where all qualities Margaret admired. What she didn't enjoy was the additional damage to Fiona. The bruises and small cuts were healing after a day but still looked painful. She had been so furious to learn what Fiona's father had done to her. More so when Fiona played it off as a minor matter. A positive note for Margaret being Fiona was still handsome to her.

Much as she hated to do it, Margaret needed to interrupt them. "There you are Finn," she said entering the kitchen and striding toward the table. Fiona promptly stood. "Good morning, Sunny. How's the reading assignment coming along?"

"Fine, Miss Margaret," Sunny replied. She lowered her head submissively, her first instinct when singled out for attention. Margaret hoped, with time, they could break her of the horrible habit. Time might not be an option for her, or for Fiona. Placing a hand on the back of Sunny's chair to make certain Sunny stayed where she was, Margaret turned her attention on Fiona. "I've been presented a task, which begins me worrying, since it involves you, Finn."

"Anything I can do for you," Fiona said, sincerity visible in her tone and expression.

"Well, it's a good thing I found you both here." She looked down at Sunny. "I'll need you to join us." Sunny paled, another expected reaction to the unknown requiring her participation.

"What's the task?" Fiona asked. Having also sensed Sunny's discomfort, she reached across the table and squeeze Sunny's hand.

Setting her tone to playful acceptance, Margaret rolled her eyes in exaggeration. "I'm taking you both upstairs, where I have the excruciating job of outfitting you in a suit, cleaning you up, and making you presentable. A daunting task if I need say so." Clasping her hands together and bringing them to her heart, Margaret stared imploringly towards Sunny, batting her eyelashes at gale-wind speed. "Please, Sunny, say you won't force me to endure the torture alone."

Color returned to Sunny's face, a beaming smile joined the warm gaze meeting hers. "Won't let you suffer," Sunny said with a soft giggle. Margaret was sure Sunny's playful tone surprised Fiona as much as it had her. Bringing attention to the reaction could set Sunny's recovery backward, so Margaret extended a hand to Sunny. "Then let us move forward with our Herculean endeavor." A wide grin filled Sunny's face with delight, as she hesitantly took Margaret's hand and stood. "Onward we go," Margaret said walking toward the back staircase to the upper floors. She knew Fiona would be right behind them, confirmed when Margaret heard her mumble, "What's so hard about dressing me? I wear clothes every day."

Margaret had placed the off-the-rack suit she'd purchased earlier, at Eldon's request, in the spare room one door down from her own. This had been Eldon's room when they were younger, but he'd since moved into their parents' suite when Mother passed. Now his room lay empty, perfect for this task. She opened the door and ushered them both inside.

As her habit, Fiona promptly shoved her hands in her pockets. "Been dressing for a good many years, Margaret," she said, eyeing the suit laid out on the bed. Then Fiona frowned at the numerous boxes covering the rest of the mattress. Confusion in her gaze, Fiona said, "I don't understand."

Margaret moved forward and wrapped an arm around Fiona's waist, hoping to offer reassurance and relax her, though Margaret herself did know how to react to Eldon's request. On the one hand, Margaret liked the idea Eldon's inclusion of Fiona in more duties meant Margaret saw her more frequently. At the same time, he placed Fiona in more positions that are obvious as Eldon's employee. Though she didn't know what that entailed, Margaret knew it couldn't all be good either. She glanced toward the dresser and the twelve-by-twelve wooden box about four inches deep, the only resident, on top. Her instructions from him were "give this to Finn with the suit, and he'll know what to do with it." The statement had set her hackles to rise. What else could she do but look inside the box? Her worse fear realized, Margaret accepted that Fiona wouldn't be in this mess if she hadn't come to Margaret's aid in the first place. Margaret owed her the same protection.

She also wondered how Fiona would respond to Eldon's newest offering. Pointing toward the changing screen, Margaret said, "Take your clothes off."

Fiona startled and Sunny gasped in surprise. "What?" she asked innocently. "I'm giving you some privacy. Now, hop to it." She clapped her hands. "You need to be dressed and ready to drive Eldon to his destination in less than ninety minutes." With one last questioning gaze at her, Fiona complied. Margaret turned her attention on Sunny. "Go across the hall and fill the pitcher with hot water, grab a washcloth and towel, soap, and bring them back to me." A haunted expression darkened the girls' features. Automatically, Margaret pulled her into a hug and spoke gently into her ear. "Neither of them is here, right now. You're safe." Since Sunny's arrival, Margaret and Fiona made certain Sunny was never alone. The task had taken some creative maneuvering of schedules. If they couldn't accomplish coverage at the house, Fiona brought Sunny to Dorcas, where Finn would later retrieve her from the club. "Brigid is on the lookout and will warn us of their return. Okay?" Sunny stared at her for a long moment, probably gauging the veracity of her statement, before exiting the room to complete Margaret's request.

Lifting the tops of various boxes on the bed, all but the hatbox, Margaret retrieved a complete set of undergarments and a large roll of sturdy gauze before walking them and the dark blue suit over to the dressing screen. She bit her lip to staunch the moan wanting to burst from her lips at the vision before her. From Fiona's embarrassed expression, Margaret doubted she'd hidden the lust from her hungry gaze. Fiona had removed her shirt and trousers, even tossed her Newsboy cap on top of the clothes pile on the floor. She stood in front of Margaret in an undershirt, boxers, and socks—the left one complete with holes at the heels and toes from wear. In spite of the boys' undergarments—or because of—she realized Fiona was an incredible and enticing sight. Margaret frowned again at the bruises coloring the milky skin, these hidden beneath her clothing. Even this damage didn't detract from the vision before her. "It's moments like this I wish we were alone on an island, where I could feast upon you with my eyes, and then my hands and mouth." Margaret hadn't intended to speak the words aloud.

Gauging from Fiona's compulsive swallow, Margaret suspected she'd done just that. She wouldn't take the words back, nor would she apologize. Closing the distance, Margaret clutched the clothing in one hand, and pulled Fiona's head down with the other, taking Fiona's lips firmly with hers. Fiona deepened the kiss, mingling the hunger with her own. Margaret heard Sunny reenter the room and reluctantly pulled away. She knew from the increased intensity of each kiss they shared that Fiona returned her affection. Margaret also knew Fiona had no idea what to do with the feelings, or how to move forward with them — not on her own. The warmth pooling between her own legs told Margaret she couldn't wait much longer to take Fiona as her lover. What Margaret feared was, in her hurry to satiate her own desire, she would move too fast. Fiona was unprepared for the physical aspects and undoubtedly had no knowledge of making love. She didn't wish to frighten her.

"Wonderful, Sunny, thank you," Margaret said taking the pitcher from her and setting it on the windowsill ledge. "The washcloth, please." Sunny handed it over, and Margaret submerged it in hot water, pulled it free and rung the excess liquid. She stepped forward, all the while maintaining eye contact with Fiona. "Your face is probably still tender, so tell me if I hurt you." Fiona nodded, and Margaret wiped cloth gently across her face. When finished, Margaret flashed a playful smile at Fiona. "Take it off, Finn, all of it."

"What?"

Margaret chuckled at Fiona's shocked tone. "Relax. Sunny and I will wait by the bed. Change into the new stuff after you wash up. We'll help you with the suit." She stalked closer until only a breath could pass between them. "Unless you want me to help you wash the rest of you? Maybe bind you?" Fiona gave a noticeable gulp, and Margaret stepped back, done with her emotional onslaught to Fiona's barriers. "Seriously, let me know if I can help. Otherwise, come out when you're done." She turned to leave after Fiona nodded.

Fiona must've worked at lightning speed (fearful Margaret wouldn't keep her word to wait to be asked back to the screen, maybe?) because she hadn't waited long. Fiona stepped from behind the screen, stopping short of the bed, and dumping her original outfit into a heap at the foot of it. Margaret's heart skipped at the glorious sight. Fiona in a fitted suit made Beau Brummell more a slob than a fashion icon. The jacket's boxy cut made Fiona's chest and shoulders appear as that of a barrel-chested and muscular silhouette. The cuffed, creased, narrow legged trousers gave her legs the appearance of being longer than her average five-six height and athletic. The high cut vest was also in dark blue and showed above the jacket opening as the current fashion dictated. Under it all, a simple white shirt and blue silk tie.

"Is it all right?" Fiona asked. She finger-combed her hair back nervously.

"More than okay," Margaret said. There was no way Fiona's Finn persona would be able to avoid the hungry and appreciative attentions of women. There would probably be a few men fuming with envy. If she could put Fiona back into Finn's usual attire, Margaret would do it in a heartbeat. Her own green-eyed monster had raised its ugly head. She didn't want anyone else flirting or touching Fiona. None of that mattered because Eldon had a plan, Fiona had a mission, and Margaret had to finish her work of art. "Two more additions, Finn, and you're ready. One is my addition, and one is from Eldon, which I have to say I don't like."

"What is it?" Fiona frowned at her, her gaze perplexed.

Margaret walked over to the box on the dresser. She picked it up, brought it over to bed, and placed on the duvet. Opening the lid, she said, "Eldon wants you to be able to protect yourself, and him, I presume."

Fiona leaned over her shoulder and peered inside. Margaret heard her audible gulp. "I can't wear that thing." Inside the box were a Browning FN Model 1910, a clip, and leather shoulder holster. "I could hurt somebody, myself included."

"Think that might be Eldon's point, Finn. To hurt the bad guys who come after him or you." Margaret felt torn over the need for the pistol. Shot once, she wanted Fiona to have the chance to protect herself from another attack.

On the other hand, the significance of the weapons' addition meant Eldon would be making more demands, dangerous demands, of Finn who essentially had just turned seventeen. Was Eldon grooming Finn for more duties? She knew, of course, about the adjustments to their family restaurants modifying them into speakeasies. Less than a year had gone by, and their businesses were losing money. No one was going out to eat; and, even the local theaters were shutting down due to lost revenue. By joining some of the less desirable men in Boston, Eldon made sure to provide what the customer wanted. She suspected Jimmy's influence was strong in Eldon's organizational decisions, which made her fear for Fiona stronger. How could Fiona not protect herself?

"Or for the purpose of protecting you, Sunny, and Brigid." Fiona unbuttoned and removed her jacket with trembling hands, tossing it on the end of the bed while winking at Sunny. "Whatever it takes to keep you ladies safe." She gave a wry grin. "Good thing I didn't have this when I saw Quinn. You'd be visiting me in the slammer."

"That's not something you should joke about." Margaret

gave an indignant huff. "We would have bailed you out, and then hidden you in the cellar."

Behind her, Sunny chuckled softly, and then said, "The garage would have been too obvious." Once again, Margaret felt excitement and surprise by Sunny's interspersed humor. Sunny may not say much, or often, but was a delight when she did contribute with just enough.

"Oh, ha, ha, squirt," Fiona said, holding her heart as if wounded. Then, Fiona pointed to her face. "See, no grease stains today."

"Wasn't necessary with all the bruises," Margaret said. She held up the leather holster so Fiona could slide her left arm through the heavier leather section, which would hold the pistol, and Margaret turned her so her right arm could slide through the thinner leather section.

"Would rather see the grime," Sunny said. Her tone was warbling as if ready to cry.

Margaret reached over and pulled Sunny into a hug. "I agree with you on that one, Sunny. Bet Finn does, too."

Fiona shrugged a couple time to settle the holster into a comfortable position, as she said, "Yeah, dirt's easier to deal with, but bruises last longer."

"Mm-hmm. You realize that's such a boy comment." Margaret reached for the pistol, but Fiona stopped her. "It's not loaded yet."

"I don't care. Any danger should be shouldered by me." Fiona picked it up and slid the clip into the base, before slipping the pistol into the holster and donning the jacket again. "At least it's not bulky. How's it look?"

"Can't tell it's there unless you're looking for it," Margaret said. Despite Fiona's air of comfortable casualness, Margaret had noticed the slight trembling again in her hands. She knew the nonchalance to be for Sunny's benefit so the girl wouldn't worry. Margaret stayed her hands when Fiona bent to retrieve her Newsboy cap. "Oh, no you don't. It's time for my addition to your ensemble." Removing the hatbox lid, Margaret pulled out a black wool Fedora with a four-inch crown. Reverently, Margaret placed the hat on Fiona's head, tilting it rakishly to the right side. Her heart stopped at the impressive and debonair transformation to Fiona. Margaret had always thought Fiona mesmeric in her appearance, but now she was heart stopping. If Sunny hadn't been present, Margaret would have kissed her soundly, if only to take proprietorship of Fiona and claim her possessiveness.

Sunny drew a breath in sharply. "You're so handsome." She stepped forward until she was beside Fiona, and ran a hand down

Fiona's right arm.

Eyes wide, Fiona said, "Thank you, Sunny. Your opinion means a lot to me."

"I agree. This is one time I'll have to applaud my brother's request." Margaret stepped close enough to kiss Fiona, though she didn't, and clutched the wide lapels in her hands. "Be careful, Finn. You may have to use the Browning to keep the women at a respectful distance. The women," she glanced at Sunny, "who care for you deeply," attention returned to Fiona's warm brown eyes, "are here, in this house."

Fiona kissed Margaret on her cheek, and then kissed Sunny's cheek. "No one could replace either of you in my attention or my heart."

"Finn?" Sunny's whispered tone trembled. Fiona and Margaret both looked in her direction with concern.

"What is it, honey?" Fiona asked. She tugged Sunny into a hug.

Voice trembling, Sunny said, "Jimmy will be mad at the attention you'll get. Please be careful." Margaret stepped behind Sunny, reached her hands around her and clasping them behind Fiona's back, so it was a three-person hug. The shuddering of Sunny's body as she cried soon gave way to comforting reassurance she and Fiona hoped to provide.

"How come I wasn't invited to the group hug?" Brigid asked from the doorway. "You owe me."

If Brigid was here, someone — or all of them — had returned. "Is it time?" Brigid nodded. Margaret wrapped an arm around Sunny's shoulder. "Okay, handsome, show time."

Chapter Twenty-one

FIONA PULLED UP in front of the house, stepped out of the car, and opened the back door as Eldon and Lorraine exited the house. Placing one hand on the car's roof, and another on the open doorframe, Eldon shook his head sadly in her direction. His smirk belied the negative action. "You look good, kid. Just have one question for you."

Straightening, Fiona said, "Okay, Boss."

Removing the hand from the door, he removed her fedora as the hand from the roof ruffled her unruly hair. "Finally get you to wash your face and still don't know exactly what you look like because of the bruises. Will I ever see the real you without accessories of one kind or another?" Eldon slapped the hat back on her head and slid in beside Lorraine.

Fiona removed the fedora and finger combed her hair, and replaced her hat, sure to pull the brim low as Margaret had done.

In the rearview mirror, Fiona caught the slight movement as Eldon reached and grasped Lorraine's hand, but they stared out their respective windows at the passing landscape and hadn't turned to each other. She wasn't privy to the couple's time together often but had wondered about their feelings for the other. Maybe they truly did care for each other. Which only confused Fiona more. If he cared for Lorraine how could Eldon not see the abuse—the repeated violations—from Jimmy? How could Eldon not see Lorraine hiding her pain and shame in a bottle? Fiona bit her bottom lip at the mental chiding, answering her own question. Forced to protect themselves emotionally behind silent masks for centuries, women found alcoholism just another mask.

The silence from each lost in their own internal retrospection was broken by Eldon. "I'm going to need you inside the restaurant and not the car, Finn. You'll be at a table, having a meal, which will make my sister happy." Fiona almost missed Lorraine's grin at the remark, so quickly had it fled. "This could be a lucrative meeting. Or it could be a setup."

"You expect something to happen?" Fiona asked, reminded again of the new and uncomfortable additional weight of the gun and holster at her side.

"This is new territory for a lot of us, Finn. I'm jumping into a mighty huge bed with the biggest bad guys in the business.

Anything could happen."

Fiona nodded her understanding. "What do you suggest as a signal in case I need to alert you?"

Eldon stared at her in the mirror's reflection. After a lengthy pause, he said, "Don't know why you continue to surprise me, kid, but you do. You'll be going places if you live long enough with your old man in the picture." He raised his chin and squinted at her when she gasped. "Babs told me what he did. I can take care of it for you if you let me."

"I appreciate the offer. Truly. The way he drinks," she said, a quick glance in Lorraine's direction, "time and booze will kill him soon enough."

"Offer's always on the table, Finn. Okay. As for this meeting, I don't know. I just don't want to be surprised with the major hiccup."

"Not my business, but care to share what you're expecting?" There were so many things she hated Eldon for doing, like placing her in a position as an accessory to his crimes. Moments like this, Fiona grudgingly liked the guy. Could it be she simply gave Eldon more license because of Margaret?

Eldon raised the hand holding Lorraine's to his lips, kissed her knuckles, and then released her hand and leaned forward. "Nothing in this town remains a secret, not for long anyway. So it's a given this meeting be in a public place and known by a lot of folks."

"So, I'm gonna let you know when trouble's coming and alert you? In the case of a barrage of bullets, do I hit the floor screaming? If it's the feds, I give you a gagging gesture—or just pull a Daniel Boone?" Fiona caught Lorraine's gaze, keeping her in the conversation. "That means to throw-up, Miss Lorraine."

Eldon burst out a laugh. "Nice sense of humor kid. Probably not too far from the truth either. If it's an attack, definitely go with the hollering, but I'd like to hope you'd use the piece I gave you and participate in defending our territory." Fiona raised a brow at the statement. Our territory? Since when was she more than a bratty, often disheveled, gopher? "If it's the feds—" He paused. "You can spot them right?" Fiona nodded. "Give me a signal of some sort, and I'll think of something." Eldon turned to Lorraine. "Keep an eye on the kid, honey. Don't want you getting hurt."

Lorraine appeared surprised by the sincerity even Fiona heard in his tone. "Okay, Eldon, whatever you say."

Fiona wanted to cheer on behalf of Lorraine. Maybe Eldon wasn't as oblivious to Lorraine as she thought. But, no, he was totally oblivious where Jimmy was concerned. Jimmy. The hothead. A hotheaded bully who could spoil everything with this meeting if he felt even a little threatened. Eldon had better come up with more than "something" if he intended to diffuse Jimmy at the get-go. "Eldon, sir, may I make a suggestion?"

Frowning, Eldon stared at Fiona in the mirror. "I'm always willing to hear ideas, kid. If you're an ass, I'll tell you. I like you, Finn, told you that before this. Good ideas bring promotion. Promotion puts you one step higher on the ladder of success. You're smart for a kid off the streets." Fiona nearly jumped out of her skin when Eldon unexpectedly placed a hand on her shoulder. "Smart doesn't work by itself. A kid like you should know how to watch his back. Never become too complacent." Too complacent? Yeah, like with this whole car ride. Eldon's nice now, but ultimately could turn on her in a heartbeat.

She had to remember to bide her time and get away from this lousy place. Out of the city, out of this life. A frisson of cold fear ran through her. When she left here, Fiona knew as a certainty Sunny would go with her. Would Margaret become so enraptured with Eldon's request that she'd stay to please Eldon, have a normal life with a man, and maybe create children? The normal life Fiona could never provide her. Eldon jolted her from these inner questions clutching at her insides with tendrils of fear. "So what's on your mind?" he asked.

If you knew you'd change your opinion of me, she thought. "You know some personal stuff about the guy we're meeting with, right?"

"Yeah. And?"

"So, if the feds walk in, you still talk business, only you change the topic. You bring up restaurant business, like planning a special party or something. It's what you do." Fiona pulled up to the restaurant and turned in her seat. "This way, you don't alert the other guys to a situation—he'll know right away—and Jimmy doesn't react with his di—" Fiona shot a glance toward Lorraine, who grinned back at her. "Well, react like a dumb hothead."

Eldon gave her a wide, toothy grin. "Keep up the good ideas, kid, and I'll stop noticing how hard it is for you to wash everything at the same time. I'll be too distracted by your gumption." Eldon gave a quick inhale of breath. "Let's get this over with."

Fiona exited the car, pocketed the keys, and rushed over to Lorraine's door. She extended a hand to assist Lorraine in getting out like a respectable lady. Soft, warm fingers met hers. Fiona glanced around to make sure there wasn't an immediate threat in sight before leaning forward. "It's—" Her gaze landed on the usual exposure of cleavage, more so because Lorraine shifted at that moment and her dress shifted. Lorraine met her gaze, panic in her eyes. Incensed, Fiona nearly missed the shake of Lorraine's head. Lorraine didn't want Eldon to know, obviously. How could he not already? Fiona wanted to scream her frustration, but she didn't. "It's clear," Fiona finished.

She released Lorraine's hand, which Eldon promptly took in his when he exited the car, and Fiona followed them into Grandma Graham's *Sorriso* Restaurant trying not to wriggle to relieve the discomfort of the gun. For half a second, Fiona squeezed her eyes shut and prayed, "Please don't make me use this thing."

ELDON'S MEETING BEGAN as planned, for which Fiona was grateful. For the most part, the floor plan was open and inviting, with a bar — would it be a sideboard now? — that held a large bowl of fruit and vases of flowers. Behind the bar stood Owen Aleman, the manager, a rail-thin, hawk-nosed man with a bald spot and horrid comb over, and a nasty attitude. Fiona ignored the sneer he directed at her and returned her attention to Eldon. His principle player, "Big Bill" Dwyer from New York, had arrived, seated at a large table near the kitchen, but not near enough for prying ears to overhear. A wall on either side, giving the effect of an alcove, helped assure added privacy. Lorraine and Jimmy flanked Eldon, Jimmy's seat against the back wall while leaving Lorraine exposed and open to the room.

The New York men sat around the table, but had a bit of distance from Eldon. Three groups of two men sat at other tables dispersed around the room. Two of these groups she recognized as their people, with the third belonging to Big Bill.

Fiona sat at the farthest table from them all, at the only one-person table in front of the large window looking out on the busy street, a nearly cleared plate of corned beef hash in front of her, courtesy of an Eldon special request. The neighborhood was multi-cultural. Fiona recognized *sorriso* as smile in Italian. Eldon was neither Italian nor Irish, but food was food and if it brought in the customers, more power to him. She would laugh at her lunch, but Eldon intended the meal as a taste-of-home for his favorite driver, he'd said. She hadn't the heart to tell him her family may have eaten boiled potatoes and cabbage, but including meat was a rarity, sometimes even for special occasions. The unexpected thoughtfulness from him kept her mouth shut.

At Eldon's main table, the conversation was low and often

heated. Fiona decided to count herself lucky she had the singular task of being the lookout for trouble. The staff, less than usual probably due to the nature of the meeting, consisted of two waitresses and the manager, who hovered near Eldon's table.

Fiona felt comfortable in the knowledge the inside of the restaurant with its lime green walls and various pictures of children at play the theme, probably to provide customers a feel of eating in grandma's dining room. She focused her attention on the activities outside. Cars had parked along the sidewalk, their occupants probably out shopping or at other restaurants. There was a sign tacked to the front door of Grandma Graham's announcing "private party" to keep customers away today. Couples and families walked the sidewalks chatting, laughing, and shopping. Occasionally Fiona would see a less than enthusiastic reveler in the crowd.

As she observed the idyllic scene outside, Fiona noted the incongruities, too. The car parked three down from hers, had two men in suits. They hadn't left the vehicle, had been there for twenty minutes, and their dual scrutiny seemed focused on Grandma Graham's. Though Fiona couldn't be certain as their faces were in shadow inside the car.

Across the street at the grocery store, one of Junior's gang pilfered an apple, and also seemed focused on the restaurant. From the expression on the grocers' face, this looting was a regular occurrence. Fiona knew that often the storeowners found it easier to ignore than fight the hooligans since doing so would invite more vandalism.

Beside the grocery store was a stoop leading to a door for access to floors above the building, often used by the business owners and families, sometimes room rentals. Perched on the stoop, leaning back against the brick wall, sat Fred, his attention seemingly engrossed in the newspaper he held. Fiona smiled to herself. If Fred were nearby, Mick had to be, too. Shifting her gaze slightly to the left, she found Mick casually standing against the side of the building talking animatedly to a woman. Fiona shook her head. Mick must've recognized her since he dipped his head in a nod. She returned her attention to the men in the car. They hadn't budged.

What are you waiting for? she wondered.

Her curiosity must be their motivator. No sooner had she silently asked the question, the men exited the car, adjusted their suit jackets, and headed in her direction as if they had all the time in the world. Feds. Fiona turned to get Owen's attention, waving him toward her table. Rather than comply, Owen turned away.

Fiona looked around for a waitress. One stood close to the

kitchen's door. She waved and the woman started forward, but was stopped with a hand on her arm by Owen. Fiona knew she shouldn't leave her post, but she had to let Eldon know about the men. She scooted her chair back and heard Lorraine call for the waitress, "Sarah." Directing her gaze to Lorraine, Fiona noticed the quick nod before Sarah blocked her view. Lorraine whispered something, Sarah nodded and rushed toward Fiona.

She looked outside to gauge the distance before the men reached the restaurant. Fiona saw a car pull in front of the grocery store with about five men. She recognized the driver as Donato Giuffrida's man, Lucas. Fiona stood, halting Sarah before she spoke. Leaning toward her, Fiona whispered, "Tell her, two Feds and a car of Giuffrida's men. Go."

The girl rushed away.

Fiona peered out the window as she reached toward the shoulder closest to her, and the man, Jack, rose. She spoke before he could. "Five of Giuffrida's men across the street." He didn't question her or check for himself. With a flick of Jack's head, all three tables of men stood and started for the door.

"Have a seat, Finn," Eldon said. He nodded at her when she glanced at him. She did as she was told. Sarah reappeared with a large slice of apple pie and placed it on the table in front of her. Lorraine came to her table and sat down opposite her, as the two Feds walked in.

Three things happened simultaneously. Eldon, from his table, asked, "Will we be providing the cake at this reception, or just the food?" Owen rushed forward and intercepted the Feds. "This is a private consultation. You'll have to come back later."

Lorraine reached over and covered one of Fiona's hand, "Do I get a reward?"

The Feds surveyed the room and left. Fiona turned her attention to the street. Eldon and Dwyer's men fanned out in a semi-circle and started toward the car across the street. Lucas gunned the engine and drove off. No one had exited the car. Eldon's men stayed fanned out. Dwyer's men flanked the front door.

"So, is that no to my reward?" Lorraine asked, grinning.

"What?" Fiona's heart was pounding from all that could have happened in the last few moments. Her head wasn't keeping up.

Lorraine looked amused. "Can't I have a bite, since we scared off the Feds and bad guys together?" She expected Lorraine to be having fun at her expense, but the beautiful blonde had a mischievous glint of amusement twinkling in her eyes.

Automatically, Fiona raised her fork, scooped up a bite of pie, and aimed it toward Lorraine's open mouth. Ruby red lips surrounded the fork, Lorraine raised one eyebrow, and Fiona shook her head. "Your bewitching won't work on me," Fiona said, shaking her head.

Lorraine placed a hand to her ample bosom. "You wound me, Finn."

"I doubt it," Fiona said, taking a large bite of pie for herself. She chewed, swallowed, offered Lorraine another bite. "Thank you, Lorraine. If you hadn't helped me, I might have done something stupid, or not been able to do anything at all. I'm beginning to like you." Lorraine's response was a wink and understanding smile.

Chairs scraping across the wood floor let Fiona and Lorraine know the meeting was over. Dwyer and his entourage left, his two men outside escorting them to their car. Eldon walked over to her table. "Thank you, Finn. That worked like a charm." He turned to Jimmy. "I need you to have a word with Owen. He no longer needs this job." Jimmy didn't appear happy with the comment, but he walked over to Owen, who was shuffling into the kitchen. "You did well, Finn. I'm sorry you didn't get the assistance you needed." She shrugged. "Are we ready to go?" he asked, taking Lorraine's hand and assisting her from her seat.

Fiona glanced toward the kitchen. "Owen's fired?"

Eldon picked up the discarded fork and scraped a huge chunk of pie on it, shoving it in his mouth as if it would evaporate if he moved too slowly. "Love this stuff." He swallowed and moaned appreciatively. "Yes, he is." Eldon shoved a hand in his pocket, the other arm curled around Lorraine's waist. Voice lowered and intense, Eldon said, "Listen, kid. You work for me, just like Owen, just like everyone here and more. You had a job to do that was almost sabotaged by Owen pointedly ignoring you."

"But it all worked out okay," Fiona said. She'd been frustrated by Owen's inactions, but not surprised, and didn't want to be responsible for his losing employment.

"This time, and no thanks to Owen." Eldon glanced at the men outside. "Doesn't matter to me you're the youngest on my payroll, Finn, because I take your word and opinion just like any of them out there. Maybe I'm more accepting because you've not let me down. If Giuffrida's men had been able to sneak up on us, we could all be dead."

Lorraine leaned into Eldon and flashed a smile at Fiona. "We should get Finn to the house. He needs to drive Margaret to her party tonight, especially since he looks so handsome."

"You're right of course," Eldon said, moving to the door and opening it for Lorraine. "Why is that important?" he asked Lorraine. Fiona would have rushed in front to make sure the path was clear, but let the men outside be responsible. Besides, she wanted to hear Lorraine's reasoning.

"You want her to find a beau, right?" Eldon nodded. "What better way for a young man to present his best than to flaunt another handsome one in front of his face?"

Fiona suspected the statement was Lorraine's off-handed way to compliment her on the new attire, but worried Eldon would read more into her own interest in Margaret. When had her life slipped so out of control, she wondered? Lorraine hit on another concern for Fiona. How would she react when Margaret flaunted her male friends in front of Fiona?

Chapter Twenty-two

THE UPCOMING EXCITEMENT of the evening radiated from Margaret and could light the night sky, Fiona thought. Not that it was necessary as the evening was pleasantly warm, and the sky bright with stars as ten o'clock approached. Why did rich people entertain so late? Margaret's happiness made Fiona happy, but a small part of her pained too, as one more checkmark appeared in the column acknowledging their differences. The party that Margaret would attend in an hour didn't bring her the same joy. Fiona had watched Margaret, since her return from Sorriso, hardly able to contain her elation.

Fiona, forced to continue wearing the suit from the restaurant meeting, now waited for Margaret in front of the house, the car running in anticipation of their journey. Leaning against the car, hands in her pockets and legs crossed at the ankles, Fiona hoped to portray a picture of nonchalance. Inside, her stomach churned, feeling dread rallying, and announcing the beginning of changes that would catapult them both into the unknown.

Fiona worried about what could be keeping Margaret. Pushing off the car, Fiona prepared to go inside when the front door opened. She straightened and her mouth opened in an O of awe at the vision before her. Margaret wore a mermaid-style dress consisting of a charcoal mesh, long-sleeved overlay splashed with silver sequins and beads, with a small trail of material behind, lined by a sleek black dress. On her hands were charcoal gloves. Onyx and silver earrings dangled visibly from her ears with her hair up in the back, the front done in the Marcel waves becoming popular. She was stunning. Fiona was truly out of her depth in this woman's presence.

Fiona rushed up the stairs to assist Margaret to the car. "You're a dazzler, Margaret," she said, taking Margaret's gloved hand in hers.

"Thank you, Finn."

Fiona escorted her to the car and released her hand with a quick squeeze once Margaret slid into the back seat. Fiona closed the door, rushed around the car and got behind the steering wheel.

"You remember the directions?" Margaret asked. Fiona nodded. "Then let the games begin."

Despite the odd statement, Fiona knew Margaret was excited

about the party, having spoken of little else since her announcement to Fiona at Dr. Matthews. At first, Fiona believed it was for Eldon's benefit, and subsequently, anyone in hearing range who could inform Eldon of her mentioning it. Fiona recognized the glint of joyful expectation this gathering brought Margaret. Fiona felt changes about to happen, which confirmed her world was about to spin out of her control.

Fiona drove up the road about two miles to reach the Hartwell's driveway. If the line of cars ahead were any indication, most of the elite of Boston were attending. She waited her turn to pull in front of the house so she could let Margaret out. The Hartwell home appeared to be an earlier design than the Graham home, in the old Federal style, boxy, low-hipped roof, molding on the cornices, even fanlights over the front doors. Both homes spoke of money. This is where Margaret belonged, what Fiona couldn't provide her — another acknowledgment of their differences.

The way cleared and she pulled up in front. A young man in black trousers, white gloves, and maroon jacket with high collar rushed to the driver's side, as another opened Margaret's door. "Park over along the exit drive, if you're waiting."

"I'm waiting." Fiona turned toward Margaret. "Don't hesitate to send someone to me, if you have a need."

Margaret smiled. "Of course, Finn, but I'm sure I'll be just fine. I won't stay too long. Just make an appearance to make Eldon happy."

Fiona nodded, waiting until Margaret was assisted out of the vehicle and inside the front door before she moved the car to the designated area. Margaret may believe what she said, but Fiona suspected once inside around people of similar age and background, time would cease to have the same meaning.

THE INSIDE FOYER, sitting room, and library doors stood opened and filled with the laughter of people enjoying themselves. Margaret glanced around, noticing people from her childhood, some from college, and so far, none was her hostess. She moved to the left and entered the sitting room. Finger sandwiches, hors d'oeuvres, and a large crystal bowl with punch lined a table pushed against the far wall. Windows along the wall were open to let in the night air to cool the heating of numerous bodies. Chaise lounges, a high back couch, and padded chairs were placed around the room. The fireplace had a large vase of flowers placed in its center.

Margaret didn't immediately spot Janice, and just as she did, a warm breath brushed against her neck, as a voice said, "You're magnificent as always, dearest Meggie."

Only Janice, and her older brother of two years called her by the nickname. "Mark," she said, turning and giving the man a hug. "It's been a while." She gave him a quick once over. Mark was short for a man, not more than a couple inches taller than Fiona, thick blond hair cut neat above his ears and slicked back. His body was healthy, but thin, and he had long slender fingers. He'd be handsome if not for his huge hooked nose. "You look good as always."

"Thank you," Mark said warmly. "Compliments will get you whatever you want. May I get you something now?"

"In a little while, maybe, after I thank your sister for inviting me."

He glanced up and over her shoulder. "Here she comes now."

"Meggie, it's been too long," Janice Hartwell gushed, wrapping Margaret in a firm warm embrace. Janice, a near identical image of her brother only curvaceous where Mark was thin, her nose shorter, had always been the wild one in their friendship, often coaxing Mark and Margaret into childhood escapades.

"Yes, it has been, and entirely my fault," Margaret said, returning the hug. Janice stepped back. "I won't rely on what I see, though the answer appears positive, that you are doing okay?"

"Yes, everything is grand." Janice moved closer to Margaret. "I thought I'd seen you last week, shopping, but you'd disappeared before I had a chance to catch your attention. Then there was that awful shooting business." Margaret felt the color drain from her face, her body shiver in memory of Fiona's bullet wound.

Mark touched her elbow. "Are you all right, Meggie?"

Margaret nodded, Fiona's image as she lay bleeding on Edward's exam table flashing in her memory. "I'm fine. The bullet hit my driver while protecting me."

"I'm sorry to hear that," Janice said, placing an arm on Margaret's shoulder. "From your expression, you care for the man. I take it the driver wasn't Jimmy."

"Hardly." Margaret snorted. She looked around at the people. She could hear some chatting from other rooms. Janice was one of the very few who knew the secret of her proclivities. They roomed together for a time in college.

Having too much fun with her frivolities and parties, not caring whom she married as long as they didn't stifle her entertainments, Janice had dropped out and returned home. So far, marriage hadn't lured Janice into more stability, though rumor spoke of both Janice and Mark leaving a long line of rejected suitors.

Margaret said, "We'll do lunch soon, and I'll tell you all about what happened."

Janice studied her and seemed to suspect the story was not one for a house full of guests. "None of my guests will miss me—"

Margaret shook her head. "No, we'll find time to talk. When I leave, you both can walk me to the car, and I'll introduce you to Finn."

Frowning, Mark said, "To your driver? Whatever for? It's sufficient to know the man is okay."

"Do shut up, Mark." Janice shook her head. Despite her family's money, Janice didn't hold to social expectations as the rest of her family, including Mark, who relied on social status to deem a person's importance.

Margaret wanted Janice to meet Fiona. She suspected Janice understood the underlying intricacies of her relationship and caring for Fiona. Other than the fact Mark was male, Margaret remembered why she'd not missed their time together. She had missed Janice, and a knot of regret snarled in her belly. She'd been wrong to relegate Janice to the haphazard phone call now and again.

"In the meantime," Margaret said, ignoring Mark's comments, "let's enjoy the wonderful extravaganza you've pulled together." Having Mark around, though, arrogant as he was, could work in her favor. If spending time with him kept Eldon and Jimmy at bay, Margaret had no problem using him for her benefit.

She just hoped Fiona would grasp the matter in the same vein.

THE HOUR NEARED two o'clock in the morning. Fiona managed a light doze, but it did little to help her stay alert. Maybe some fresh air would be helpful. She pushed open the driver's door and exited, leaning against the side facing the front of the house, pulling the hat brim down to shadow her eyes, even in the darkness. Couples and singles had been coming and going in waves all night, but now seemed to dwindle to a steady flow of folks leaving for the night—more like morning, she groused silently. Fiona was about ready to despair of getting any real sleep before dawn when she spotted Margaret stepping from the front door with a man and woman.

She straightened, her gaze following Margaret's progress toward their car. They seemed safe enough, and Margaret seemed happy, but Fiona couldn't say the same for herself when she noted the man's arm draped around Margaret's waist. It's not like someone like you can claim her, Fiona's inner voice declared. Even when Margaret gave her hope they might somehow have a chance at a relationship, hope Margaret might truly go with her and Sunny to Colorado for a new life, Fiona had to admit she grasped at a fantasy. They were from two different worlds. Margaret's was about to collide with Fiona's reality.

"Finn, I want you to meet some friends of mine." Margaret latched on to the arm of the woman and leaned her head onto her shoulder. "This is Janice. We've been childhood friends, and went to college together for a time."

Janice extended a hand and demurred to batting eyelashes. "Finn, hmm, the pleasure is all mine, I'm sure." Fiona shook the offered hand. "You're quite handsome, aren't you?" she asked, stepping closer and placing a possessive hand on Fiona's chest.

"Enough, Janice." Margaret removed the hand on Fiona. "Leave him alone."

"Yes, do stop playing with the children, sister," the man said.

"You're just jealous, Mark," Janice said, her tone blasé, but her hungry gaze focused on Fiona. Fiona wanted to squirm under the uncomfortable scrutiny, but didn't want Mark to note her discomfort. "There's nothing childlike in Finn." She whisked a gaze in Margaret's direction. "Not that anyone cares, but I certainly approve. I must admit I'm a bit jealous, too, Meggie, knowing this gorgeous young man actually took a bullet for you."

Goodness, what had Margaret told them? Fiona wondered. Uncomfortable with Janice's attention, Fiona cleared her throat. "Are you ready to go home, Miss Margaret?" She was in a hurry to leave the hot, from Janice, and cold, from Mark, responses of the Hartwell's.

"Yes, take the child home. I'm sure his nappy needs changing." Mark snickered. "I'd say get him to bed, but Janice might offer to assist in that endeavor on your behalf." He leaned in and kissed Margaret on the cheek—a little too long for Fiona's comfort.

"Don't be so crass, Mark," Margaret said tiredly.

Mark shrugged drolly. "So he took a bullet, it's his job, right? I'm certain the boy's well paid for performing his duties. He's the hired help, after all."

Nope, Fiona didn't like this pompous ass one whit.

Margaret stepped closer to Fiona, who opened the door to the back of the car. "Thank you for a wonderful party, Janice. I had a wonderful time." When Margaret turned to Mark and smiled, Fiona stifled the urge to punch him in the kisser. "Don't be a stranger, either of you."

What? Fiona had to bite the inside of her cheek to keep from speaking the word aloud. Margaret slid into the car, and Fiona closed the door. Pinching the brim of her Fedora, Fiona nodded in Janice's direction. "Good evening, Miss Janice." Fiona pointedly ignored Mark, as she settled into the driver's seat and started the car. Hired help was she? Well, take a little snubbing from servants, mister high-and-mighty-rich-guy.

Fiona expected Margaret to call her on the bad manners, but she didn't. They drove the short distance home in silence, and Fiona believed the matter dropped. Until they reached the house and Fiona pulled up in front. "Mark had no right to speak to you as he did, but I need him, Fiona."

"For what?" Fiona stared at Margaret in the rearview mirror. If she turned to look at her directly, and someone inside was watching, it would be obvious they were doing more than discussing employer to employee directions. "He's an ass."

"Yes, and one who will convince Eldon Jimmy's out of the running for spousal intentions, when I spend time with him. It's just for a little while," Margaret said, her voice soft.

Pain flared in Fiona's chest. "Fine. But if you still need me —"

"Of course I need you. You'll still be my driver."

The pain blazed hotter. "Margaret, I don't know if can."

Margaret's brow drew together in confusion. "Why not?"

Didn't she realize how difficult that would be for Fiona to watch Margaret with someone else? A man, no less. Mark already took liberties with Margaret's person, physically with both kissing and waist holding. Maybe their relationship wasn't the same for them both. Fiona heaved a heavy sigh. "Forget it, I'm out of line."

Shifting forward in the back seat, Margaret placed her gloved hand on Fiona's shoulder, and she turned around, even as she suspected Margaret was about to remind her of her place, her position. "Believe me, honey, it won't be any easier on me," she said. Fiona realized Margaret understood her hesitation. "Mark's safe insofar as a friend and the perfect cover for my true affections — you. Between Sunny and Mark, Eldon and Jimmy won't be expecting it when we all run away." Margaret shrugged. "Trust me when I say I intend Janice to be with us for each outing with Mark."

She had no right to question Margaret, but explaining herself made Fiona feel a bit reassured. Fiona squeezed her eyes, before she got out of the car, opened the door for Margaret, and waited until she entered the front door. She drove around to the back of the house and parked the car. The bright side of Margaret's plan being Fiona wasn't allowed in the establishments Margaret, and the Hartwell's would be frequenting. She wouldn't have to see Mark possibly get fresh, but lord help him if she caught him getting out of line.

Chapter Twenty-three

EXCESSIVE BANGING ECHOED in her bedroom, and Fiona groggily opened her eyes.

"Get up, runt. I have work for you to do," Jimmy announced from the other side of her door.

Sunny rushed from Brigid's room, ready to play her part as a lover, should the need arise. Fiona shook her head. Sunny sat down at the end of the bed. Fiona glanced at the clock. It was only a couple minutes after six in the morning.

"What the hell, Jimmy?" she hollered. "I'm not working for Eldon today." Not to mention she'd only gone to bed little more than two hours ago, a fact Fiona suspected Jimmy was well aware of.

Another heavy thump sounded. The chair she'd placed under the doorknob vibrated but didn't budge. "You'll fucking do what you're told when you're told. Get your ass out here in ten minutes, or I'll break this door down and beat you with it. Do I make myself clear?"

Yeah, crystal clear you pecker-head. Aloud she replied, "I'm coming."

"Glad the little bitch is good for something." Jimmy guffawed, his meanness forgotten in his crudeness. "Hurry it up."

Fiona sneered at the door. "Disgusting creep," she mumbled. Sunny gave her a sympathetic smile. Reaching across the bed, Fiona caressed Sunny's cheek. "I can make every effort to keep him away from you, but I can't stop his garbage talk."

"I know. Better get ready," Sunny said. "It'll be worse for you if he has to wait."

Tossing back the covers, Fiona got out of bed and hurriedly dressed in her Finn guise—not the fancy suit for chauffeuring. She pulled the chair away from the door. She reached out to Sunny, placing a hand on the back of her neck. "You've been patient, Sunny. We won't be much longer in leaving this town."

Furrowing her brow, Sunny asked, "Miss Margaret, too?"

She couldn't answer that question. Margaret stated she would, but the more nights Fiona drove her and the Hartwell's to various clubs, the less certain Fiona was of Margaret's intent. More often than not, Margaret had exited these establishments a bit tipsy, alerting Fiona they'd been down to the speakeasy parts of the businesses. On the positive side, Margaret had only once strayed from Eldon's businesses.

Since Fiona was only the lowly driver, she'd been outside with the car when the three had hastily exited the Cuckold Beasts, barely long enough for a drink. Not that she was complaining. Fiona much preferred when they stayed with establishments where she had some knowledge of either the managers or the employees. And, now, she wanted to respond to Sunny with some assurance, but couldn't.

"She's been invited, but I just don't know, honey."

"Fall's coming soon, and you believed we'd go about now," Sunny reminded.

Fiona raked her fingers through her hair, pushing the locks into some semblance of neatness. "Look okay?" she asked.

Sunny nibbled her lower lip. "Bruises are at the yucky yellow stage. You'll need to go back to smudging with dirt soon."

Dropping a kiss on the top of Sunny's blonde head, Fiona started for the door. "Thanks for keeping an eye out for me, sweetie. Be good today, and I'll see you—"

"When pecker-head allows it?" Sunny said. Her tone innocent, but the mischievous sparkle in her eye belied it as such.

Fiona snorted. "Yeah, until then."

She found Jimmy pacing in the kitchen.

"'Bout Goddamned time. I need you to wait in the office of The Fishing Net." He shoved a brown paper wrapped bundle, about the size and shape of a brick, toward her. "A woman, Jane, will be there at seven o'clock. Give this to her." He handed her a key. "Unlocks the office door." She pocketed it. "Then you do whatever else until nine when I need you to run your old delivery route. Your temporary replacement has been screwing up, and I haven't anyone to fill in."

A myriad of questions buzzed through her head, but Fiona mostly ignored them. It was safer that way. The package couldn't be life-saving medicine. The woman's name was Jane, and she conducted business too early in the morning for legality's sake. And after Terry, there was no way Fiona was going to ask about what may happen to the temporary driver. Too much knowledge was a dangerous thing to both her sanity and her life.

"Any special message for Jane?"

"If there were I'd'a told you so. Don't push me. Get your ass going. Time's wasting."

A short time later, Fiona let herself in the restaurant with her set of keys. She left the back door to the kitchen ajar so she'd hear anyone entering, and Jane would know someone was here. Using the key Jimmy gave her, Fiona entered through the door with the frosted window, the word office stenciled in the center. The room was small and held too much furniture for its size. There was a small three-by-three barred window facing the alley, a dingy yellow towel covering it. A desk placed in front of the window faced the door and sat flush with the wall to the right, an armless desk chair pushed against it.

On top of the desk lay three metal in-boxes, each overflowing with papers and manila folders, an ashtray heaped with ash and spent cigarette butts, a few pencils and pens haphazardly placed as if tossed. Against the left wall, three metal four-drawer file cabinets, their tops also cluttered with piles of unfiled papers and folders. The wall with the door had a chair in the corner, a cardboard box of what appeared to be soiled towels and table linens on the seat. A simple clock hung on the wall, letting her know she had fifteen minutes before the seven a.m. meeting time.

Fiona moved behind the desk, pulled out the chair, and sat down on the worn leather. She reached for one of the pencils, intent on using it as a distraction, but stopped herself when she noted the grease and dried food caking the item. Instead, Fiona began lifting the corners of papers in the center inbox, finding receipts and invoices from various businesses clumped together, with no apparent timeframe separating them into any reasonable filing system.

"Damn, Owen," she mumbled, "how the hell do you find anything in this mess?" It appeared he hadn't actually accomplished anything for a while. She frowned, realizing she hadn't seen Owen around since Eldon's meeting with Dwyer. Fiona shook her head, not wanting to focus on the implications. She gave up riffling through the paperwork and started pulling out desk drawers. A couple were empty, the center one had more dirty writing instruments and an opened pack of cigarettes, a silver Zippo, and pack of mints. She wrinkled her nose and closed it. The largest and last drawer to investigate, on the lower right-hand side, had a lock. Fiona tugged at it, not expecting it to budge, but it slid with only a minor squeak of protestation.

Considering the size of the drawer, it was strange that the only contents were two thick leather-bound volumes resembling the standard register for accounting. Fiona pulled them both out and lay them side by side. She opened them, scanned the entries, and began comparing them against each other. In no time at all, Fiona had concluded one volume represented the restaurant's accounting of incoming and outgoing expendables. The other, though nearly identical, reflected the true reckoning of funds. Someone was skimming from Eldon. But who? And, why keep these books together? If a person were going to steal from their employer, would it behoove them to secure the volume away from prying eyes and exposure?

What appeared to be the case hit Fiona like a punch to the gut. Jimmy. Only he could be responsible if he had access to the damaging records and this office. Had he intended this as a trap? Having her caught with both volumes? For all intents and purposes, these notations went back way before she'd started working for Eldon, negating her duplicity with doctored books. But, would that really matter when shown in the light of day? Did Eldon know this was still going on, even after killing Terry?

Fiona felt nauseous. Whether a set-up or not, Fiona didn't intend to be caught unawares. Shoving the registers back in the drawer, Fiona exited the office and locked the door behind her.

Leaning against the locked office door, Fiona tried to appear bored and sleepy—not too hard there—as she waited for Jane. It wasn't long when a heavy-set, middle-aged woman with greying hair, her bosom the size of cantaloupes leading the way, entered through the back door. Fiona pushed herself off the door. "Jane?"

Jane appeared mildly surprised, raising a single eyebrow. "I'd have met you in the office."

Feigning confusion, Fiona said, "This is the office. What I'm supposed to give you was handed to me by Jimmy, not from in there." She tilted her head toward the door. Then, she pulled the package from her pocket and handed it to the older woman.

"I see." Did she? Had Fiona scuttled the plan Jimmy had made? Jane accepted the package. She inhaled deeply, her massive breasts rose like the cresting of a boat on the swells of a turbulent sea. Fiona stifled the urge to laugh when an image of an infant, nestled in her cleavage while Jane breathed, flashed in her mind. Talk about a joy ride, Fiona thought, wrestling her gaze from bosom to face. "Thank you. I won't keep you any longer."

"You're welcomed," Fiona said simply. "Have a good day." Jane turned to leave, and Fiona followed, locking the restaurant behind her. She managed to get into the delivery truck without incident, pulling away from the building only after Jane made her way to the sidewalk and turned right onto the streets filled with the waking of the day's business.

"Managed to dodge another bullet," she mumbled, "both figuratively and literally."

FOR THE FOURTH night in a row, Fiona waited for Margaret and friends to wind down their frolicking so she could drive everyone home. She was exhausted.

Each morning Jimmy made certain she rose at dawn,

complete with excessive door pounding, to conduct a busy schedule of errands and deliveries. She didn't dare complain to Eldon, not knowing if he was already aware, and considered it part of Fiona's duties.

Also, she didn't comment to Margaret, since she was having fun. It was good to see the happy, exuberant Margaret, even if they spent little to no time alone anymore. Besides, complaining to Margaret might translate as jealousy of Mark. Not that that could ever happen since, other than the amount of time he shared with Margaret, Fiona witnessed little in redeeming qualities in him.

She'd considered flirting with Janice, but feared the attention would backfire. Janice apparently was known as the love 'em and dump 'em character. Of course, Fiona didn't have the heart, or the comfortable ease, to disrespect Margaret that way. No one would know since outsiders saw a young boy and his sophisticated employer's sister. But she'd know. Her heart belonged to Margaret, whether she reciprocated or not.

Tonight Fiona parked in the backdoor delivery spot of Fishing Favors, making it easier for Margaret and friends to enter and leave. Plus, no one would question Finn Cavanaugh's presence as one of Eldon's employees. Music drifted out from the upstairs restaurant, a few casual diners — hired for this purpose — ate dinner, danced to a quartet of musicians, and chatted; while, downstairs in the sound-proofed basement, the real crowd laughed, drank, danced, and was entertained by Fatima and the girls.

Fiona had hung around the dressing room for a while, catching up with the people who'd accepted her from the beginning. The problem was, they knew her too well, could tell how the strain of her insecurity concerning Margaret affected her. She loved their support, but didn't want them thinking less of Margaret and the perception of feigned attentions. Molly hinted earlier, having spotted Margaret in the crowd, at her upset of toying with Fiona's tender heart. Much as she denied having a tender heart, or alienation of Margaret's affection, Fiona couldn't hide all her emotion from her face or her friends.

So, she'd decided to bide her time in the cool night air. Clattering of pots, utensils and the like from the kitchen resonated into the night letting her know she wasn't alone — even if feeling a tad lonely. This was hard for her. Fiona needed to know if she delayed her departure needlessly, waiting for something, someone, with no intention of running away with her. She should put her foot down, demand an answer, and adjust her plans accordingly. Part of Fiona feared Margaret wouldn't leave;

and, as long as the question lay unspoken, hope existed, and hope was all Fiona had anymore.

The night was still early, just this side of midnight, and Fiona considered pursuing the habit of smoking to pass the time, remembering the opened pack in the manager's office. But she'd wasted no time giving Jimmy back the key. Also, to do so would give away being inside the office if she acknowledged the pack's existence. Nasty habit anyway.

"Finn," Margaret's voice rang out in the night, sounding tipsy. Fiona turned to see her three charges gliding out the kitchen door. Margaret tilted her head, listened to the music for a moment, and rushed to Fiona's side. "Dance with me, Finn."

"Why do you insist on leading the riffraff on?" Mark groused from ten feet away.

"Finn isn't riffraff," Margaret defended, hands on hips, appearing suddenly sober. Had she been drinking? Or was it all an act for the Hartwell's benefit?

"Really? Then why's his face covered in bruises and scars telling otherwise?"

"You don't know anything, Mark."

Impulsively, Fiona placed a hand on Margaret's shoulder. "You don't have to defend me," she said, meeting Margaret's gaze. A painful blow landed on her jaw, rocking her head back, and forcing her a step backward, more from surprise, than any real force. "Sonofa—"

"You jerk," Margaret shouted, as she slapped Mark hard across the face. "You've just added to Finn's bruises with a stupid move like that."

"Filthy scum shouldn't have touched you." Mark covered the red mark left from Margaret's palm. From the way he swayed, Fiona knew Mark was thoroughly inebriated. "I get tired of the rabble insinuating themselves into the good graces of those of us with better upbringing and resources."

Janice walked passed Mark and close to Fiona. "Let me see." She reached up to gently clasp Fiona's chin, tilting to examine her jaw.

Catching the fury glinting in Margaret's eyes, Fiona pulled her face out of Janice's grip. "I'm fine. Little girls have hit me harder."

"I'm sure they have," Janice said, smiling. She stepped back. "Give Meggie her dance, Finn. I'll make certain Mark doesn't interfere."

The soft notes of a song Fiona was unfamiliar with wafted through the night. Margaret strode close, took Fiona's left hand in her right, placed her left hand on Fiona's hip. "Please?" she asked, her gaze pleading as they met Fiona's.

Helpless to deny Margaret anything, Fiona led her into a dance. Mark was correct. Fiona was out of her league. But holding Margaret in her arms felt so right. Their steps matched perfectly, their nearly even height fusing them in all the appropriate places. She hoped the music played forever. Her nerves jangled, Fiona became acutely aware of her perspiring palm. "I'm sorry, I'm sweating on you."

"Oh, Finn, I don't care. Plus, gloves remember?" Margaret breathed, her warm breath skimming across Fiona's ear. "How do you always make me feel safe?"

Fiona knew it as a rhetorical question, but she responded anyway, nestling her lips against Margaret's ear so not to be overheard. "My sole wish is to care for you. I wish it could be forever."

"One day soon, it will be." Fiona quickly squeezed her eyes shut, reveling in the moment, learning her one hope would become a possibility—in time. "I want to kiss you right now." Fiona missed a step, and Margaret said, "Much as I'd like to drop Mark a peg, I won't give him the opportunity to berate you anymore." All too soon, the song ended, and Margaret pulled away. "Thank you, Finn. You can take us home now."

Fiona stood speechless for a moment to catch her breath and then helped the women into the car before slipping behind the wheel and driving off. As expected, Fiona dropped the Hartwell's off, left Margaret at the front door, and drove to the servants' entrance.

Chapter Twenty-four

MARGARET WAS SO focused on replaying her dance with Fiona in her head, it took a moment for her to realize she wasn't alone in her room. She recognized Sunny sitting in a chair with her arms folded across her chest, in the corner of the window. "Sunny, what's wrong?"

The young girl glared at her. "Why are you doing this to him?" To protect Fiona, Sunny also maintained the masculine pronoun. Sunny, Brigid, and Margaret agreed it the best way to prevent an accidental slip.

Margaret was at a loss as to what she had done. "I don't understand." She pulled the elbow length gloves from her left hand, then her right, tossing them on the dresser. "What have I done?"

Sunny didn't meet her gaze, lowering her head and focusing on the floor. "Jimmy bangs Finn awake before the sun's up after Finn's just gone to bed only minutes before. You keep Finn out all night when Jimmy's worked him all day." Sunny lifted her curly blonde head, swiped away at tears running down her cheeks. "Miss Margaret, what will happen to us if Finn gets sick? How can he protect us, protect himself?"

Hurrying forward, dropping to her knees in front of Sunny, Margaret clasped the girl's hands in her own. "Oh, honey, I didn't know."

Sniffing, and then curling her lips into a snarl, Sunny said, "How could you? You get to sleep after you come home. The help doesn't have the same luxury."

Margaret flinched. "I deserve your anger, Sunny. But I hadn't ignored the situation on purpose." She wiped away the fresh tears from Sunny's face with the pad of her thumb. "Eldon told me Finn would work on my schedule. Jimmy wasn't supposed to be able to order him around."

"What if something happens, Miss Margaret? What if someone shoots Finn again and...you know?" Sunny's shoulders shook with her renewed sobs. "Why can't we leave now, before Finn dies? Or is flaunting your conquest more important?"

"Oh, Sunny, Finn isn't going to die," Margaret said, pulling Sunny into her embrace. When Sunny's breathing evened out a little, Margaret asked, "Who said I was flaunting a conquest?" It didn't sound like something a child, even one who'd gone through what Sunny had, would come up with without an adult associated.

"I heard Lorraine and Eldon talking. Eldon laughed and said Jimmy was pissed, watching you flaunt your conquest." Sunny raised her gaze, wiped at her runny nose with her sleeve, and asked in a barely audible whisper, "Don't you like Fiona no more?"

Inhaling deeply, Margaret stood up and turned away. "That's not something I'm comfortable discussing with you, Sunny."

"Do you like the man better?" Sunny persisted.

"You really should go to bed. It's getting late." Why hadn't she denied involvement with Mark? She had just let Sunny get the wrong impression, of not only her affections but also that she might not accompany them to Colorado.

Sunny rose from the chair. Head and shoulders bent, she shuffled to the door. "I'm sorry. Please don't make me go away. I don't want to leave Finn."

"That will never happen. Finn loves you."

She paused in front of the closed door, hand on the doorknob, and said, "Finn loves you, too." Sunny flicked her gaze toward her, resignation in her eyes. "You're gonna hurt him, aren't you?" She opened the door, stepped across the threshold, and closed the door behind her, not waiting for an answer.

Margaret was too stunned to have provided one. Was she the one responsible for Fiona's delayed departure? Could Fiona be waiting for Margaret to acknowledge a firm date for leaving? Yes, she used the Hartwell's—Mark in particular—to deny Eldon the opportunity to arrange a husband for her. It had been so long since she'd enjoyed herself.

No, that wasn't true. She hadn't really been enjoying herself. Maybe a small part of her truly was frightened to run away, not knowing what to expect. Wasn't staying here just as unpredictable? If she remained, Eldon would insist she consider marriage, no matter who Margaret selected as the potential groom.

She should let Fiona go. Margaret could always follow later when she'd sorted out her jumbled emotions. Margaret could do that, right?

No, she definitely couldn't let Fiona go. Especially after their dance tonight, the way Fiona had felt in her arms, felt pressed flush to her, Fiona's warm breath brushing across her flesh with her whispered words. Nothing had ever made her feel that remarkable before, even getting her teaching license couldn't compare. No one had ever made her feel so special, so treasured. Only Fiona had, even in her boy's attire, looking handsome. Fiona in a suit was heart stopping.

Damn, what was she to do? "Right now, get ready for bed?" she said aloud. Margaret removed her dress, grabbed her gloves off the dresser, and stepped into her walk-in closet. In no time, Margaret had changed into her black nightgown. Her hand stopped short of yanking her bathrobe from the back of the closet door, as something Sunny said replayed in her head.

"Finn loves you, too."

Could Sunny be right? On Fiona's part, did she see more to their relationship beyond shared attraction? Why wouldn't she? You offered to leave Boston and go to Colorado with her.

What did she feel for Fiona? Could she live without her? Her heart thudded heavily in her chest as if in response. No, Margaret might exist, but she wouldn't be living. She needed Fiona. Pulling her robe free, Margaret hurriedly slung it on, left her room, and rushed down the servants' stairway.

"LOOK WHAT DRAGGED itself home," Lorraine said. She sat at the kitchen table, drink held in her right hand and resting on the tabletop, her feet bare and propped up on the chair in front of her.

"Dinner party over so soon?" Fiona asked, tiredly dragging a chair out from the table and falling into it.

Lorraine snorted. "Seems the Misses didn't care for the Mister ogling his business partner's girlfriend for most the evening."

"At the risk of being distasteful, I don't blame Mister for ogling."

A short burst of Lorraine's laughter filled the room. "You know, Finn, I would let you ogle and not feel dirty afterward."

"That's always good to know," Fiona said. Then, more serious, she asked, "Are you okay? Jimmy still...well, hurting you?"

Pain crossed Lorraine's face. "I appreciate your attempt to be delicate, Finn, for both our sakes. We can lay that spade card on the table, though. Is Jimmy raping me regularly? Yes. Has Eldon noticed, or does he care? No, and probably not. But hey, on the plus side, he's leaving your precious girlfriend alone," her voice lowered, "and the kid, Sunny." Lorraine took a swig from her glass. "Finn, you really need to get the kid out of here, take her somewhere else, somewhere safe. Don't you have any family?"

"No family that matters, and I'm working on it," she said, rubbing a hand over her eyes to relieve some of the burning.

"Don't wait too long, hun. Don't want getting away to

happen too late for the kid."

Fiona couldn't keep the anger from her tone. "We both know it's already too late for Sunny. I'm doing all I can to keep it from happening again. What about you, Lorraine? One of these days Jimmy's going to go too far. He could hurt you badly with his temper. You're already bruised from his roughness." She slammed a fist on the table. "How can Eldon not see the evidence?"

Sighing wearily, Lorraine said, "Guess he's like you in that way."

"What the hell does that mean? I see Jimmy's abuse."

"You see what you want, Finn. Eldon doesn't see the bruises because he doesn't want to acknowledge them because he might have to face a situation he isn't ready to address. You don't see that little-miss-high-and-mighty is jerking you around by her chain."

"Don't talk about Margaret that way," Fiona said, dropping her tone menacingly. "She's not like that. There isn't any chain jerking."

"Come on, kid. Don't be delusional." Lorraine finished her drink, and slid the glass to the side, facing Fiona full on. "I see the way you look at her. Finn's heart is hooked. You're young, and your pecker's going to lead you astray. We're the underprivileged, the crap under the rich guy's shoes. Disposable. Some of us are willing to put up with a bunch of crap for even a few moments in the high-life. There are no Cinderella stories for us."

"Not looking for rich, I'm looking for forever."

Lorraine snorted. "You think the Graham princess will give that to you? You're more self-deceptive than I thought. Not only haven't you reached the legal age," Lorraine squinted at her, "albeit there's something confusing about you, I think," she leaned back in her chair, "but if she cared even an iota, why would she brandish the homely rich guy in front of you."

"She isn't brandishing," Fiona said weakly.

"Then why does she have you drive them around? Don't they have their own driver?" Lorraine raised her hands in the air. "And what's with the condition you're in? Can't she see you're running ragged on no sleep?"

"Because there was already an attempt on her life. I have the bullet hole to prove it. I'm more likely to notice something out of place."

"Seriously, Finn? Out of all the muscle working for Eldon, a little guy like you is Margaret's best defense?"

"Most people underestimate me," Fiona said. She regretted it immediately, as it came out sounding defensive.

"They're rich, which makes them users—especially toward us low-lifers. I've gotta tell you honestly, Finn. Under different circumstance, even as young as you are, I'd be honored to receive even a portion of the adoration and attention you show Margaret." Lorraine clasped Fiona's hands in hers. "Save yourself, save Sunny, and quit believing happily-ever-after happens to us."

"I'll be sure to take your comments, harsh as they felt, under advisement." She smiled and winked to take the bite of sarcasm out of her tone. In all fairness to her, Lorraine had said aloud the feelings recently plaguing Fiona. Maybe she should focus on counting her money and her blessings, grab hold of Sunny and run fast and far. What had she to lose?

How about the owner of her heart?

Chapter Twenty-five

ANY OTHER TIME, if Margaret realized she was overhearing a private conversation, she would have quietly left or loudly announced her presence to alert those she would interrupt. However, hearing Fiona's voice, laced with exhaustion, cemented her feet to the floor. Sunny had been correct in her reprimand of Margaret. As to listening in, how else was she supposed to know what was going on? It wasn't like Fiona would complain about her ill treatment. She had a plan, a purpose, and Fiona would do whatever was necessary to accomplish her goal. Even to Fiona's own detriment.

What Margaret hadn't expected was learning she'd been as oblivious as Eldon to what Lorraine endured in their absence. She'd seen an inkling of her abuse, though she hadn't understood at the time, the night Eldon had stationed Fiona as her bodyguard outside her bedroom. No matter what she learned, Margaret's concern needed to focus on Fiona. Fiona, who filled her thoughts so often this last week that Margaret concentrated on little else.

During Margaret's time with Mark, comparing him against Fiona, she realized he always fell short. She'd hoped he had changed and found reason to mature, but he hadn't, not that any maturity would have allowed her feelings other than friendship for him. But it would have made their time together more enjoyable. She silently thanked the powers that be that Janice had joined them on each occasion, even if she tended to make herself scarce for long stretches of time.

Tonight, she'd apologize; try to make it right with Fiona. Forcing her legs to move forward, she pasted a surprised expression on her face, Margaret entered the kitchen. "Ah, Finn, there you are." She glanced at Lorraine. "How are you Lorraine?" For half a second, Margaret felt uncomfortable dressed only in her nightgown and robe.

Raising an eyebrow in surprise, Lorraine said, "Dandy. And you?"

"Fine, for the most part, thank you. I hate to interrupt, but I need a private word with Finn." She focused on Fiona, noticing now the dark circles under her eyes, the sunken cheeks, her slumped shoulders. Had she lost weight, too? "It's late, I know, and I'll try not to take up too much of your time."

Fiona gave a shake of her head. "That's okay. But, can we do it in my room? Sunny can be your chaperone, if you'd like." She glanced toward Lorraine. "Will you be okay?" At Lorraine's nod, Fiona got up from the table, walking passed her and toward her room. Margaret followed.

Once inside the room, which she hadn't been in since Fiona first brought Sunny to the house, Margaret felt a little less sure of herself. She couldn't say why that was the case. The room held the bed, a bedside table with a small, winding alarm clock, an armchair along the wall near the bed. At the foot of the bed stood a small four-drawer dresser, a hurricane lamp, and box of matches on top. Fiona lit the lamp, and stood facing Margaret.

"Want me to wake Sunny, or maybe Brigid?" Fiona asked, her tone and body posture sullen. She removed her jacket and tossed it on the armchair.

Margaret shook her head. "No." She hesitated a moment. "I need to apologize, Fiona. I had no idea what Jimmy was playing, waking you and working you right after we'd returned from the clubs. Eldon gave me the impression your availability was exclusively at my whim. I'm sorry."

Shrugging, Fiona said, "Jimmy does whatever suits his agenda. Screwing around with my life is only a small part of his motivation."

"I'm also sorry for putting you in the position that enabled Mark to unleash his cruelty on you." She took a few steps toward Fiona. "However, I'm not sorry for the dance, for holding you in my arms and having your body pressed to mine. I wish we were able to do it always. Someday maybe we will."

"I won't always be here, Margaret. And, honestly, I don't know if you truly want to leave." Fiona turned away, fiddling with the lamp key to lower the light, as if trying to hide away in the darkness. "Even if you're not interested in Mark, you enjoy the nightlife, and your own kind. I can't give you that."

"I don't want that, Fiona." Margaret moved closer until she was standing behind Fiona. "I had hoped to keep you away from whatever dealings, illegal I suspect, with the clubs, by suggesting you be my exclusive driver. Jimmy being Jimmy screwed that up, and I didn't expect my plan to backfire." Margaret closed the distance and wrapped her arms around Fiona's waist, lay her cheek against Fiona's back.

Fiona stiffened for a moment, then gradually relaxed even if she didn't completely give in to calm. "You aren't responsible for other people's actions. I'm a big girl, Margaret, and can take care of myself." Of course she could. Margaret watched it every day. Fiona took care of herself, Sunny, and so many more people, herself included. She wanted to be the one to take care of Fiona.

This close, Fiona in her embrace, Margaret had a hard time thinking of anything but the feel of Fiona, her hard muscled arms and torso, the soft pliant flesh. "You should get some rest. It's been a long day," Fiona whispered.

Margaret pressed herself tighter against Fiona's back and felt their warmth joining in a perfect bonding. She tugged at Fiona's shirt, pulling it free from her trousers. A gasp escaped Margaret's throat. "Oh, Fiona." Her fingers dug into the soft flesh of Fiona's stomach. "I never wanted you to suffer so because of me. I care for you. A lot."

"You heard?" Fiona tried to pull away, but Margaret held tighter.

"I didn't intend to, but you saw me before I could leave." Margaret spun Fiona around and placed a kiss to Fiona's shoulder. "I needed to apologize to you. Now, all I can think about is touching you. Please, let me." She slid her hands up the front of the Fiona's shirt, and unfastened the buttons, skimming fingertips across the tender skin, stopping when she reached the binding. "Will you take it off for me?"

Fiona nodded, her hands visibly trembling as they complied with Margaret's request. "Margaret—"

"Hush," Margaret whispered, pressing a finger to Fiona's lips. "There are no expectations, no excuses, honey. Just the two of us, our feelings, and the journey we take exploring and sharing them." Binding removed, Margaret continued her discovery of tender flesh in the small mounds of Fiona's breasts.

They both groaned as Margaret squeezed the left one, then the right. Margaret nearly lost herself to her own orgasm from the exquisite pleasure of Fiona's flesh, her breasts full and malleable in Margaret's hand.

Margaret gloried in how hard Fiona's nipples were against her palm. While Fiona made no overt sound at her fondling, Margaret sucked in her breath and let her hands wander across the warmth of her flesh. Margaret was sinking fast into feeling more intensity than any she'd felt with other lovers, and this exploration had barely begun. Lust, arousal, burning desire flooded in her loins, driven by this woman's captivating essence. Margaret wrapped her other arm around Fiona's torso, inhaled the scent of her neck, taking in large wafts of the clean scent that was Fiona's own. Margaret smiled inwardly at the thought, Fiona's dirty face flashing in her mind's eye.

Part of Margaret wanted to devour this remarkable woman like a wanton beast, but Fiona deserved her slower, tender ministrations. If the skin was soft to the touch, it was more so to Margaret's lips, as she suckled Fiona's throat while simultaneously pinching her nipples. "Ah..." Margaret wanted to crumble to her knees, her squeezes becoming harder and her lips marking the perfect skin. Her mouth left behind red blotches, and guilt tore through her. She was no better than Fiona's father, and others who had bruised Fiona's sensitive flesh. "I'm so sorry. I've marked you."

"The intention isn't malicious, so I don't fault you." Fiona's voice was husky with emotion.

Margaret wanted her, needed her, even. The burning sensation in the pit of Margaret's stomach told her so. "Please, Fiona, get undressed and lie down." Margaret removed her own clothing as Fiona shed hers. When she lay upon the bed, Margaret joined her.

Fiona groaned, mouth slightly open, as Margaret ran her hand up one side of her thigh and reached for her other thigh. "I feel on fire," Fiona whispered, her eyes closed tight as if the admission would make Margaret think less of her. "What if—"

Pressing her lips firmly to Fiona's, Margaret silenced her. The kiss started as a slow exploration, gradually cresting to mutual hunger. "Don't hide from me. Open those luscious caramel eyes, babe. There you go." Like the rest of her, Fiona's flesh was warm and gloriously wet when Margaret touched Fiona on her mound, sliding down and across her lips, eliciting a startled gasp from Fiona.

All control escaped her. Margaret wanted their first time to be tender and last all night long. Faced with the responsive woman beneath her, Margaret lost herself in need.

Margaret found Fiona's sweet nectar and pushed her finger into it. All that mattered was the way this handsome woman whimpered in acquiescence when Margaret wrapped her arms around her, rhythmically pumping, in-out, in-out. "You feel so good."

Fiona leaned her head against Margaret's shoulder and gazed toward the ceiling. "Oh, I never thought—"

Fiona was even more captivating with her body seductively undulating against Margaret's fingers. Her skin glowed in the soft light from the hurricane lamp, from jaw to breasts, gently bouncing to their shared rhythm. Just touching Fiona was enough, but when Margaret put her lips to Fiona's throat and held a kiss there, her own body became aroused. Would each time be this incredible? Filled with insatiable need?

She nudged Fiona's legs wider, placing her thumb on Fiona's nub, rubbing in firm circular stokes. Margaret pushed deeper into her warm recesses. Soon enough Fiona's inner walls clamped on Margaret's fingers, and she came.

Long, anguished moans of pleasure filled the room as Fiona's nectar coated Margaret's hand. Every time Fiona inhaled deep breaths, trying to stifle her verbal exhalations, Margaret sucked her flesh as her fingers eased in and out of her. First, entering in gentle sliding strokes, and then gradually increasing the speed and depth. Soon those stifled moans turned into shallow breaths, and Fiona stopped her trembling before falling limp in Margaret's arms.

Margaret lightly dropped kisses along Fiona's brow, her cheeks, just behind her ear, until Fiona's breath steadied. "You're incredible, Fiona. I adore everything about you."

Fiona chuckled nervously on a long exhale. "Shouldn't I be giving the compliments after the way you just made me feel?"

"This isn't tit-for-tat," Margaret said, brushing a lock of dampened brown hair back from Fiona's brow.

"Hmm, actually, I think it is." With a look of longing, Fiona caressed the side of Margaret's face with her strong hand. It never failed to amaze her that Fiona could be so strong and tender simultaneously, the perfect conundrum. Margaret turned to face her. Fiona grabbed the back of her neck and kissed her, hot and a little bit rough, desire sending shivers down her spine. Margaret let out a moan, which made Fiona kiss her deeper. Fiona's tongue roamed over hers, sensually probing Margaret's mouth. Fiona pulled away, nibbling at her lower lip before kissing Margaret soundly again.

Fiona's hands roamed over Margaret's ribcage, sliding along her heated skin. Margaret's body shook with pleasure every time Fiona's fingers roamed close to her quivering breasts. They pulled away from each other. "Ah, you're perfection, sweetheart. Nirvana," Fiona murmured breathlessly. Fiona shook her head, her eyes burning bright in the near darkness. She pulled Margaret closer to her in another sweet, thorough kiss. Her right hand grazed Margaret's breast, and she gasped against Fiona's mouth. In the back of Margaret's mind was the thought, "Let this last forever."

Fiona's warm, soft mouth moved to her earlobe and silenced all thoughts. Fiona drew Margaret's earlobe between her lips, sucking gently and then scraping her teeth over it lightly.

Margaret groaned and clutched Fiona's back. Her heart pounded in her chest, so loudly she was surprised Fiona didn't hear it. She hoped the sound hadn't left the confines of this room. Her whole body burned with desire. Fiona moved from her earlobe to her neck, nibbling at the sensitive skin before deftly drawing her tongue across it. Margaret whimpered and arched her back. Even Fiona's lightest touch was making her whole body shudder.

Fiona ran her fingers over Margaret's lips, "You're shaking."

"You make me feel."

"Feel what?"

"Simply feel. I can't stop thinking about you, Fiona." Margaret sighed, unable to stop the truth from leaving her lips. "I've never felt this way about anyone." Fiona pressed her mouth to Margaret's, and the two immediately fell into another earth-shattering kiss.

"Margaret?" Fiona murmured against her lips, "Please shush. I don't want to mess this up."

"You never could, babe." Margaret leaned back as Fiona trailed kisses down her neck. She trembled at Fiona's touch. Fiona's hands roamed over her burning flesh, pausing to encase Margaret's breasts. She let out a moan at the instant hardening of her nipples before Fiona rubbed her thumbs over them, and then pinched the hard nubs, rolling them between her fingers. Margaret's moans echoed loudly in the room, and she trembled.

Her body's reactions to Fiona's touch brought a rush of thoughts. Margaret's heart wasn't just pounding with the intense sensual responses and desire she felt for Fiona, but also for something more. Her heart throbbed for Fiona's smile. For the laughter, shared together, and shared with Sunny, Brigid, and Mrs. Baumann. Margaret's body was flush from the pleasure quaking through her, brought on by the touch of this remarkable woman. Margaret realized she loved Fiona. She loved every nuance and molecule that made up Fiona, loved her with every fiber of her own being.

Fiona pressed Margaret's full breasts together and slid her tongue between them. "Ah, sweet goodness," Margaret cried out, clutching Fiona's head to her breasts, unconsciously grinding them against Fiona's face. "Getting a bit brazen, are you?"

Pulling away, Fiona flashed a wicked grin. "Complaining?"

"Never."

Fiona's long fingers delicately tugged her nipples. Her tongue roamed over Margaret's sensitized skin, and she moaned again, her hands clutching the back of Fiona's head. Her legs jolted as Fiona's expressive lips wrapped around one pouty nipple, tugging lightly with her teeth while her hand twisted the other. Her tongue spiraled rapidly over Margaret's breast, and her other hand gently stroked the inside of her thigh. She bit her lip and threw her head back, letting the waves of pleasure completely overtake her.

Her moans became more urgent as Fiona's hands and tongue moved more and more quickly over her flushed skin. Fiona raised her head and pulled Margaret into yet another warm kiss, her hands stroking Margaret's breasts. "Please, Fiona." Margaret heard the huskiness of desire in her own voice. "I can't stand much more. Take me."

Fiona shifted, her eyes traveling slowly over her, settling on Margaret's mound, her legs. She knew what Fiona intended. "You don't have to do that," Margaret said.

"I do." Fiona stroked her hair, leaned down to kiss her deeply. "I hope I do this right."

"Nothing you do to me could be wrong." Margaret reached to caress her cheek, hoping to provide reassurance through her touch if not her words.

Fiona's kisses shifted away from her mouth, moving over her jaw, her throat, and collarbones. She lavished attention on Margaret's breasts, covering their sensitive flesh with kisses, stroked the outer curves of the breasts with exploring fingertips, nuzzled her face into the cleft between them. When Margaret writhed beneath her, Fiona moved farther down, dropping kisses across her ribs, next to her navel, on her hips. Finally, Fiona kissed Margaret at the juncture of her thighs. Margaret jerked with surprise and pleasure, squeezed her eyes shut, her mouth opening on a gasp.

Smoothing her hands over Margaret's thighs, Fiona spread them apart and slid herself between them. She stroked her hand across Margaret's mound, and her nether lips. Margaret knew she was wet, felt Fiona's fingers easily glide across and between her folds. Her touch felt marvelous. Margaret was helpless to restrain a moan of loss when Fiona pulled her hand away.

Fiona bent and pressed her mouth to Margaret's clitoris. Her tongue swept across Margaret's bud, down across her lips, deep in the folds. Margaret's hips jumped upward to press more firmly to Fiona's mouth. Fiona clasped her hips to hold her down, but Margaret couldn't seem to stay still, squirming under the almost painful pleasure of Fiona's ministrations. Fiona had no difficulty holding her still enough to continue with the glorious assault upon her senses. Her tongue laved the entire length of Margaret's lips repeatedly.

Margaret shook and gasped, but Fiona only pressed her tongue harder against Margaret's folds, sliding between them to enter her. Margaret's hands flew to her mouth, biting the heel of her hand to prevent herself from screaming out, announcing her pleasure to the whole damn house.

Fiona ceased pleasuring with her tongue and Margaret moaned at the withdrawal. She wanted more. Fiona placed her lips to her clitoris and sucked, continuing the onslaught of hot pleasure. Margaret's back arched up off the bed like a drawn bow, and even with her hand at her mouth she couldn't entirely suppress a shout. Fiona continue to kiss her nub even as Margaret thrashed and keened. Fiona's lips and tongue flicking and sucking until Margaret felt as though she would explode. The whole world seemed to burst into bright white light, and Margaret fell into an incredible spiraling climax.

Afterwards, she lay still, filled with a warm lassitude.

"Are you all right," Fiona asked, moving to lie beside her on the bed.

"Perfect," she mumbled. Margaret felt content. "You need to sleep."

"What about you? You don't want to be found here," Fiona said, panic lacing her words. She jumped from the bed, pulled up their clothing from the floor, arranging Margaret's neatly at the bottom of the bed. Fiona then replaced her binding, shirt, and trousers. Margaret had hoped to hold Fiona's flesh close to her for a little while longer, but could settle for holding her any manner allowed.

"I'll just rest for a bit, and leave once you've fallen asleep." She yawned, wriggled into a slightly more comfortable position. And swiftly fell into a deep sleep.

Chapter Twenty-six

"FINN, WAKE UP." Fiona could feel someone shaking her shoulder, but was too tired to move. Until remembering Margaret had fallen asleep next to her last night, and she hadn't slipped the chair under the doorknob. Was Margaret in trouble of being found out? Groggily, she opened her eyes. It wasn't Margaret, however, who hovered above and quickly kissed her.

"Sunny?"

No sooner had she spoken the name than the bedroom door burst open. "Damn you to hell, Finn," Eldon yelled.

Fiona pulled Sunny closer as she reached for the switchblade on the bedside table. "What the hell?" she mumbled, staring at the doorway and finding a livid Eldon, a frightened Lorraine, and Jimmy nearly salivating as his gaze settled on Sunny.

Fiona focused on Jimmy first. "I'll stick you, Jimmy, if you ever act on what your face says you're thinking right now." She turned to Eldon, hoping her expression showed righteous anger instead of the confused shock she felt. "Have I done something to piss you off, and that can't wait until morning to discuss, sir?" She added the last word in hopes to soften her surly attitude, despite the situation calling for it.

"Where's Margaret?" Eldon stammered. Then Fiona knew what the mass invasion was about; and wondered when Margaret had left the room.

Frowning, also glad she'd dozed off while wearing most of her clothes, Fiona reached for the robe at the foot of the bed, put it on, and stood. Tucking the blanket firmly about Sunny even though she wore a heavy nightdress, Fiona raised Sunny in her arms, surprised at how small and light she still felt. She walked to the armchair and sat down, gathering Sunny tight to her chest. "I would assume Margaret's in her own room, sleeping, probably."

"Look, I'm sorry, kid." Eldon waved in the direction of Jimmy and Lorraine. "They had this strange idea they heard Margaret from inside this room."

"Can't imagine why anyone would think that. Seems they're rather offensive toward Miss Margaret, and suggests I'm not happy with your gratitude," Fiona said with an elevated eyebrow. She placed a soft kiss on Sunny's forehead and then smiled wickedly as she laced her fingers through Sunny's right hand. "Don't believe we were loud enough for Brigid to hear, let alone anyone from the main part of the house."

As if the implications just dawned on him, Eldon said, "Yes, it does beg the question, and maybe much more." His scowl took in Lorraine and Jimmy. "You two go wait in my office. I'll be there in a bit to discuss whose hearing is so keen." He watched them until they were out of sight. When Eldon returned his attention to Fiona, he gave a smug smile. "Glad your birthday present is working out for you kid. I have a couple unhappy clients 'cause of my gift to you."

Fiona clenched her jaw before responding. "Don't wanna hurt your business, Mr. Graham, but honestly, can't say I'm upset 'bout it either." She flashed a smile at Sunny, then kissed her lips gently. "Best damn bauble a fella can get."

Eldon nodded, but his face held disgust. "Glad she's more receptive to you. Must be an age thing, you both being young. I couldn't even get a grunt from her." So today will be a "hate Eldon" day. Sunny gave a small cry of discomfort into Fiona's ear and realized she'd squeezed Sunny's fingers painfully in her own. Leave it to a creep like Eldon to remind her she had his used goods that didn't get the approval of the original user. "Sorry to have bothered you, kid. See you in the morning," he said before pulling the door closed.

Fuming from his remarks and the coldness of her own, Fiona took deep breaths before she looked at Sunny. She noted the lone tear at the corner of Sunny's eye. "Sweetie, I'm sorry if I hurt you." Fiona raised Sunny's injured hand, placed a kiss on her knuckles, and said, "With my grip and my words." Fiona felt the small shrug and pulled her closer into a hug. She placed a finger under Sunny's chin and raised it until their eyes met. "You know I don't think of you as a bauble, right? That I really care about you?"

"Mm-hmm," Sunny replied softly. A corner of her lip raised in a semblance of a smile.

Fiona gave her a quick peck on the lips. "All right. Let's get you to bed." Sunny giggled. "Your own bed, squirt." Sunny wrapped her arms around Fiona's neck as she brought them both to a standing position, wincing a bit from her bruised muscles and tender skin. As Fiona walked them toward the bathroom separating her room from Brigid's, Fiona asked, "How'd you know they were coming?"

"Brigid heard them. She woke Miss Margaret while I took her place." She scrunched up her face in distress. "Are you mad I kissed you?"

"No, sunshine, I could never be mad at you," Fiona stated honestly. Reaching Brigid's room, Fiona tenderly placed Sunny on the bed. The quarters were tight, but safer for them all to stay close to one another. Once Sunny's head hit the pillow, Fiona pulled the bedclothes over her and gave one last kiss to her forehead. "Sleep," she commanded.

"Everything okay, Finn?" Brigid asked, raising herself onto an elbow.

"Yeah, thanks to quick thinking from you two." Fiona caught Brigid's gaze. "Is Margaret—"

"Okay. She used the service stairs. Mr. Graham refuses to use or even remember them." Brigid smirked. "I watched her all the way to her room, while they were all peeking in on you."

"I should go check on her."

Brigid shook her head. "Not wise, Finn. You've satisfied the brother. Anything you do now would only taint the waters. Go get some rest, you're still looking battered and bruised."

Fiona gave a feigned look of shock. "What? You don't think it adds character to my boyish charm?"

"Be serious," Brigid said. "We count on you to be able to look after us. Margaret does too. I see the worry in her eyes when you aren't around her."

"I won't let anything happen to any of you," Fiona said solemnly. "I just need a bit more time before we can leave." She'd offered to take Brigid too, but Brigid stated she needed to give this idea some consideration.

Sunny grabbed her hand. "You aren't safe, Finn."

Fiona glanced down at her, then over to a nodding Brigid, who said, "You aren't doing it on purpose, but you keep messing up Jimmy's plans to make you look bad. He's dangerous, more than even Mr. Graham, and he wants both your girlfriend and your birthday present in a bad way. You stand between him and his desires for Margaret and Sunny."

Sitting on the corner of Sunny's bed, Fiona said, "Jimmy wouldn't hesitate to take his anger out on either of you. Even Margaret isn't safe." Soberly, Fiona shook her head. "Okay, I've got some thinking to do. Remember I don't want either of you to ever be caught by Jimmy alone. Sunny, try not to let Eldon catch you alone, either. His moods are too mercurial and I never know when he's Jekyll or Hyde. Stay close to each other. See if Margaret will confirm it's her idea that you do." She jumped up from the bed, yanked the side chair from the corner, and wedged the back under the door handle. "Make certain you do this, every night." Fiona turned toward them. "I need you both, and need you safe." She heaved a weary sigh. "Any luck and we only need to hold out for a little while longer, a month at most."

"Just watch your back, Finn." Brigid smiled weakly. "We can

be on guard when you're here, look out for each other when you aren't. But out there, no one is watching out for you."

With a final smile, Fiona asked, "How'd I get to be such a lucky fella to have such beautiful dolls for protection?" She turned and went back to her own room.

MARGARET WAITED IMPATIENTLY in her room, expecting Eldon to send for her at any moment; or at least have a bed check done by one of his underlings. She'd put on her nightdress, washed up, and still no one. As more time passed, the silence unbearable, she decided to check for herself if Finn was all right. The more time that passed, the more she worried the worst had happened. Although, she hoped the silence was a positive sign that Finn was okay.

Tossing on her bathrobe, Margaret opened her door, and was about to head down the service stairs, when she heard the angry, though muffled, voices of Lorraine and Jimmy in the foyer. She peered over the railing in time to see them enter Eldon's office.

Quietly, she rushed down the stairs thankful her slippers silenced her progress. As she approached Eldon's office, Margaret noted the door ajar, heard footsteps coming, and rushed into the library before anyone saw her. Margaret opened a tiny supply closet door, entered, and gently closed the door behind her. From here, she could hear everything said in her brother's office.

"All right you two, one of you tell me what the fuck is going on," Eldon raged loudly. "And I don't care which one it is, start talking."

"Jimmy thought—" Lorraine began.

"Shut up, bitch," Jimmy said. Even through the wall, Margaret could tell someone had, presumably Jimmy, slapped Lorraine hard. She gave a muffled cry, and Jimmy used the opportunity to continue. "I was just following suspicions from your girl," Jimmy said. "Some cockamamie idea your sister was in here with the runt. That they've been conducting an affair right under your nose."

Lorraine's voice was low. "I never—" A pause. "Sure, I taunted Jimmy because he was whining about Finn again. But whatever he told you, I had no part."

Margaret heard pacing, suspected it was her brother. "I thought you said you heard Margaret's voice," Eldon said.

Jimmy gave a snort. "You know how it is, boss. One bitch in heat sounds much like another." Margaret suspected his trademark smirk was present. She wished someone would swipe it permanently from his face. Wish she had the nerve to be that someone. "Kinda like our girl here."

Surprised, Margaret pressed her ear closer to the wall. Had Jimmy just subtly announced having an affair with Lorraine? She knew they had, especially after the night a drunk Lorraine tried to seduce Fiona. Since then, Margaret had seen signs of more nefarious deeds, by Jimmy, applied to Lorraine. What she never expected was his admission. She wondered if Jimmy realized what he'd announced.

"Our girl?" Eldon's tone calm, which meant the opposite.

"Wait, it's not exactly what you think, boss," Jimmy said. Margaret could hear the strain in those few words of denial. "It's kinda like—"

"What's it like Lorraine?" Eldon's voice was hard as steel. "Have you been sleeping with Jimmy, too?"

"It's not like I had many options, Eldon," Lorraine said, her voice low and pained. She didn't care for Lorraine's drinking, but she didn't mind Lorraine, who'd been gentle and playful with Sunny. Lorraine softened since Sunny moved in and Fiona started staying around. Moreover, Margaret knew what Jimmy was capable of doing. If he'd threatened her with her position as Eldon's girlfriend, there's no doubt Lorraine would have succumbed to those demands. Most likely, Jimmy also took what he wanted by force.

"You could have said no," Eldon said.

"Jimmy didn't exactly listen."

"What's your side of it, Jimmy?" Eldon asked.

"The bitch came on to me," Jimmy said easily. Margaret knew he lied. Right now, she felt sorry for Lorraine. The boys club would stick together. Lorraine was on her own. Margaret shouldn't be surprised by what Eldon said next.

"I want you out of here Lorraine. Pack your shit tonight, and get out of this house. I never want to see you again."

Margaret heard a tearful wail, followed by Lorraine's pleading. "Please Eldon, it was a mistake. It'll never happen again. Just tell Jimmy to stay away from me. I didn't want him and this wasn't my fault."

"No I suppose it wasn't," Eldon said, but Margaret couldn't hear sympathy in his tone. "Regardless who's at fault, I'll be removing the temptation out of my house." Margaret heard the office door open, and Eldon's voice colder than she'd heard in a long time. "I don't care what you do with her Jimmy, just get her out of this house, along with everything belonging to her, within the hour."

"Eldon, please listen," Lorraine begged. The woman must've

rushed to Eldon to plead her case and been physically rebuffed by her brother. Margaret heard the sound of a body falling to the floor. Then Lorraine asked, "Why am I the only one being punished?"

"Because you should've come to me if Jimmy forced you. You should've told me." Eldon heaved a loud sigh. "I would've understood you had no choice if you had told me what Jimmy had done. I know sometimes a man's needs become too difficult for him to control. Now, you can't be trusted, and I'm going to have to watch Jimmy a little closer when he's around my sister. Because know this Jimmy, any thoughts I had leaning toward you as the best candidate for Margaret have just been destroyed."

"Now Eldon please," Jimmy said. "What has this to do with that?"

"If you can't be trusted with my girlfriend," Eldon said, "how the hell can I trust you to properly take care of my sister? Much as I want her to move on with her life, Margaret deserves someone who'll look after her properly."

Jimmy barked a laugh. "There's a difference between a wife and piece of ass. No man can be forced into being monogamous just because he's married."

"I suppose not. I wouldn't have expected it, not even for my sister. But you could have used a little more discretion."

Margaret heard the office door slam. Inside the office, she heard Lorraine sobbing right before the sharp cry of pain. She suspected Jimmy, in his anger, was taking it out on Lorraine as he complied with Eldon's orders. Margaret waited in the closet, afraid to leave until everyone had gone. When she believed the coast clear, she carefully and slowly made her way to the kitchen, up the servant entrance, and snuck back into her room. As she got back into bed, Margaret gave a silent prayer for Lorraine's safety.

AS USUALLY HAPPENED when Fiona received the command to appear in Eldon's office, the cold fingers of dread ran up and down her spine. She and Eldon had been on polite and friendly terms, since she took a bullet in defense of protecting Margaret. Sometimes she wished things would be different, but Fiona knew men like Eldon never changed and didn't intend to let her guard down. Although she believed the bullet had been intended for her, Fiona wasn't stupid enough to sock a gift horse in the snout.

She knocked on Eldon's door and was commanded to enter. Jimmy was already inside and seated.

"You wanted to see me, sir," Fiona said.

"Yeah Finn," Eldon said. "There's a special job I need you to do with Jimmy. Are you up for the task?"

"Always, sir." Although a niggling of certainty was the last thing Fiona felt. What she felt was intense fear. Because Jimmy wasn't only evil, he was determined to get Fiona out of the way. "What'd'ya need me to do?"

Eldon leaned back in his chair, crossing his arms over his chest. "Had some problems with the few shipments coming from New York way. Jimmy here," he said pointing unnecessarily toward the couch. "He's to concentrate on any activity which isn't part of my operation. And you're one of our best and most cautious drivers." He gave a half smirk. "Plus, as Jimmy has reminded me, I need to be assured of your loyalties." There was a quick spark of annoyance directed for half a second toward Jimmy. "Honestly, Finn, this is more for him than me. I believe you have the best of intentions to the Grahams. But business is business."

"We're jake." Difficult as it was, Fiona kept her expression blank, knowing the only loyalties that should be in question were Jimmy's own. Someday, Fiona hoped to provide Eldon with enough evidence of Jimmy's duplicity. Not that she cared about what happened to Eldon, but anything pertaining to Eldon would affect Margaret. "I always have and will be loyal to you."

"Good, good," Eldon said. "The operation is tonight. I'll need you to leave with the men at dusk."

Jimmy gave a snort, and Fiona turned toward him. Jimmy leered, his gaze raking her from head to foot. "Maybe the runt here needs to take a nap. I wouldn't want him nodding off for staying up too late."

Eldon uncrossed his arms and leaned forward in his chair. "Knock it off, Jim. You've harassed Finn enough, and he's proven nothing but good for us."

"Only because he's trying to look good in your sister's estimation," Jimmy said. Fiona didn't miss the angry gleam in his eye. She hoped Eldon noted it too.

"Seems to me you both should have the same mission in mind, and that doesn't include bed gymnastics." Eldon put his arms on the desktop and weaved his fingers together. "This is an important matter tonight for the Graham businesses. I expect the two of you to act together and civilly. Any dislike or arguments you have with each other, save it for some other time. Tonight, you're the best of friends. I want tonight to go off without a hitch."

"I'll do my best Eldon," Fiona said, hoping the use of his given name would cement her sincerity. "Just tell me what you need."

Eldon smiled at her, this time with a spark of teasing in his eye. "I believe you will, kid. Jimmy here may have the right of it. Take the rest of the afternoon off, get a good meal, and rest up. I want you in the best condition for driving." Both his expression and his tone became more serious. "Much as I want this to go well, something in my bones tells me it's not gonna be that easy. Be on the lookout, Finn, it's going to be dark, and anything can happen. Not only do I want my shipment picked up in one piece," he said, "but if anything should happen to you, I don't want to have to explain to my sister, or your bed warmer."

Just when I get all warm and fuzzy he's a decent enough guy, he gets crude, again, she thought.

Fiona had been tiptoeing around Eldon since he'd sent Lorraine away nearly four days ago. Margaret had also curbed her nightly clubbing with the Hartwell's; and, she, Fiona and Sunny had spent those nights reading together in the library. She and Margaret hadn't made love again, but under the watchful lookout conducted by Brigid and Sunny, managed a few moments of intense kissing.

Fiona couldn't say anything in response to the last part. She wouldn't have done so with Jimmy in the room, and still wasn't sure where she stood overall in the pecking order with Eldon. It felt good, no matter how inappropriate to know he'd noticed Margaret worried about her. It was one of the things she loved about Margaret; her ability to make Fiona feel cherished, cared for.

On the other hand, Fiona thought, maybe that's why Jimmy was so pissed off at her.

Chapter Twenty-seven

THE NIGHT WAS cool, for which Fiona was grateful. Jimmy sat stoically next to her and stared out the passenger window. She couldn't name it, but there was something in his manner making her nervous. Jimmy was up to something. Fiona only hoped she could figure it out before whatever issue presented itself. They were coming closer to a small seaport just outside of town. From what Eldon disclosed, this is where the meeting would take place to pick up the shipment Eldon purchased.

"Just park over there," Jimmy said. Fiona did, noticing the trucks behind hers did likewise. She parked in a small cove, the water in front of her, trees and beach grass dotted the sandy shore around and behind them. A well-worn path led from the water's edge, where a long wood dock extended out into the water, and toward the area cleared for vehicles. "Now's a waiting game, and you get to wait in the truck." Jimmy glared at her. "I'll let you know if I need you." He gave her a quick once over and sneered. "Can't imagine what use you'd be. Eldon's a fool to put such trust in a scrawny runt like you, barely wrenched from your mother's teat."

Good thing Fiona hadn't spoken about her family because if her mother's given name had slipped from Jimmy's thick lips, she'd not be responsible for her violent actions against the man. Instead, Fiona just grunted her affirmative reply to his order. There was no use buying more trouble with him. She was already on thin ice where he was concerned. She wasn't stupid. No way would she leave the truck, and therefore the safety of other eyes. Being found alone with Jimmy didn't place high on her must-do list. She watched Jimmy walk the path, stopping at the end of the dock. Please fall in the water, please fall in the water, Fiona prayed the mental manta. Much to her frustration, he didn't.

Glancing in the rearview mirror, Fiona caught the cherry-red glow from the lit tips of cigarettes dotting the night, as the men accompanying them smoked their boredom away. Occasional clouds moved in, blotting out the moonlight, as it did right now. Despite having relaxed today, spending time with her girls and presented with another outstanding meal from Mrs. Baumann to fill her stomach, the gentle lapping of waves against the sand created a lulling and made staying alert challenging.

She rolled down her window to allow the cool air to buffet

her skin. Movement in her peripheral caught Fiona's attention. Using her index finger, Fiona nudged the bill of her Newsboy higher on her brow. Not sure if there had been something to see, Fiona sat straighter and peered into the darkness. About to chastise herself for letting her imagination run rampant, the movement came again from within the three-foot high beach grass clusters. Then the moonlight returned. The water's reflection sending sparkles of light off the water to glitter like sparks darting through the tall stems. A slightly darker shape shifted and blotted the sparks of reflection.

Adrenaline shot through Fiona. This was not good, not good at all. Casting a quick glance toward the dock, Fiona saw Jimmy still stood at its end, his focus locked out on the water. Then, she caught the distant sound of a boat engine. Their delivery was close. Concentrating on the surrounding darkness, Fiona watched, recognizing five odd distortions positioned around them on the left. So far, she hadn't caught movement on the right side. A chill raced down Fiona's back. This had to be a set-up. She suspected Jimmy was behind it, but had no proof. Capture during a shipment gone badly wasn't something Fiona intended to experience.

Pushing open the driver door, Fiona got out, moved around the back of her truck, and headed toward the cluster of trees and grass on the right.

"Get back in the truck, Finn," Jimmy hollered from the dock. A boat appeared, slowing making its way to the dock.

"Need to take a leak. Prefer to do it privately," she announced, not deterring from her course. He spat a few expletives in her wake. When she reached the relative safety of the trees, Fiona dropped to the ground behind the thickest tree, about six feet from the water, and watched the tragedy, which nearly included her, unfold.

Jimmy signaled Eldon's men, and they all left their vehicles, congregating in a group beside her now empty truck. A man jumped from the boat, conversed amicably with Jimmy. Jimmy nodded. The boat-man raised an arm above his head. When boat-man fisted his hand, the shadow's she'd observed in the beach grass transformed into men with tommy guns, bullets blazing, tearing down their men.

Some were quicker to scatter into the scenery realizing their slaughter imminent, tripping, and jumping over the men who dropped like stones where they stood. Before long, both sides alternated firing a barrage of bullets. Fiona, focused on the carnage, neglected to keep an eye on Jimmy's position.

Until now.

Ten feet away from her position, pistol pointed at her head, Jimmy glared down at her. "Well, you little shit. Your luck just ran out. I'm about ready to remove the painful pain from my ass. No one's here to save you this time."

Body trembling, Fiona slowly rose to her feet. She'd be damned if he'd shoot her lying down. "Can I ask a question?"

He smirked. "Am I gonna look after your sweetie bitch? Sure, kid, I'll console her real good."

"Fuck you."

"No, I'll be fucking her."

Fiona clenched her fists so tight her blunt nails pierced her flesh. Don't take the bait, breathe, she pleaded with herself. If he killed her, Fiona would come back and haunt him until eternity.

She didn't intend to die tonight.

Maybe even a little distraction would give her the opportunity to conceive an escape. "Tossing your hat in with Dwyer? Or is this your plan to go solo?"

"Why the hell do you care?"

She shook her head. "Are you afraid to brag about your smarts? You have the gun. Where am I gonna go? Wait," she said when he started to retort. "Okay, other than me going to hell, of course."

"Fine, I'll tell you. We've time." Gunfire still sounded around them. He lowered his gun but kept it pointed in her direction. "Both are accurate, actually. I take over operations here as the extended arm of Dwyer. In return, Dwyer gets Giuffrida off my back, and this town answers to me."

Fiona smirked. "All it costs are loyal men."

Shrugging, Jimmy said, "These guys weren't loyal to me."

"Won't it be suspicious if you're the only survivor? Or that Eldon will suspect your perfidy?"

"My per...what? Never mind. I've men waiting elsewhere, so won't be the only one left alive." He snickered. "Eldon and Margaret will be too busy comforting each other over the loss of you. Guess you can be good for something, runt." Jimmy raised the gun toward her head again. "Time for—"

"Jimmy," a voice hollered. A man Fiona didn't recognize came up behind him and whispered in his ear.

While listening, Jimmy turned his head slightly, gaze following and off Fiona, though the pistol stayed aimed in her direction. No way would she ignore this opportunity, meager as it was, by not acting. Spinning around and charging toward the beach, Fiona made for the ocean.

She was ankle deep in the cold water.

Knee deep.

Ready to dive under.

A loud report sounded behind her, just as a burning ache burst through her head, the force throwing her forward and under the water. Fiona gasped, ocean water filling her mouth. Gagging, unable to breathe, Fiona clawed her way toward air. Coughing, gagging, wheezing as she sucked in the fresh air, Fiona heard more gunfire. One round so close, droplets of water hit her face. Inhaling a deep breath of air, Fiona dived under.

Head throbbing, lungs protesting, Fiona swam to the right, away from the dock, the delivery, and Jimmy Bennett. Dizziness made swimming under water more difficult with every stroke. Right before consciousness left, Fiona stopped, relaxing all her muscles, and let herself bob out of the water, hoping she'd gone far enough.

Damn, I lost my favorite hat.

THE PAIN IN Fiona's head was eclipsed by the startling coldness of the water. She shivered uncontrollably. She angled her way toward where she observed a shack sitting on a long dock, raised five feet above the water on pylons, level with the elevated beachfront. Her lungs strained, demanded air. Fiona grabbed the pylon tightly, despite the mossy growth slick beneath her hold. Slowly raising her mouth from the water, Fiona sucked in deep gasping breaths. The gunfire grew sporadic, shouts raised from both sides. She hoped the continued noise would cover any she might make.

Fiona glanced around and upward, now able to breathe steadily though still painful, and investigate her surroundings. She noted a small trapdoor from the dock to the flooring of the shack. Despite her shivering from the ice-cold water, Fiona made her way up the rickety stairs, until she reached the door. She gave a slight nudge to determine if it was unlatched. Nothing barred the trapdoor.

Little by little, Fiona raised it, trying to take in what might await within the shack. From her lower position, she noted a door on the far side, a rickety cot, and little more than that. From here, Fiona couldn't tell if anyone occupied the room. She had a sense of someone, but couldn't hear movement or breathing. Easing the trapdoor all the way open, Fiona made her way onto the floor, belly-down. That's when she heard the low rasping breath and held her own.

Attempting to make as little sound as possible, Fiona gradually raised her upper body placing most her weight on her forearms and elbows. The sight before her sent an awful chill racing through her body. Tied spread-eagle to the bed lay Lorraine, naked and abused. "Oh, dear God," Fiona whispered. Assuring herself they were the only two in the shack, Fiona got to her feet and rushed to Lorraine's side.

Lorraine was unconscious, her breathing severely labored, her beautiful body beaten and showing signs of other forms of torture. Fiona knelt beside the cot, brushing filthy matted hair off Lorraine's brow. She was burning up with fever. "Lorraine?" Fiona whispered. She didn't want to frighten her. "Lorraine, open your eyes. I need you to look at me."

An eternity ticked by before Lorraine lifted one swollen eyelid. In spite of the horrid pain she must be suffering, Lorraine smiled, causing her split and chapped lips to bleed. "Handsome," Lorraine said, her breath coming out in a wheeze. "Fancy you here." Not considering the condition of her shirt, Fiona impulsively tugged the sleeve down, and used the wet cuff to blot at the trickles of blood.

Fiona fought back the tears. Sonofabitch, what Lorraine must've suffered—still was suffering. "I never expected this could happen to you."

"You had nothing to do with it."

"Who did this to you?" Fiona asked. Anger and bile rose simultaneously. She swallowed both down.

"You know who." Lorraine tried to shift.

The action made Fiona aware of how little movement Lorraine was allowed with her bindings. "Yeah, I guess I do," Fiona said. She untied Lorraine, wincing at Lorraine's whimpers of pain as the blood flow returned to restrained limbs. Fiona glanced around the room hoping for something to cover the poor woman. Tossed in the corner of the shack, Fiona noticed a torn dress and a wool blanket, which had seen some better days. Fiona slid an arm beneath her shoulders when Lorraine was free from her bindings. As carefully as possible, Fiona raised her to a sitting position. She stilled her motions as a cry of pain tore itself from Lorraine's bloodied lips. "I am so sorry. But I need to get you out of here, Lorraine."

"Oh, no." Lorraine looked at her with shock-filled eyes. "If they find you with me, they'll hurt you. Or worse."

Gritting her teeth, Fiona said, "Jimmy's busy." She pointed to her head and the wound from the bullet's grazing. "So far, he thinks I'm dead. At least, I hope he does. That gives us a little time to work. I've gotta get you to a hospital." Careful not to cause any harm to her swollen, cut face, Fiona cupped Lorraine's cheek and gazed into her eyes. "Do you think you can move, maybe stand?"

"If it means getting out of here," Lorraine said. "I'll do my damnedest."

"I know this is going to hurt in the worst way, but I can't carry you the whole way. You'll need to put as much weight on me as you can, until I can at least get us to some transportation. Wait, gimme a sec." Fiona released the hold on Lorraine and went to the room's main door. She peered out and realized, from this angle, they were too close to Jimmy and the others. Unfamiliar vehicles were driving up and down the road. Escape out the front door would be noticeable. She returned to Lorraine. Her options were limited. She couldn't escape out the front, and in Lorraine's condition, she didn't think to exit the way she entered was a viable option. "I dunno Lorraine. It might be best for me to go get help and come back for you. You're in no condition to travel."

"Don't leave me here, Finn," Lorraine pleaded. Fear clouded her eyes, and her body began to shake violently. "You have no idea—"

"Shush. Calm down," Fiona said, moving to sit beside her, and gently hugging her. Unfortunately, she had many ideas of what had happened to this woman during her confinement. The sight of Lorraine confirmed just how heinous Jimmy could be. "I don't want to leave you here. I also don't want to inflict more pain on you, which will happen if we make an escape."

Tears fell unrestrained down Lorraine's cheeks, giving a grizzly appearance as it combined with her blood. "I'd rather die to escape with you than die in here alone—or because they find me unbound. That would beg questions I'm in no shape to answer."

"But Lorraine—"

"Hush. I'm dying, Finn. Don't make it happen here."

"Don't say that." Sobs caught in Fiona's throat. No one deserved what Lorraine had gone through. No one deserved to die here in the shack, either. Fiona didn't know how she'd do it, but Jimmy would pay for this atrocity. She nodded. "Okay, but you need to tell me when the pain is unbearable." Fiona bit her lip and shook her head. "Stupid, huh? Pain's unbearable already. Let me know when to stop, okay?"

Lorraine gave a weak smile. "Okay."

"Right, stay put," Fiona said. Lorraine snorted weakly. "Sorry, I'm scared, and talking dumb." The throbbing headache wasn't helping, either.

"You're doing fine," Lorraine whispered weakly.

Fiona prayed Lorraine was wrong about dying. Her appearance confirmed the self-diagnosis. She needed to get Lorraine to the hospital. "We're leaving the way I came in. First, I need to check that it's safe. We'll be in the ocean. It's cold but it'll be easier to move while in the water than across land. What I want to do is take a car and get you to the hospital. Understand?" Lorraine nodded faintly. "I'm telling you this, not only so you understand the plan, but because any part of that could go wrong. And, if it goes right, the ride to the hospital could be just as painful, hun."

"You won't leave me?" Lorraine asked, soft tone pleading.

"Not while I'm still breathing. Promise."

"If I do stop breathing?"

Fiona inhaled deeply. "I don't want that to happen, Lorraine."

"Don't always get—" Lorraine cried out in agony, clutching at her stomach. Amidst the damage to her face, Lorraine paled.

"Let's do this." Fiona hurried to the trap door and opened it, her upper body hanging out through the hatch. The way appeared clear. Returning to Lorraine, Fiona knelt in front of her. "Ready?" Lorraine nodded. "I'm going to carry you to the opening, and then put you down. Once I'm on the ladder, get on my back and hold on tight."

"Wait. You can't carry me, Finn. You're—"

"Stronger than I look. Here we go." She carried Lorraine to the trapdoor and lowered her so Lorraine's feet dangled through the opening closest to the ladder. Fiona took a few steps down until hers and Lorraine's shoulders were level. "Climb aboard," Fiona said. "Hold on for as long as you can."

Mindful of the moss and dampness of the rungs, Fiona made slow, deliberate progress. Lorraine's grip remained, but Fiona sensed her strength weaken. Submerged up to her waist, Fiona walked backward until the water reached her chest, Lorraine's legs bobbing at her waist. The moon hid behind a few clouds. She hoped the moonlight would remain hidden as to further shadow them from prying eyes. Using the water to buoy Lorraine, Fiona began the slow trek back the way she had come. Fiona stopped about 200-feet from the cove and its dock. Voices drifted into the night, and from the resonance, Fiona suspected the men were finishing the loading of the trucks. Her heartbeat quickened when she noted a car sat away from the activity, just ahead of where she stood in the ocean. Please let it be empty.

Twisting her upper torso, Fiona reached around and gripped Lorraine by the waist, and pulled her across the water and into her arms. The water suspended most of Lorraine's body, but Fiona held her close, cradling her like a child. Lorraine, although barely conscious, met Fiona's gaze, but where Fiona was worried, Lorraine seemed resigned. Fiona placed her lips close to Lorraine's ear, "How you holding up?"

"Cold."

Fiona kissed her forehead. "Me, too, but hang in there. I have to leave you for a moment." Lorraine's body tensed in her arms. "Shush. I'm going to swim us over to some brush, were no one will find you." She nodded her head toward the road. "There's a car just a few feet ahead. I'm going to check out the area, make sure it's safe enough for me to get you in the car. Okay?"

"Please be careful, Finn."

She nodded. "I'm getting you out of this, Lorraine."

Once she had Lorraine hidden in a patch of three-foot beach grass, Fiona belly-crawled her way to the car until she lay a couple feet away from the trunk. She paused long enough to catch her breath, listen for any indication she wasn't alone, before making her way around the passenger side of the vehicle. Bit by bit, Fiona raised herself to peek into the window. No one was inside. A fedora and a jacket lay tossed on the passenger seat. In the backseat, a folded blanket behind the driver's seat, a thermos resting on top. She looked through the front window and her suspicions were confirmed. The loading of the alcohol shipment was nearly completed. Jimmy stood off to the side, talking to the stranger from the boat, beside him Owen in his shirtsleeves with hands shoved in his pockets. This was Owen's car. From the fervor of the body language among the three, Fiona imagined their argument might occupy them for a while.

Fiona sent a silent prayer to the heavens. Thank you, but please keep the good luck coming.

Chapter Twenty-eight

FIONA SETTLED LORRAINE across the back seat of the car as gently as possible. She tossed the thermos on the floor, draped the blanket over Lorraine, and scrunched up the jacket to pillow Lorraine's head. She heard voices advancing on their location. Her heart beat rapidly. Please, God, I beg you, let me get Lorraine to safety.

"Bottom right drawer, false bottoms," Lorraine whispered.

"What?" Fiona asked, not certain she heard correctly.

"Jimmy hides the real books in the desks."

From her previous office visit to Fisher's Net, Fiona knew doctored accounts existed. Lorraine was confirming her observation. "Okay, sweetie, hang tight."

"Use information against Jimmy." Lorraine's eyes closed.

Fiona gave a quick peck to the top of Lorraine's forehead. "Hold on and you can use it yourself." She silently closed the car door.

She brushed her back flush with the car while walking from a squat position, then slid in behind the steering wheel. No sooner had she eased the driver door closed, the engaging *click* sounding exceptionally loud, a truck approached. The truck's headlights illuminated the car's interior like a fireball. Fiona threw herself onto the seat, hoping the truck's occupants hadn't noticed her and Lorraine. Using the noise from the truck, Fiona popped up, started the car, and followed it.

There was a shout, but it didn't appear anyone pursued—yet. She reached her right hand to the side, clutched the fedora, and plopped it on her head. Owen had a huge head. The hat slipped down nearly covering her ears; she tipped it back to uncover her eyes, hoping they'd assume Owen was driving. As soon as Fiona reached a place in the road safe to do so, she pressed hard on the accelerator until she shot pass the truck ahead of her.

Fiona drove as fast as the road conditions and basic safety dictated, not driving too quickly, as she feared to be pulled over by law enforcement. How would she explain the severely injured woman in the back of a stolen car? Plus, Fiona needed to be able to watch for Jimmy or his cohorts in case they managed to follow. Still, she needed to hurry to get Lorraine to the hospital.

From the rearview mirror, even in the haphazard lighting from businesses and the occasional moonlight, Fiona couldn't miss the death-like pallor to Lorraine's skin, the trickle of blood from her lips. Worst of all, the fact that Lorraine was now hemorrhaging between her legs, the stain of blood noticeable when she'd twisted in another bout of pain and dislodged the blanket.

Her head throbbed from the gash at her forehead, her eyes burned from salt water and exhaustion. Fiona had about given up hope of arriving at the hospital in time when she sighted it just up ahead. She slammed the car to a halt under the awning of the emergency room entrance, and set the brake. Yanking open the back door, Fiona half-climbed inside, pulling Lorraine into her arms with as much gentleness as she could, cradling Lorraine close to her chest.

Just short of the doors, a male nurse caught sight of them, tossed his cigarette to the ground, and rushed toward them. "Here, let me carry her." Fiona gratefully allowed the transfer, shuddering at the sharp cry from Lorraine, who then appeared to have passed out. She noticed his nametag read Perry.

"What happened?" Perry asked, placing Lorraine on an empty gurney.

"Found her like this," Fiona said, trying to stick as close to the truth as possible. It was easier to remember later. "Out by the docks and found her hurt like this." As she explained, two female nurses came forward and assisted Perry, inspecting Lorraine, taking vitals, and cutting off clothing stiffening from the drying of the salt water. They efficiently assessed the damage.

"Is Dr. Matthews available tonight?" Fiona asked.

One of the women turned a suspicious glare at her. "How do you know this woman?"

"I work for her fiancé. Um, about Dr. Matthews?"

With a head nod from the first nurse, the second nurse left the area. "What's her name?"

Fiona felt a modicum of relief at the nurse's departure, believing she would bring the doctor posthaste. "Lorraine Mills. Is she gonna be okay?"

"Who are you?" Perry asked.

"Finn, Finn Cavanaugh, and I work for Eldon Graham." Fiona felt herself start to panic. Granted they were preoccupied with helping a severely injured woman, but they weren't answering her questions. She considered leaving the room to ask someone about Edward, but couldn't leave Lorraine alone. What if she woke up and found herself surrounded by all these strangers? Lorraine would need a friendly face. Right now, that was her.

After what seemed an eternity, in reality only a few minutes, the second nurse returned with two large men, one slightly shorter than the other. Both tall, husky, buzz cut heads of brown hair, and with sour expressions, stating roughing up a kid would be welcomed activity to their evening. The female nurse returned to Lorraine and the two men approached Fiona. "We need you to come with us," one man said.

"No, I won't leave her," Fiona said, taking a step backward and hitting the wall, which effectively halted her movement. "Oomph."

"Don't make this harder than it has to be."

"I didn't do anything."

The shorter man said, "We just have some questions for you. Outside. Let these fine folks do their jobs to help this poor woman." He grabbed her by the arm, just above the elbow, his grip stronger than necessary, fingers biting into her flesh. The other men followed suit. Without effort, they dragged her from the room. Fiona didn't put up a fight at first, not wanting to interfere with Lorraine's care. When she realized they were dragging her toward an empty room, panic set in fast. She struggled, managing to land a kick to one groin, before the other man twisted and pressed the side of her face into a wall. "Hold still, you little bastard. The cops are on their way."

The head wound was already painful, and the drying salt from the ocean water made her skin feel pinched, but the pressure on the side of Fiona's face was nearly her undoing. She couldn't fight them, and they all knew it. "Please," Fiona begged. "Don't let her be alone." She let herself stop struggling, though Fiona knew going to jail would end badly for her. She squeezed her eyes shut trying to resign herself to her fate.

"Finn?" a voice called out. Fiona recognized the voice but couldn't place it. "What the hell is going on?"

She opened her eyes to see Fred striding angrily in her direction.

"We're holding this hooligan—"

"Shut up, and release this boy," Fred demanded. He put a hand on Fiona's shoulder and turned her to face him with a hand to her chin. "Damn kid, your dad hit you again?"

Fiona started to shake her head in denial but realized he'd provided her the perfect excuse for the current situation. "Yeah, so I ran away to the docks. Found Miss Lorraine—"

A bloodcurdling scream of panic rent the air. Just then, one of the female nurses opened the door and glanced frantically up and down the hallway until her gaze landed on Fiona. "Bring that boy back in here."

Fiona didn't waste another moment. She sprinted toward the nurse, brushing by her a little rougher than etiquette warranted, and entered the room.

Lorraine was hysterically struggling with the male and female nurses in an effort to get up from the gurney. They had replaced her clothing with one of those awful hospital gowns, which did little to cover her, more so with her struggles. Fiona could see the horrible toll her action was taking. Rushing to the bed, Fiona grasped one of Lorraine's thrashing arms, and then clasped their hands. "I'm here, Lorraine," she said cupping a hand to Lorraine's cheek. She was burning up, her eyes glazed in fever and pain.

"Finn? Thought you left me." Lorraine stopped struggling.

"I'm here now," she said softly. "You need to lie back and let the folks take care of you."

There was a slight pressure in Lorraine's grip, and Fiona recognized the return squeeze to be of reassurance. "Don't leave me, Finn. I don't want to die alone."

Fiona felt the first onslaught of tears race down her cheeks. Much as she wanted to deny that event would happen, based on the grave looks from the hospital staff, Lorraine's death was inevitable. But, they hadn't tried everything yet, had they? Couldn't the doctors operate?

There was a commotion at the door. Fiona glanced up in time to see Fred slide into the shadows of a corner and Perry hold the door open for Dr. Matthews, who entered with purposeful steps while absorbing every detail of the room. He pushed his glasses up his nose, and rubbed at his mustache. "Nurse, morphine, please. The rest of you go about your business. You may stay for a little longer, officer." He stood by the bed now, placing his left hand on Lorraine's shoulder and his right on her forehead. Edward grinned across to Fiona. "Young man, if this is your attempt to keep me so busy I can't retire soon, I must say it's having the opposite effect." The nurse returned with the syringe, which she inserted into Lorraine's arm just below where Edward held Lorraine's shoulder. Edward didn't do more than shift so the nurse had access, as if he wanted Lorraine to know he was here for her exclusively. "You can leave us, Nurse."

"But, Doctor?"

Edward shook his head. "Take the officer with you," he said taking his gaze from Lorraine's long enough to glance at Fred. When Lorraine, Fiona, and Edward were all that remained in the room, Edward released a heavy sigh. "Are you feeling any better, young lady?" he asked Lorraine. She nodded in reply. "Good."

"When are you taking her to surgery?" Fiona asked.

"Finn." Edward's tone indicated the answer should be obvious.

Lorraine squeezed her hand, the pressure weaker than a

moment ago. "There's nothing these people can do, Finn, other than make my last moments comfortable." The words seemed to sap the rest of Lorraine's strength. Her breath labored as if each inhale was agonizing.

Edward removed his right hand and gave another squeeze to her shoulder with his left. "I'll leave you to it with Finn here, then." Fiona didn't have to question what he meant to either of them, his meaning starkly written in his eyes.

"Thank you, Doctor," Lorraine said simply. Just like that, Fiona realized, painfully, Lorraine accepted her fate.

To her, Edward said, "Take all the time you need, Finn. No one else will bother you." His parting gaze was full of meaning for her, telling her he would be here for her, and confirming the gloomy diagnosis. He couldn't save Lorraine. All he could do was make her comfortable in her last moments. Fiona didn't need to watch him leave.

Fiona wanted to sob in denial, demand more effort by these alleged professionals, but her full attention had to be for Lorraine. Alone, Fiona squeezed Lorraine's hand. "Is there anyone I can get for you? Anyone at all?"

"No."

"Eldon?" she asked reluctantly.

Lorraine barked a harsh laugh. "No, Finn, just you. You've been my only true friend. Sad as that is."

"Sad, huh?" Fiona said, giving an indignant sniff, mostly to hide the tears. "Never expected to be caught dead with the street rat?" Fiona initially cringed, then tried desperately to enter just a bit of levity into her tone, no matter how morbid it made the moment.

"I guess not, but wouldn't change the fact." Lorraine held her gaze for a moment, then turned away, tears pouring down her cheeks, the trembling, and quick rise and then fall of her chest the only indication she sobbed in silence.

Fiona considered pulling Lorraine into her arms, but feared injuring her further. She's already dying, you dolt. The inner chastisement was all the incentive Fiona needed. Climbing up on the bed and positioning herself behind Lorraine, Fiona pulled the older woman into her arms and flush against her chest, much like an infant or a lover. Lorraine broke down and cried in earnest. Silently, Fiona joined her.

Fiona didn't know how much time had passed, but true to Edward's word, no one disturbed them. As Lorraine's crying lessened, Fiona realized how labored and shallow her breathing had become. "Thank you, Finn, for staying with me."

Caressing the stiff and matted blonde hair, Fiona looked

down, her gaze met by an ice blue eye, the other eye swollen shut. Bruising, multiple scratches and cuts, and swollen split lip had replaced the flawless skin and beautiful visage that was Lorraine Mills. "Is there anything I can do for you, before—" Fiona bit back the sob trying to escape.

"Answer a question and provide a favor." Lorraine focused her one good eye on Fiona as she waited.

Something about the way Lorraine said the sentence had Fiona's stomach clench in suspicion. What if Lorraine asked a question where the answer brought her pain? Did Fiona want Lorraine's moments to be filled with emotional torment, as well as physical? If the situation reversed, would Fiona want honesty, no matter how distressing? Yes, she would. "Okay."

"What is it about you? You're not like any other boy." Lorraine squeezed her eye shut. "Not that I'm complaining."

Fiona bit her bottom lip. She and Lorraine had started on shaky ground. But, even if not best friends, they shared an understanding. Lorraine deserved honesty. "Because I'm not. A boy that is."

Lorraine stared at her for a tense moment. "Does Margaret know?"

Fiona gave a lopsided grin. "That's two questions. And, yes, she does."

"That explains a lot," Lorraine said. She shifted and her face contorted in pain. Lorraine closed her good eye, gave a soft whimper, and inhaled deeply through her nose. The small adjustment must have been excruciating. "Kiss me?"

"What?" Fiona wasn't certain she heard correctly. She felt her face flush.

"The favor is a kiss." The corner of Lorraine's lips rose slightly in amusement, apparently at Fiona's surprise.

Frowning, Fiona stated the obvious. "I'm a girl."

"I don't care." A stray tear fell from the corner of Lorraine's good eye. "Please, Finn, I've been curious since the first day I saw you. Give me this?"

Fiona nodded. Gently, trying to avoid the worst of the injuries to Lorraine's face, Fiona brushed a finger to Lorraine's cheek, then cupped Lorraine's chin. Lowering her head, Fiona brought her lips to within a breath of Lorraine's. Holding the blonde's gaze, she whispered, "Fiona," before tenderly pressing a kiss to Lorraine's battered lips. Not too quickly, but with a feel of slight panic when Lorraine's breathing became more shallow, Fiona pulled away and broke the connection of their lips.

Lorraine closed her eyes. "Thank you, Fiona."

"You're—" Fiona realized Lorraine wasn't breathing. "Lorraine?" She gave the woman a little shake. "Lorraine, talk to me, sweetie." Nothing. "Lorraine?" Lorraine was dead.

Deep wracking sobs consumed her.

Chapter Twenty-nine

MARGARET HADN'T BEEN surprised to find Eldon and Jimmy unavailable when the call from Edward Matthews came in. The information Edward provided had been minimal, but two things stood out starkly — Finn and hospital.

She arrived to find Edward speaking to two men in the corridor outside a private room in the emergency wing. "Edward," she said. All three men turn before Edward met her part way. "Finn?"

"He's fine," Edward said, placing his hands on her shoulders. "Miss Mills, however, is not." Edward's voice dropped as he explained Lorraine's condition. He shook his head sadly. "She won't be with us long."

Then Margaret heard an agonizing cry come from inside the room. Fiona. She started for the door, but was stopped by the two men barricaded themselves in front of the entrance. "Miss Graham?" the taller, older one spoke. "I'm Ian Donnelly." She frowned, recognizing the name but not understanding why. "Nana is my mother, and you've met my sister Claire. This is my partner, Fred Morton."

Recognition dawned. "Yes, of course. They are well?"

Ian flashed a wry grin. "Yes, thank you for asking," he replied, continuing the charade of civility. "Cavanaugh will be done soon. We all need to have a chat."

Margaret nodded. Her focus concentrated on listening to the changes inside the room. The tormented crying became hiccupping sobs. She wanted — needed — to be there for Fiona, hated these men for stopping her. Just as her nerves became too taut to bear, the door behind Ian opened. Her first glimpse of Fiona had her heart racing in panic and anger simultaneously. Fiona's clothes were stiff and discolored by a milky-white substance — dried sweat, salt? The short length of her dark brown hair stood at angles atop her head. Margaret's stomach jolted, ready to heave, when she saw the open gash that extended from above the left eyebrow and up into the hairline, where the reddish coloring of exposed tissue and flesh from within could be seen. Pushing roughly through Ian and Fred, Margaret reached Fiona's side. The misery of Fiona's eyes nearly stopped her from pulling Fiona into an embrace. Nearly. Would she ever be able to wipe this pain from Fiona?

"Lorraine's dead," Fiona said into her ear.

"I know." As a few more tears escaped Fiona's eyes, falling to dampen the side of Margaret's cheek where it pressed to Fiona's, Margaret steadied her own myriad emotions and focused on just one. Anger. Maintaining her hold on Fiona, she turned to Edward. "Can we get someone to tend to Finn's wound, please?"

"It's okay," Fiona said, straightening, gouging at her eyes with the butt of her palm to erase the tears.

"No, it's not okay, Finn. My God, what's going on?" she demanded of Ian.

"Let's all calm down a little, and take this to my office upstairs," Edward said. "Margaret, I'll take care of Finn while we discuss recent events." Ian and Fred hesitated, waiting for Margaret and Fiona to follow Edward before following her.

Once inside Edward's office, Margaret led Fiona to a chair pushed against a wall. There was a desk littered with papers, folders, a stethoscope tossed on top. A small table stood in the corner with a pitcher, tall glass, and pile of hand towels. Ian and Fred flanked the door. Opening a white and glass cabinet filled with medical vials and tools beside his desk, Edward pulled out items, placed them atop the desk, and picked up a small, wheeled stool and placed it in front of Fiona. "This will hurt like the dickens."

Fiona nodded. "Just do what you need to."

Margaret couldn't watch, but she clasped one of Fiona's hands in both of hers, and decided to distract herself. Glaring at the men at the door, she asked, "Will someone tell me what's going on?"

Fred shrugged. When Ian spoke, he kept his voice low so no one outside the room could hear. "We know about as much as you, so far, Miss Graham. Fred was here on another matter, luckily, and took control of the matter from the hospital security. The doc here called you when Fred called me in. One thing we know is Miss Mills was hurt badly when Fiona found her. She…ah…appropriated a nearby vehicle and drove them here to the hospital."

So, Ian and his partner were aware of Fiona's disguise. She hadn't expected that, but suspected it stemmed from their childhood friendship. The knowledge was a plus. Margaret stared Ian directly in the eyes. "Before we get into too many details, Ian, I need to know what kind of trouble Fiona's in."

Leaning his back against the door, hands shoved into his pockets, Ian smiled at her. "Miss Graham."

"Margaret."

"Very well, Margaret it is." He winced just as Fiona squeezed her hand painfully. She refused to let go, but couldn't look down to see what Edward was doing, either. Knowing Fiona was hurting was a tad easier than witnessing her pain. "No trouble with us, but we need to establish what happened so we can help her, should trouble arise."

"The car she drove belongs to Owen Aleman. Can't tell how he'll react to his missing vehicle," Fred said.

This time, Margaret did look down at Fiona, only to have her stomach lurch at the sight of the needle piercing flesh as Edward methodically stitched the gash closed. "Just a couple more," Edward said. "Then she'll be able to answer all your questions." He dipped his head conspiratorially toward Fiona. "I have some whiskey, strictly for medicinal purposes of course."

When he finished and scooted his stool back, Fiona said, "Thank you, sir." Her body slumped in the chair. Margaret could see the strain in her posture and her features.

Edward leaned forward and patted Fiona's knee. "You're always welcomed."

Fiona gave a tired smile. "'Bout that whiskey?"

Barking a laugh, Edward stood, shaking his head. "Sorry, Fiona, but I can't give you alcohol with a head wound. Best I can do is wash the stitches with it, but I'm not that generous with my spirits." He opened the cabinet again, shook out a couple pills from a bottle, and poured water from the pitcher into the glass. He brought them to Fiona. "These will help a little."

As Fiona swallowed the pills and then water, Margaret, still holding her hand, shifted so her hip was flush to Fiona's shoulder. Fiona subtly leaned into Margaret, who released one of her hands from Fiona's and wrapped it across Fiona's shoulder. Margaret wished she could give more of herself to Fiona, but any other physical or emotional support needed to wait until she got her home. She looked down at an exhausted Fiona. "Can you tell us what happened last night?"

Faintly, Fiona nodded. She told the events from leaving with Jimmy to pick up a shipment coming by boat, to arriving at the hospital with Lorraine. Margaret was horrified, especially concerning Lorraine, but not surprised by Jimmy's perfidy or that Owen Aleman was also involved.

Lorraine's implication of doctored account books had surprised her. Eldon had believed someone was stealing funds from the restaurants, but said he'd fired Terry Whitehouse for the crime. Were Owen and Jimmy the true culprits? Occasionally during the recounting, Margaret glanced to Ian, trying to gauge just how he reacted to Fiona's participation in obvious illegal activities. During one of those shared glances, Ian winked at her.

When Fiona finished and fell silent, Margaret turned to Ian. "What now? It won't be safe for her to return to the house, not with Jimmy around."

Pushing his glasses higher on the bridge of his nose, Edward said, "I believe I can assist. After all, Finn here has a head wound, probably a concussion. Those tend to cause amnesia. The kind of amnesia lasting a little while, or a long time."

"Enough time to get my things, Sunny, and plan to leave?" Fiona asked in a whisper. She glanced at Margaret. "You're coming too, right?"

The desperation in Fiona's eyes was nearly Margaret's undoing. She squeezed Fiona's shoulder. "We'll talk about that later, honey." Carmel eyes darkened in her withdrawal, and she felt Fiona stiffen and pull away from her. There were things they needed to discuss, and this room wasn't the place for it. She didn't know how to make Fiona understand with just a gesture.

As if sensing their tension, Ian moved away from the door. "Okay, so young Finn has amnesia. He doesn't know how he and Lorraine ended up in the hospital. Whatever happened at the beach last night isn't even a glimmer of a memory." He put a hand on Margaret's shoulder. "We should get Finn home to rest. I'll come with you, and explain about Lorraine's death. Also to make sure that the welcome isn't a violent one for our Finn, if Jimmy Bennett is there."

"Do you think those hidden books would prove Jimmy," he paused with a reluctant gaze at Margaret, "and Eldon, are in collusion with Dwyer and his attempts to expand?" Fred asked.

"I don't know," Ian said simply.

Margaret didn't want to see her brother in trouble, and couldn't be part of gathering evidence against him. Yes, she knew about the speakeasies he'd installed in the restaurants, but who were those truly hurting? They had even suited her needs when she was out with friends, keeping Fiona close by, finding reasons to be her driver. "You're welcomed to the books, but I won't be a party to getting them for you. Honestly, I care about two things. One is getting Fiona home, maybe fed, and certainly resting. Two is making arrangements for Lorraine's burial."

Fiona stood, her balance a little uncertain as she steadied herself by tightening the hand held in Margaret's. "The Galloway's can help. Talk to Frank or, better yet, his sister Siobhan, since she's the mortician." Fiona tugged her hand from Margaret, who knew she'd upset Fiona. She had faith they'd get beyond this once Fiona had some sleep.

"Well, then, let's break the news to Eldon Graham." Ian focused his attention on Fiona. "Are you up to this, Fiona? I can take you to Nana and Claire."

"I'll be okay at the Graham's. Sunny can look after me until I decide what we're gonna do."

Margaret frowned as the pain of rejection filled her. Did Fiona believe she didn't intend to leave with them ever? She did, just not so soon, not now. Surely, she could make Fiona understand. Couldn't she?

FIONA DRAGGED HER feet, reluctantly following Ian and Margaret into Eldon's home office. As expected, Jimmy was there already, and didn't look at all pleased to see her. His heated glare confirmed the observation, as did the steady clenching and unclenching of his fists. She stopped behind Margaret.

"What's going on?" Eldon demanded of Margaret as he stood from his chair.

Ian glanced between Eldon and Jimmy. "Be nice if you could tell me," he said, his tone friendly. "We found this kid in the early hours and, lucky for him, Doctor Matthews recognized him. Miss Graham was the only one we could get hold of to confirm that, and we're bringing Finn here, where I understand he lives. And works as your driver?"

"Yes, he does. Is he in trouble?" Eldon asked, flashing a confused glance at Jimmy. Fiona wondered what Jimmy had told Eldon about last night. Did he know she'd found Lorraine?

Margaret spoke up. "Someone shot him. Again. I told Officer Donnelly Finn sometimes makes deliveries for the restaurant in the early hours."

"What does the runt say?" Jimmy asked.

"Who are you?" Ian asked. He didn't even try to hide his dislike of Jimmy.

Jimmy straightened. "Jimmy Bennett. I work with Eldon, here."

"The head wound has affected Finn's memory, Eldon. He recognized me when I got to the hospital, but couldn't remember my name or why he knew me. Edward believes his memory may come back, but can't say for certain, or when that could be if it were to." Margaret turned to look at Fiona, and gave a wry smile. "He needs to rest."

Although the alleged amnesia was to make the situation, and Margaret's part in it easier, Fiona didn't know if she'd be able to playact this lie. She'd never be able to forget so much of this night. Margaret wasn't entirely fabricating the matter. Fiona was tired, and her head pounded like the devil struck it with a hammer while laying on an anvil, even after Edward had given her the medicine.

Jimmy stepped forward. "So what happened — "

"Mr. Graham," Ian said, interrupting Jimmy. "Finn was found outside the hospital, along with Lorraine Mills. Someone had just dumped them outside the building and left. Miss Mills died in the hospital from her injuries." Fiona could hear Jimmy's audible gulp at the mention of Lorraine. She wondered what he'd told Eldon he'd done with her.

"Lorraine? But she's supposed to be back in the mid-west?" Eldon said. His furrowed brow and lips tightening as if he were trying to reconcile the confusion he felt.

"Who told you that, Mr. Graham?" Ian asked.

If Eldon intend the information to be private, his instinctive glare at Jimmy belied the fact. "Jimmy?"

Jimmy took a couple steps away from Eldon and the desk. "I got her out of the house, just like you asked."

"Where'd you take her?"

Fiona expected Jimmy to be better at fabricating a story, but he appeared to be at a loss for half-a-minute, as he continued his slow progress toward the office door. "Bus station. Let me go check on that for you, Eldon."

"That won't be — " Eldon didn't finish. Jimmy left the room; his hurried footsteps and the slamming of the front door letting them know he'd left the house. Under other circumstance, Fiona would have laughed at the absurdity that his actions proved anything but his guilt. Eldon fell back into his chair as if all the air left him. "What happened to Lorraine?" he asked.

"You'll need to talk to the hospital. I don't feel comfortable sharing that with you," Ian said. Eldon raised his head quickly, his frown questioning. "It wasn't a pleasant death by any means, is all I can say."

Fiona wanted to scream at him, "A little too late to care about her." Instead, she glanced between Margaret and Ian. "Can I go now?"

"Yes," Eldon said.

Ian stepped toward the door. "I'll let myself out."

Margaret absently rubbed a hand up and down Fiona's back. She considered pulling away, but the action showed Margaret did care for her a little. Even if she wouldn't run away with her.

MARGARET CLOSED THE door behind her once they entered Fiona's room. She was tired, stressed, and heartbroken at how withdrawn Fiona had become since the hospital. The reason became apparent as soon as Fiona spoke. "Leave with me,

Margaret. Tonight. Please." Fiona turned to face her. "It will only take a few minutes for Sunny and me to pack, but we'll wait for you. I'm still jake with Old Man Chambers and I know he'll give me one of his old trucks."

Tonight? "Honey, I can't leave now."

Fiona's expression was crestfallen. "Why not?"

"I have obligations, Fiona. I can't just run off willy-nilly."

"Obligations?" She took a step forward, but Fiona moved to put the bed between them. Fiona snorted loudly. "So, I'm not important enough as either your lover—one time granted—or even important enough to be an obligation."

"That's not true, Fiona. I'm just asking for a little time."

Fiona crumpled onto the chair by the bed. From the quivering in her shoulders, Margaret realized she was silently crying. On impulse driven by her heart, Margaret rushed to Fiona and dropped to her knees, clasping Fiona's hands in hers.

With an anguished whisper, Fiona said, "I don't know how I can. I don't want to be part of this charade anymore. I want to be me, Fiona." Her head rose and watery brown eyes met Margaret's. "I can't be part of these horrible—"

Squeezing the hands in hers, Margaret said, "I understand. I'll do my best to keep you away from Eldon and Jimmy." Margaret suspected Jimmy would do his best to maintain distance for a while, rather than explain what happened with Lorraine. "I'm not saying never, just that I can't leave this soon. Please, stay with me for a while longer?"

"What are your feelings for me?" Fiona asked, her voice sounding small and hurt.

How could she not know Margaret's feelings for her? They'd made love, hadn't they? Looking at the torment in Fiona's eyes had her questioning what was really going on with her insecurity. "Honey, what are you afraid of?"

Fiona looked away. "I'm afraid I can't protect you, can't protect Sunny. After Lorraine—"

Edward had skimmed over the explanation, but the expressions from him and Fiona had her realizing she didn't want to know the specific details. Margaret cupped Fiona's cheek, the pad of her thumb brushing across her chin. "If I didn't care for you, Fiona, I wouldn't be asking for time. If you need to leave, I'll be sorry to see you go, but will understand. I wish you would stay."

"What if I can't protect you?"

"Nothing's going to happen. I love you, Fiona. Please trust me." After a short hesitation, Fiona nodded. Margaret stood and pulled Fiona with her. "You need to rest."

"Will you stay?" Fiona sat on bed and removed her boots.

Margaret placed a gentle kiss to Fiona's lips. "Let me lock the door."

With the door secure, Margaret started to pull back the duvet, only to have Fiona stop her. "I'm tired, but I'm filthy," Fiona said. "I'll just lie down on top of the duvet."

"I understand." Margaret sat next to her to do likewise, but jumped up at the hard feel of something under the thin mattress. She raised the corner of the mattress and found the gun and holster Eldon had given Fiona. "Why is this here?"

Fiona shrugged. "Makes me nervous, but I didn't want to leave it in the open."

"You could have hidden it in a dresser."

"Nah, that's the first place someone might look. I want it close in case I need it."

As Margaret returned it to the original hiding place, Fiona lay back on the bed. She looked so worn out, and still so beautiful to Margaret. She climbed up on the bed and snuggled close to Fiona's side, her head on Fiona's shoulder. "Let me protect you for a little while." She knew from the steady, shallow breathes, Fiona had already fallen asleep. "I love you, Fiona." Margaret just wished Fiona didn't doubt that.

Chapter Thirty

MARGARET CAREFULLY LET herself out of bed so she wouldn't disturb Fiona. Margaret stared at her sleeping form. Since Jimmy's hasty departure from Eldon's office, she worried what he'd do next. Margaret's turn to protect those she loved had arrived. She managed, grudgingly, to get Fiona to postpone leaving. Margaret wasn't ready to leave Boston yet, but was more reluctant to leave before she gave Ian Donnelly the evidence he needed. Problem was that the evidence would implicate Eldon, too. She had to work a deal. For that, Margaret needed assistance.

Moving to the side of the bed, Margaret continued to stare down at Fiona. This wonderful woman with the heart of gold was trying to singlehandedly safeguard those she loved, like a knight of old. Well, Margaret would pick up the gauntlet.

Placing a light kiss to Fiona's forehead, Margaret silently left the room. She headed for the kitchen, surprised to find Mrs. Baumann already at her cooking. "Good morning, Mrs. Baumann."

Mrs. Baumann gave her a glance from head to foot, and frowned. "Is everything all right, dear? I've coffee ready."

Doubting the family business would be private much longer, Margaret chose to make some explanations. "Actually, no. Someone hurt Finn again." Partial truths were always easiest to remember. "And Lorraine's dead. I'll need to make arrangements for her."

Hand pressed to her heart, Mrs. Baumann appeared ready to cry. "I'm sorry about Miss Lorraine." She swallowed as if the words had lodged in her throat. "Finn, he'll be okay?"

Margaret nodded. "In time. He's resting now." She poured herself a cup of coffee. "I need to make arrangements for Lorraine today, and don't believe Eldon's up to it. May I ask a favor?"

Mrs. Baumann's face grew stern. "As if you need permission. Just ask."

"Keep an eye on Finn? His injuries have left him with partial amnesia. He remembers things but not specifics. He was with Lorraine when she died and I'm not sure how all this is going to affect him."

"Oh, that poor boy. I'll do my best, Miss Margaret."

"That's all I ask." Margaret drank her coffee, ate the plate of food Mrs. Baumann placed in front of her, and mentally formulated her course of action. She needed to find Ian Donnelly, needed to arrange for Lorraine's burial, and most of all needed to sort out her plans for the future—plans involving Fiona.

Before she could begin, Margaret would need transportation. She couldn't take Fiona's truck. Jimmy was out there somewhere and could be targeting it with killing Fiona in mind. Eldon's car was out of the question. She had no idea what his plans were and if he'd need it. Besides, she needed a dose of familiar support. Walking to the phone on the wall, Margaret picked up the receiver and requested Chatham555. After the call picked up at the other end, Margaret requested to speak to Janice, stating the call an emergency when told the hour was too early to disturb her.

"This had better be good," Janice's tired voice snarled.

"I need you to be my chauffeur," Margaret said. "I'll explain when you pick me up." Margaret grinned although Janice couldn't see through the phone line. "Will the chore be easier if I promise to include a handsome, and single, detective?" She prayed Ian would forgive her for whatever Janice might do.

"I'm on my way." Despite her turbulent emotions, Margaret smiled.

FIONA AWOKE, INSTANTLY aware Margaret no longer slept beside her. Not surprised, but her absence hurt Fiona nonetheless. Her head pounded painfully and caused her stomach to churn, but her bloodied, damaged, ocean-stiff clothing needed addressing first. She needed a bath.

Forty minutes later, Fiona was ready to start her day. She smiled at the knowledge Sunny had been checking on her progress during that time. Sunny had been quiet as a church mouse, but Fiona could sense her, once when she removed Fiona's soiled clothing, and again as she peeked into the bedroom after Fiona had dressed. She felt more than heard when Sunny went to tidy their shared bathroom. From the doorway, Fiona said, "I can take care of this later, Sunny."

"We do for each other," Sunny said, her gaze darting to the stitches at Fiona's forehead.

Fiona walked into the room and pulled Sunny into a hug. "I'm okay, honey. Leave this till later and come get something to eat with me." Sunny nodded against her shoulder. "That's my girl."

They greeted a busy Mrs. Baumann, who poured a cup of coffee for Fiona and a glass of milk for Sunny as soon as she noticed them in the hall. "Hear you had another adventure," Mrs.

Baumann said, sliding a plate before each of them as they sat at the table. "You attract trouble like a magnet."

"I aim for a simple life. Guess my aim is well and truly off." Fiona took a bite of food, marveling at the exquisite taste the woman always produced. "How'd you hear about it anyway?"

"Miss Margaret told me before she left."

"Left?" Fiona's heart raced in panic. Where would she go? It wasn't safe, not with Jimmy who-knows-where out there.

Nodding, Mrs. Baumann said, "She called her friend, Hartwell I believe the name was, and mentioned the police."

Her insides felt like a sledgehammer just shattered what was left of her hope. So, Margaret had made her choice and it was Hartwell, not her. Suddenly, the delicious food of a moment ago tasted like sawdust. Fiona pushed the plate away, no longer able to eat. Sunny reached over, placed a hand on top of hers, concern in her eyes. Fiona just shook her head.

She was about to retreat to her room, but Eldon entered the kitchen on unsteady legs, his gaze narrowing in on her. He looked...off. Was he finally feeling guilt for the way he'd treated Lorraine? She wanted to shake him, tell him it was way too late.

"Know you're supposed to be resting, Finn. Need you to do that later. Right now, I want to go to Favors."

Fiona nodded. "Yes sir. I'll bring the car around front in fifteen minutes. That okay?"

"Yeah, fine." Eldon turned and left.

Doubtful he witnessed when Fiona clenched and unclenched her hands, with Margaret running around with that awful, stuck up Hartwell, her having to traipse around with the hangdog Eldon, and Jimmy in the wind, Sunny wouldn't have her protection at the house.

"Mrs. Baumann, a favor please?" Fiona asked.

"Anything, Finn." Mrs. Baumann moved to the table and stood next to Fiona as she stood from her chair.

Expression stern, Mrs. Baumann latched Fiona's chin in a vice grip of finger and thumb. "Who is looking after you? No one." She gave a nod in Sunny's direction. "I'll care for your girls, Finn. Just watch your back."

"Yes, ma'am, I will," Fiona agreed.

The usual fierceness of the older woman was replaced with a quick softening. She released Fiona's chin. "Be sure you do, Finn. These girls may survive without you, but I can tell you they won't be living a proper life without you in it."

"As long as they're safe, they'll get by just fine."

Mrs. Baumann stepped back and clucked. "That's where you're wrong, Finn." She returned to her stove. "Now get on with you before you get Mr. Eldon's dander up."

A quick kiss to Sunny's forehead and Fiona went to get the car. Duty called.

IT WAS CLOSE to six o'clock in the evening when Sunny and Brigid heard, from the couch in the library, the houses front door bang open. She'd seen Margaret use a small closet to listen in on Eldon's meeting with Finn. Sunny tugged on Brigid until both stood nestled inside, and the door closed behind them.

From their hiding spot, Sunny could make out the banging sounds of doors roughly pushed open, stomping from two sets of heavy feet, ending with loud cursing voices from Eldon's office.

"Where the hell is everybody?" Sunny recognized Jimmy's voice. She tensed and Brigid pulled her into an embrace, offering comfort.

"Guess this screws up your plans, huh?" She didn't recognize that voice, but could tell he was younger than Jimmy.

"No, Junior, it doesn't." Slamming of desk drawers echoed. "Margaret's probably with her friends, so she can wait a bit. I'll come back for her after I take care of Eldon. I wanted to make the runt suffer by using his little bitch as bait. Guess I'll have to find another way."

"Can you use his old man?" Junior asked. Sunny's heart began to slam against her ribs. No. Finn's father would surely ruin and tattle about her secret. Quinn wouldn't have forgotten about Finn's last beating, where Quinn would have felt humiliated.

"You know where to find him?"

"Yeah. And word around is there's no love lost between them."

Jimmy laughed, and it was an awful thing to Sunny, all wicked and dirty. "It's about time for the clubs to open. Let's go get the runt's dad and plan a little family reunion."

Sunny had to do something. Finn — her Fiona — was in serious trouble. Soon as the front door once again slammed closed, Sunny exited her hiding place and raced to their quarters.

"Sunny, what are you doing?" Brigid asked from behind her.

"Gonna protect Finn." She reached Fiona's room and went straight for the bed, pulled up the mattress and removed the Browning Fiona kept hidden. She also took the small change purse that Fiona hid for Sunny, so she could use it when Margaret or Brigid took her to town.

"With that? Are you crazy?" Brigid reached for the gun. Sunny jerked her hand away and raced into their shared room, slamming the door between them to prevent Brigid from following. "Sunny, what are you doing? Let me in."

During one of their shopping excursions, Sunny had talked Margaret into a set of boys' clothes like Fiona wore. She'd readily agreed believing it another way for Sunny to idolize Fiona. In truth, Sunny understood why Fiona liked the clothes, as the outfit was freeing and gave her more maneuverability. Once dressed, Sunny stuffed the Browning in her pants pocket, just as she heard Bridget use her key in their door. Rushing back into Fiona's room, Sunny made her way down the hall and out the kitchen door.

Sunny was halfway down the road before she heard Bridget call out to her. "Please, Sunny, come back, it's not safe for you out there. At least wait for me."

She turned just long enough to holler to Brigid. "They were going to Favors." She remembered Fiona had told her the real name was different. "Finn's at The Fisher's Net. Find Margaret, we've got to protect her." Then she was jogging toward the street, trying to find a taxi to help her save the only person who ever cared for her.

FIONA PACED THE concrete floor of the Favor's barroom. Eldon had closed the restaurant, and sent word for everyone to stay home. Then, he proceeded to imbibe of bottle after bottle of bootleg spirits. The place felt odd without the wait staff or the entertainers buzzing around. This gave her too much time to think, to obsess over what she'd do now that Margaret had made her choice to stay in Boston.

First, she tried to reconcile with Margaret asking her for a bit of time. She'd been willing to do it, knowing Margaret would move west with her and Sunny. They'd be like a family—away from people trying to see Fiona dead.

Second, Fiona tried to shake the repeated images of Lorraine's tortured body playing in her head. With what Jimmy had done to Lorraine, because Eldon had picked Jimmy over his own girlfriend, Fiona couldn't feel sad for him. Hell, this was one of her hate Eldon days. He'd professed caring for Lorraine, had been a gentleman the day of the restaurant meeting with that fella from New York. Fiona had hoped it was a positive sign in their relationship. Obviously, she was wrong. Fiona held her tongue, mostly because she was supposed to be suffering amnesia. However, the more Eldon drank, whining to no one in particular, the more Fiona paced—and fumed.

Eldon raised his head and braced by an elbow on the table. "I was good to her, Finn. She didn't appreciate what I did for her."

Fiona loosed the hold on her temper. "Like what, Eldon? You certainly didn't protect her, did you?" She stomped over to his table, towering over him as she looked down on him with as much disgust as she could muster. "Did you ever see the bruises and ask her how she got them? Did you never suspect what Jimmy was demanding from her? And she put up with it because she cared for you, wanted to be with you, the high-and-mighty Eldon Graham, bootlegger and wannabe gangster." She slammed a fist on the table, setting the bottle to wobble precariously and the glass in his fist to shake. "Jimmy's been playing you. Terry didn't steal from you. Jimmy's been doing that, while he goes behind your back with creeps like Dwyer in New York and Wallace here in town. Hell, maybe he's making a deal with Giuffrida, too."

"He wouldn't do that to his partner," Eldon said, not looking at her.

Who in the hell was he trying to convince, because she wasn't falling for it. "Bullshit. You're a means to an end, Eldon. An end Jimmy doesn't need anymore." Fiona turned away from him. "You never should have gotten into this business. You're an ass, Eldon, but I don't think you're as despicable as Jimmy."

Eldon filled his glass and gulped the contents, wincing as he swallowed. "You don't know what I'm capable of, Finn. I'm stronger than I look."

"Really? Let me be the judge of that, Eldon. How 'bout I tell you what Lorraine went through before she died, and judge by your reaction."

"How 'bout we do show-and-tell instead?" Fiona's blood froze in her veins when she heard Jimmy's voice. She spun around and with crystal-clarity knew her time had run out. On Jimmy's left stood Junior Detweiler, on his right side none other than Quinn Cavanaugh. Gleaming pretty-as-you-please in Jimmy's hand was a Colt M1911 automatic pistol, Armed Service issue, pointed directly at her heart.

Sitting straighter in his chair, Eldon asked, "What are you doing here?"

"Coming to teach lessons, like I already told you." Jimmy glared at her, his lips curling in a sneer. "Gonna love this lesson more than I originally thought. Aren't I Fiona?"

"Fiona? Have you lost your—" Eldon's comment was cut off by a bullet fired into his stomach. One hand clutched his gut, while the other clawed at the table for support to stay in his chair. "Fuck."

"Eventually," Jimmy said. His gaze returned to her as she'd tried to make her way to an exit. "Stop where you are," he said, swinging the gun in her direction. His gaze never left her. "Junior, get Cavanaugh that bottle we promised him."

In her peripheral, Fiona saw Junior retrieve a bottle from behind the bar, and then walk over to where Quinn sat at the table behind Eldon. He'd no sooner slammed it down, before Quinn latched on, uncorked it, and downed a third of the contents. Slowly, he put the bottle on the table and wiped his mouth with the back of his hand. Junior twisted a chair around backwards, and plopped down resting his arms across the back as if ready for a show.

Fiona had no doubt what Jimmy intended for her. She took a step back, Jimmy a step forward. She swung her gaze to Quinn. "Da, please, don't let him do this."

Quinn smirked. "Need to learn your place girl." Another long swig from the bottle, before he added, "Jimmy here's just the man to do it, too."

She'd rather be shot in the back then succumb to what was intended for her, shocked her father didn't seem bothered by watching, or that Junior would be also. Fiona spun around, and dashed for the raised stage, hoping to escape. Another shot and a fire burned in her left thigh, the leg giving out under her. Fiona fell short of the stage.

Jimmy was on her in an instant, slamming a foot down on her wounded leg. Then, he wielded a kick to her abdomen, another, a third, fourth. Her breath escaped her lungs, the pain so severe Fiona couldn't draw even a small inhale of air, stars danced in her vision. Grabbing her shirt into his fists, Jimmy jerked her upright, and smashed her into the lip of the stage. A fist hammered into her face until a mix of blood and swollen flesh darkened the edge of her vision. He continued the onslaught until she felt teeth loosening and her jaw break. At least she'd be unconscious for the worst brutality.

"Oh, no you don't," Jimmy said. He must have made some signal to Junior, because next Fiona knew, the harsh burn of liquor splashed into her open cuts and damaged flesh. She hissed at the contact. "Now for the part I enjoyed most with Lorraine."

From elsewhere in the room, Fiona heard Eldon's faint mumbled protest. "Don't do it, Jim."

Jimmy snickered. Fiona felt the sharp edge of cold metal biting into her clothing, her bindings, and her skin. Please, she prayed, let me die before he finishes. Her prayers were unanswered. Once he'd cut away her clothes, bruised flesh bared for all, Jimmy picked her up, slammed her down on a table, and cruelly spread her legs. Unable to fight, her muscles too tormented to defend herself, Fiona recited the mantra in her head,

"Please let me die now."

As fingers brutally bit into the flesh of her thighs, a sharp spear of agony caused her to cry out. After the repeated pain of entry, Fiona heard another gunshot, before finally finding unconsciousness.

Chapter Thirty-one

MARGARET FELT A rush of relief when Janice pulled up in front of the Fisher's Net, the last of Eldon's businesses, and the final set of doctored books. She hadn't been able to get Fiona out of her head, worried about leaving her in her weakened condition. "Last place." She opened the passenger door as Fred appeared out of nowhere, racing toward the door. He had just kicked it open, when Ian jumped from the car and followed. "What's going on?" she asked, not expecting an answer, which was a good thing, as she didn't receive any. Somehow, Fred had located the entrance to Favors. A gunshot rang out from below.

What she found in the Favor's barroom had her speechless, and then terrified. An older man sat at a table drinking from a bottle and staring at a retreating Jimmy, Fred following. In front of him, a pale and bleeding Eldon sat, clutching his stomach and openly crying. Ian roughly pushed Junior's face into the wooden front bar top while handcuffing him. Sunny moaned mournfully as she cradled the nearly naked and beaten body of Fiona on the floor, torn clothing pooled limply around her body. A toppled table lay beside Fiona's head, what looked like her Browning atop Fiona's stomach, Sunny clutching the weapon in a death grip.

Immediately, Margaret rushed to Fiona and Sunny, dropped to her knees, ignoring the discomfort. The first thing she did was make sure Fiona was breathing. She glanced around the room until she locked gazes with the horrified Janice. "Please, find me something to cover her with." Margaret carefully covered the hand Sunny clutched the gun in. "Sweetie, let's get rid of this," Margaret said. Sunny removed her hand, and then used the arm to pull Fiona closer. A folded tablecloth appeared over her shoulder. Margaret shook it open and covered Fiona with it. They needed to get Fiona to the hospital. Though she wanted to scream and cry, Margaret realized the necessity to maintain the appearance of calm.

On silent feet, Ian appeared beside her. "We need to get Fiona and Eldon to the hospital. I need to appropriate your vehicle, Miss Hartwell."

Janice nodded.

Ian bent to one knee beside Margaret. "Fred lost Jimmy. But

he can take custody of our prisoners and get them to the station."

Margaret went behind Sunny and crouched down, wrapping her arms around her and speaking into her ear. "Sunny, Ian has to carry Fiona to the car. She needs the hospital."

Sunny nodded, reluctance showing in the slow release of her charge. Sunny's hand absently reached for the gun, and when Sunny stood, she placed it in her pocket. Margaret would have to take the gun from her at some point. "I tried to kill him. He ran away when you came." Sunny spun in her arms her body shaking with the fresh burst of emotions. "I was too late. He hurt her bad, Miss Margaret."

Margaret stroked Sunny's hair as the young girl cried on her chest. "I know, sweetheart, we'll take care of her now." Ian stood with Fiona cradled in his arms. He walked to the exit. Margaret and Sunny followed until a hand on Margaret's arm stopped her. She turned to Janice, noting blood on her hands.

Janice looked down, too. "Better clean up before Mark sees me." She gave a wry grin. "Eldon needs to speak to you before you go."

She glanced toward her brother. He looked paler than when she arrived. "We can talk at the hospital." Margaret was angry with him. Fiona and Lorraine were both seriously harmed because of him, one dead and another dying.

"Says he's not going," Janice said.

"But I don't—" Janice stopped her with a raised eyebrow. "Fine. Ian, get Fiona to the hospital. Dr. Matthews will be waiting, I hope. Go." She turned her attention to Sunny. "I really need your help. Will you look after her until I get there?" Panicked eyes met hers. "Fiona needs you right now, Sunny." The words were the catalyst to get Sunny moving. She raced after Ian.

"Why aren't you going to the hospital?" she asked her brother. She wanted to hold him and hit him at the same time. "Would you rather I sent for an ambulance?"

Eldon shook his head. "No, but if the cop is a friend of yours, we should get me upstairs to the restaurant. Don't think you should be associated with this part of my business." With Janice's assistance, she was able to get Eldon upstairs and placed in front of another table. Fred had followed with Junior and the other man. Eldon swayed in his seat.

"Eldon—"

He shook his head, eyes becoming glazed and unfocused. "Do you know who the man is?" Eldon asked.

"Not the older man. But Junior's the one from the alley."

Eldon groaned. "Should've guessed Jimmy would hook up

with him." Eldon coughed and blood dribbled from the side of his mouth. "The other is Quinn, Finn's father."

Margaret turned to glare at Quinn. "He watched and did nothing?"

"So she would learn her place." A tear trickled down his face, then another. "I was so busy being a big shot. I didn't realize I was out of my league. Please tell Finn and Thelma—Sunny I guess you call her now—I'm so very sorry."

Margaret kneeled in front of him. "Tell them yourself. After you get fixed up at the hospital."

"No. Listen. I need you to do something for me." His gaze was pleading. Margaret was torn between demanding he go and doing as he wanted.

"What is it?" she asked. He leaned toward her and whispered. After a few moments, he pulled away, gave her a smile that could only be termed as macabre with the blood. Margaret nodded. Her agreement seemed to release Eldon. His head dropped to his chest, and his body slumped across the table. Eldon, her last living relative, was dead.

Janice, standing behind her, pulled Margaret to her feet, much as she had done for Sunny earlier. "I secured the doors to downstairs. We should go to the hospital now. I'll call a cab."

"I'll have someone drive you." Margaret had almost forgotten about the other man with her. Fred held a squirming Junior who somewhere along the way acquired a dishtowel stuffed into his mouth. She turned to them and without breaking eye contact with Quinn, whose gaze was darting erratically around the room, Margaret pulled a key from a small pocket in her dress. "Janice, go to the office and call Dr. Matthews." She gave her the number, and Janice hurried from the room.

Margaret walked to the men. She pointedly dismissed Junior. He was a bully who had found a home with bigger bullies like Jimmy Bennett, and the darker side of mobster life. Quinn confused her. How does the father sit and watch his daughter raped and beaten? Balling her hand tightly, Margaret punched him with all the anger—and fear—consuming her. He fell to the floor and neither she nor Fred assisted in helping him stand. Quinn didn't seem in a hurry to get up.

"There's a unit coming," Fred said. As if on cue, two uniformed officers raced into the room, Quinn and Junior given into their custody. Fred asked one to call the coroner for Eldon. Janice returned, standing beside her with an arm around Margaret's waist.

"I'll get you ladies to the hospital now," Fred said, as another group of uniforms entered the restaurant.

Margaret nodded as she and Janice followed Fred.

THE NURSE IN emergency forwarded them on to the waiting area for the operating room. Ian was there, joined by his sister, Claire, and Nana Donnelly. Ian gave her a nod of welcome as Nana pulled Margaret into a reassuring hug. Sitting in a chair, her knees pulled tight to her chest, rocking back and forth, sat Sunny, apparently oblivious to the others in the room. Margaret went to her, crouched beside her, and placed her palm to Sunny's cheek. Sunny's face turned to her slowly, and as recognition dawned, Sunny dropped her legs, slid from the chair, and clasped her arms around Margaret's neck. Sunny's head dropped to Margaret's shoulder and she sobbed. With gentle reassuring pats to Sunny's back, Margaret held her until she was spent. During that time, Molly, Dorcas, and Frank joined the group waiting on Fiona.

Over four hours later, into the early hours of morning, Edward trudged into the waiting room. He would normally put on a clean lab coat, but appeared not to have taken the time on this occasion. Margaret realized how stressed and tired he was, his features showing every day of his fifty-plus years. Edward glanced at all the expected faces and said, "Fiona's out of surgery."

"So she's alive," Nana said. "Blessings be."

Edward stared at her with an expression she couldn't quite read. Then it dawned on Margaret he was asking how much to tell. She shook her head. He nodded. "She's in recovery, but not stable yet. If Fiona makes it through the night, there's a chance she could recover."

Most of the occupants in the room broke down in sobs. Edward gave her a look that said she should follow, as he turned and walked into the hall. Margaret did, walking silently beside him until they reached the far end, well away from the waiting area. Edward placed gentle hands on her shoulders and looked her directly in the eyes. "It's not good, Margaret. In simple terms, Fiona has multiple bruising and lacerations. She has well over one hundred sutures, three broken ribs, two lost teeth that she nearly suffocated on. There was damage to her spleen. She may have some vision problems, from damage to her left eye." Edward paused and swallowed hard. "Are you sure you want to hear the rest?"

Margaret knew it had to be bad if he needed to ask. Her mind screamed no. "Go ahead."

Edward inhaled deeply. "He didn't just rape her." He pulled

something wrapped in plastic from his lab coat pocket. A gun. "The bastard also used this. We found it tangled in her clothing. Could be the gun used to shoot Eldon."

Margaret held up a hand and bit back a cry. She took deep breaths to get her turbulent emotions under control. "Give that to Ian Donnelly." There was no way she could touch it to do so herself. "Make sure the others don't hear you tell him what you just told me." She squeezed her eyes shut, trying to keep down the bile rising in her throat. "When can I go to her?"

"Because she may not make it, I'd like to say you can take turns." He shook his head. "But that may not be wise considering how she looks. It may frighten them more. Especially the young girl."

"Sunny needs to see Fiona most of all." Margaret bowed her head. "She has more right than I do." She leaned against the wall, swallowing hard.

Edward didn't ask her to explain. "I'll come get you when Fiona's more stable and out of recovery." He left her standing where she was and returned to the waiting room, calling Ian into the hall. As Edward explained, handing the gun over to him, Ian shoved it in a pocket and stared down the hall at her. As they locked gazes, all the emotion she'd restrained until now, broke free. Margaret slid down the wall landing roughly on her backside and broke into body shuddering sobs.

FOR SIX DAYS, Margaret and Sunny stood vigil beside Fiona's bed. They took turns getting away long enough to wash up and shower, but they did so in the hospital, approved under special directions of Edwards. During her time away, Margaret made phone calls and set plans into motion if — when — Fiona was well enough to leave. It was predawn of the seventh day, Sunny slouched in the chair on the opposite side of the bed, when Margaret asked the question she'd been afraid to broach. She suspected the answer, but had no idea how a private, self-sufficient Sunny would respond. In truth, Margaret realized she let the opportunities to know Sunny and Fiona better take a backseat in her attempts to please Eldon and discouraged Jimmy.

She focused on Sunny, who seemed to sense the attention and returned her gaze with the questioning one. When the silence dragged on, and Sunny's inquisitive expression turned to a frown, Margaret asked, "Would you like to change your name officially?"

Sunny's frown turned into a suspicious squint. "Officially how? And to what?"

Margaret squirmed in her seat until ready to answer. "As soon as Fiona's ready, we'll be leaving for Colorado. I have a friend who can assist in getting you a birth certificate with a new name." She paused, inhaled and exhaled. "With the name of Sunny Cavanaugh. He can use Fiona's information to make you her younger sister."

"Isn't that illegal?" Sunny asked. She stared at Margaret suspiciously, but there was excitement in her posture as she straightened in her chair.

"How will anyone know? I'm not going to tell."

"Josephine," Sunny blurted.

"Who?"

"Sunny Josephine Cavanaugh. Josephine's after an aunt who treated me good, before my parents took me away."

"So it's okay? You don't mind?" Margaret wanted to be certain. This was a life-altering step, after all.

Sunny glanced at the bed, staring at the figure nearly hidden beneath layers of gauze. Fiona's head alone was entirely concealed, save an opening where her right eye gazed out—if she ever opened it—and a slit for her mouth and nose. "No one will know about her bastard father where we're going."

"Only know Fiona and I are sisters?"

"That's right, honey."

A toothy grin split Sunny's lips. "I'd be proud." Just as suddenly, her expression turned to panic. "What if Fiona doesn't want that?"

Margaret left her chair, stood behind Sunny's, and gave her a hug from behind her. Both were gazing at Fiona's still form. "She's already thought of you as her family. We're only making it official."

"What about you? Will you change your name, too?" Standing straighter, but keeping her hands on Sunny's shoulders, Margaret said, "I did give it honest thought. I've the impression from my phone conversations with the realtor in Colorado he'd prefer to sell to a married couple. I considered having a marriage certificate made using Fionn's name."

"Fiona's dead brother?"

"Yes. Fiona could play Finn or rather Fionn 'Finn' Cavanaugh from the hospital bed. Only we would know. Ian and Edward could be witnesses."

"Why don't you?" Sunny asked, glancing up at her from over her shoulder.

"Because that could hurt Brigid. She cared deeply, I'm told, for him." Margaret squeezed Sunny's shoulders. "I'll figure something out, we've got a little time." Margaret started back to her chair and froze when she saw Brigid in the doorway. "Brigid, how—"

"Just because you'll all be Cavanaugh's doesn't mean you can treat me like the old maiden aunt of this family." Brigid came into the room and took Margaret's place behind Sunny. "I stay as Bridget Connor, cousin extraordinaire." She beamed, apparently proud of her announcement.

"It's all settled then." Margaret sat down, relieved to have her plans falling into place.

Now, if only Fiona would wake up.

Chapter Thirty-two

THE PRIEST HAD just finished performing the ceremony. Sunny, Ian, Peter and Edward present for the occasion. "Are you certain I shouldn't perform the last rites?"

Margaret stiffened at the insinuation. It was day eight. Fiona, though stable, had yet to wake. "My husband is pulling through." As concerned as she was, Margaret felt elation at knowing, though not legal, she had married Fiona. She wished Fiona awake to share in their moment.

"Thank you for your time, Father," Peter said, guiding the man out the door. Margaret flashed him her gratitude. He returned less than two minutes later carrying a picnic basket and thermos. "Finger sandwiches, small snack cakes, and lemonade." He placed the basket on a side table. In a stage whisper, he said, "I thought of sneaking something with more of a kick, but worried the guard would have imbibed and we'd be found out." He snorted. "Man already globbed down a sandwich and two cakes."

"Lemonade is fine, Peter," Margaret said, placing a peck on his cheek. "I appreciate all you've done."

Edward stepped close, flashed a loving smile at Peter. "The beast that put Fiona here is still loose. I could have her transported to our house. Better to keep her safe."

"I don't know, Edward. That's an awful imposition."

"Congratulations everyone." Margaret turned to find Frank and Siobhan Galloway enter the room, closing the door behind them.

Margaret felt a moment of unease, having the owners of the mortuary in the same room as Fiona felt like a bad omen. If Margaret hadn't come too actually like Siobhan, she'd take umbrage to their presence. However, despite the business Margaret brought to the Galloway's with Lorraine and Eldon, she also appreciated Siobhan's friendship and kindness, and knew Frank felt the same for Fiona. "Thank you for coming," Margaret said.

"You're part of our friends and family circle," Frank said. His tone laced with sincerity. "The moment would be perfect if we had a little bit of Finn attitude interjected here." Frank's gaze settled on Fiona.

As if on cue, Sunny jumped off the bed where she'd been

sitting, holding Fiona's hand. "She twitched." Sunny's gaze darted around the room until they landed on Margaret. Tears clouded her eyes and dripped down her cheeks. The room became deathly silent. "Has she come back?" She reclaimed Fiona's hand.

Margaret rushed to the side of the bed, leaned close to Fiona's bandaged head. "Fiona, honey, can you hear me?" She thought she heard a groan. Gently, she placed her forehead to Fiona's bandaged temple. "Oh, honey, I've missed you so," she whispered. Louder, she said, "Don't panic, honey. You're bandaged pretty excessively. You're going to be all right. We're all here for you." Fiona mumbled something, but Margaret couldn't make it out.

Edward stepped forward with a cup and straw. He nudged the straw between Fiona's lips. "The water will help. Sip slowly."

Barely audible, Fiona said one word. Tired. She fell asleep. Margaret, and the entire room of people, was nearly giddy in their excitement. Fiona continued to sleep, but at least they now had hope.

Siobhan clasped Margaret's elbow, getting her attention. They moved away from the others. As Margaret stared at her, flicking furtive glances toward Fiona, Siobhan cleared her throat. "We both know Jimmy's out there, and mad as a wounded bear because Sunny shot him, and Fiona's not dead." Margaret nodded. She didn't like thinking about Jimmy—liked his still-breathing status even less. "Do you trust me?"

Margaret looked at the tall woman. In height and physique, Siobhan and Frank were nearly identical. Even Frank as Fatima didn't compare to the hidden beauty of Siobhan. Her eyes radiated such depths of emotion, currently warmth, that it surprised Margaret most people only saw stoic, cold hardness in her. Margaret saw, and felt, so much more. "Yes, Siobhan, I trust you," she said, hoping her honesty was evident in the words.

"Good," Siobhan said. She smiled and her dark green eyes shone bright. "I have a plan." Margaret leaned toward Siobhan. As she whispered to her, Margaret's own smile widened.

SIOBHAN LED THE way up the back stairs to the room Fiona occupied, and Margaret followed silently. "You'll be close to the stairs, furthest from incoming customers and activity. I placed Sunny and Brigid in the room across from you."

Margaret glanced around at the beautiful molding and wallpaper. The banisters and doors were sturdy cherry walnut. There were windows at each end of the hall. They were large enough to allow a lot of light, and plain, unlike those on the first level, which were fully or partially stained glass pieces. Siobhan pushed open the door to the right just beside the stairwell.

Directly facing the door was a huge four-poster bed, leaving little room for the armoire on the left and a small make up table with cushioned stool on the right. The window above the table was smaller than the windows in the hall, but covered in a beautiful lace and stitched-flower design of a light lavender color, identical to the duvet covering Fiona. Despite numerous objections, Fiona had demanded the removal of most of the bandages. She still had one large bandage covering her eye, and surrounding her crown to cover stitches in the back of her head where it rested on the pillow. Fiona's uncovered eye was closed, and Margaret assumed her sleep. Although the sleep helped Fiona heal, Margaret worried it also provided too much time to focus on what put her in that bed.

"I'll leave you to orient yourself. Help yourself to anything you need." Siobhan turned to leave but stopped, flashing another grin. "By the way, I took your advice and spoke with Mrs. Baumann. She'll be cooking dinner tonight, as the new—only ever—Galloway cook. Frank, needless to say, is happy to pass on the reins."

Margaret smiled. "You weren't the family cook?"

"My talents never extended into that part of the house." Siobhan grinned. "Don't worry, none of the tools of my trade did, either." She left.

Slowly, so as not to disturb Fiona, Margaret made her way to the side of the bed were Fiona lay. Careful to sit on the edge, Margaret took up Fiona's hand and held it in both of her own. Fiona flinched. She didn't know if the reaction was automatic, or if Fiona were awake, but Margaret held on. Margaret wanted to apologize for what had happened, but knew the words could never be enough. Instead, she whispered, "No matter what else goes on in your head, honey, know this. I love you."

Margaret felt Sunny enter the room before she saw her. She watched with a smile as Sunny slowly crawled on the bed and nestled beside Fiona. Fiona's body tensed for a moment before relaxing. Margaret wondered if Sunny noticed, suspecting if she did, she expected the reaction and was determined to provide comfort and support nonetheless. Eyes closed, Sunny asked, a grin on her face, "How's my sister today?"

Margaret gave a soft chuckle. "Saying that pleases you, doesn't it?"

"More than you know," Sunny said. Sunny opened her eyes, her expression losing their earlier jovialness. "We buried Lorraine and Eldon at the same time. I'm happy I didn't have to attend a service for Fiona."

Reaching across Fiona, Margaret caressed Sunny's cheek. "I am, too, honey. She's safe with us now. Soon as Fiona's ready, we'll be on that train to Colorado."

"Margaret?"

"Yes, honey." Margaret saw a flash of panic in Sunny's eyes.

"Do you think she'll be mad I didn't kill Jimmy, that I only wounded him?"

Margaret thought she saw Fiona's brow furrow, but it was smooth in an expression of sleep now. "If she's mad about anything it will be you taking her gun in the first place."

"I did it for her, because she'd do it for me."

"That'll be the only reason she'll ground you for four years and not twenty."

Sunny grinned, levered onto an elbow, and planted a loud kiss to the forehead over Fiona's good eye. "As long as she gets better and isn't mad about my new certificate."

"She'll get better, sweetie. You officially being Sunny Cavanaugh will make her proud." Margaret sensed, rather than saw, Fiona tremble, and realized she was listening. Fiona was also holding back her emotions. "Sunny, could you go make a cup of tea for me, please? I'll sit with Fiona for a while. Get yourself a sandwich first, and take your time."

"Okay." Sunny kissed Fiona again before carefully hopping off the bed and out the door.

Margaret got up and closed it, before turning back around. "Welcome back, love."

FIONA HURT EVERYWHERE. It took three tries before her vision, only one eye, adjusted to the lighting in the room. She'd been conscious off and on for the last day or so. Unable to track time had her uncertain how long she'd been lying here. This last time it took all her willpower to stay still and not react to Sunny's words. As soon as she heard the door close, Fiona cried. It started with the release of a few tears, but they continued to build until Fiona lost control.

Margaret returned to the bed and Fiona could tell she took great care to be gentle when she sat, Margaret pulling her into an embrace. Fiona's first reaction was to pull away, the contact initially frightening her. If felt like forever before Fiona's emotions were spent, her body fatigued. Margaret must have sensed it, because she slowly released her hold and returned Fiona to the pillow. When she felt she could speak again, Fiona asked, "How?"

Margaret gave a shrug. "Brigid's father, a few favors, and...well, a few greased palms." Margaret placed a hand over Fiona's. Shifting with the pretense of getting more comfortable, Fiona extricated her hand and clutched the blanket to her chest tightly. If the hurt expression on Margaret's face were any indication, Margaret knew it was intentional.

"What else have I missed?" Fiona asked.

Sitting back silently, Margaret was quiet for a long time. When Margaret reached to lay a hand on Fiona's again, Fiona flinched before she could contain her reaction. Margaret inhaled deeply, stood, and rushed to the door. "I'll leave you to rest." She turned the knob and opened the door.

Fiona knew inaction or remaining silent could push Margaret away for good. Part of her believed that would be the best for Margaret—for her. She would need to give Margaret up, but couldn't do it yet. "Please, give me time, Margaret. I just—" Her emotions were so confused, she had no words.

With the barely perceptible nod, Margaret left.

"ISN'T THIS A pretty picture."

Margaret woke from a half-sleep to a voice she'd hoped never to hear again, but knew she would. She shifted carefully to a sitting position, mindful of a still healing Fiona beside her. Jimmy stood in the doorway with a smirk, a revolver in his hand and pointed in their direction. Margaret and Siobhan had made their exit from the hospital easy, hoping Jimmy would follow. What she hadn't expected was that it would be so soon. She wasn't ready. "It's my have and haven't yet, both already in bed together. How convenient?"

"What are you doing here?" Margaret asked. She suspected the answer, of course, confirmed by his comment. She needed to stall, plan an escape safe for her and Fiona. Margaret needed time. Involuntarily, her gaze darted to the gun on the nightstand, and then to the baseball bat leaning at the foot of the bed. She hadn't planned smartly. Fiona stirred beside her.

"You'll never reach either in time." Jimmy stepped into the room, as if this were a meeting of friends. He gingerly rolled his left shoulder, flipped on the light, and stabbed the gun in Fiona's direction. "Then I'm going to pay her little tramp back for shooting me."

"Over my dead body," Fiona whispered, paling as she tried to sit up. Was it from the strain or seeing Jimmy after what he'd done to her?

Of course, Jimmy would hear her. "Gladly," he glared at

Fiona, then smirked at her. "When I'm done."

Margaret knew she had to distract him. More than that, she needed to keep Jimmy away from Fiona. She stood. Jimmy swung the gun barrel toward her. With his attention on her, Margaret asked, "Why'd you have to kill Eldon?"

Jimmy smirked. "He'd outlived his usefulness. I've made the connections I needed." He licked his lips with the crude smacking noise. "Soon, I'll be richer than him. I'll be able to buy and sell bitches like you. Maybe I'll even take over your place. Figure you're gonna sell. Saw the trucks emptying the place."

"Too late," Margaret said. Fiona moaned, having shifted to the side of the bed. "Sold the place already." Luckily, she'd been able to sell to Janice, who was familiar with the place and wouldn't destroy the more pleasant Graham memories.

"Well, I'll get bigger and better," Jimmy assured her.

"Gaudy's more like," Fiona said, her body swaying even in her sitting position. Margaret appreciated Fiona sharing the diversion of Jimmy's attention, but Fiona's complexion was turning a frightening shade of green.

Jimmy growled. "What would you know, you stupid bitch? Couldn't figure out you ain't no man." He smirked and Margaret could almost feel the malice rolling off him like drops of ice. "At least now you know how to be female."

Fiona gave a pain-filled cry, stood up and nearly toppled over. Having sensed Fiona's reaction from the moment Jimmy started speaking, Margaret launched herself across the bed, coming to her feet on the other side in time to catch Fiona. She noticed a shadow behind Jimmy about the same time he was mere inches from them.

Jimmy gasped, growled, and then dropped to his knees, his free hand clutching at the back of his thick neck, his gun thudding to the floor.

"Nighty-night," Siobhan said, lowering the needle held in her hand. "Better get her back in bed."

Margaret looked at Fiona then. Sweat was beading on her brow, her nightgown dampened, and her body trembled. "Hey, hey, honey." Margaret helped her sit, and then lay down, before pulling the covers over her. Fiona didn't fight, not even when she placed a kiss to Fiona's lips. "Rest now. Jimmy's taking a trip where he won't hurt anyone again."

"But—"

"Shush. Trust me." There was a soft knock on the door, and Margaret waved Fred inside. "He's all yours, Detective Morton."

Fred snorted. "For what I'm about to do, I'm just plain old friend Fred." With Siobhan's assistance, they dragged Jimmy from the room.

Margaret turned her attention to Fiona. "Do you need a pain pill, honey?"

Fiona shook her head slowly. "Make sure Sunny's okay?"

"I will."

"Margaret?" Fiona paused, eyes shifting side to side as if trying to focus on one of too many thoughts. She said nothing else.

Margaret hurried from the room and went to the bed in Sunny's room. She shook her until Sunny squinted tired eyes at her. "Fiona needs to see you."

They returned, Fiona glancing between them. "Stay with me?" she asked. Sunny climbed onto the bed and promptly fell asleep. Fiona shifted so she was closer to the middle. Margaret reached for the light switch. "No." Fiona's voice was full of panic.

"Okay, honey," Margaret said. She started toward the bed, but stopped. Fiona hadn't wanted her too close, pulled away or flinched if she did. Margaret couldn't stay, couldn't be the one to hurt Fiona further. "Um, I'll just stay in Sunny's room with Brigid."

"Please stay," Fiona said, hesitantly meeting Margaret's gaze. "Don't leave." As Margaret approached the bed, Fiona turned on her side toward Margaret, wincing. Fiona flashed her a crooked smile. "Still tender."

Margaret lay down, twisting to her side and facing Fiona. "Tell me if I need to leave."

A sob escaped Fiona's lips. "Please, Margaret, be patient."

Margaret placed a hand to Fiona shoulder. She hoped her next words would come true. "We have forever together." For a long time they both just lay there. Finally, Fiona fell asleep. Margaret followed soon after.

Chapter Thirty-three

AS IF BY design, the cemetery yawned open and empty of visitors. Fred knew where Donato Giuffrida would be. Clutching the flowers in hand, he followed the path to Donato. He sighted Donato, a salt and pepper haired man with matching bushy moustache, heavy-set frame standing at five-foot-ten, seated on a bench before the Giuffrida mausoleum. Two men stood a discreet distance away. Kneeling in front of the headstone next to Donato, Fred placed the flowers in the holder, and bowed his head.

"I've information on the package we discussed," Fred said quietly. Part of Fred hated himself for doing this, talking to a known criminal and setting up what Fred suspected would be a hit. Until he reminded himself who they spoke of and the atrocities he'd conducted, the barbaric attack on Claire's friend, inadvertent murder of Lorraine Mills, and the attempt to assist in the annihilation of the man next to him, his uncle. "Package will be picked up at six tomorrow from the mortuary, crated and transported to the train station. Further travel to New York. Big Bill Dwyer will be on a train leaving at eight-twenty."

"Status of package?" Donato asked.

"Alive, medicated to keep...civil."

Donato nodded. "The package will have air?"

"An Oxygen Concentrator will be attached to the container." Fred shuffled his feet, for circulation and for the niggling of guilt at being here and disclosing this information. His friends wanted to punish Bennett, not kill him, and make him severely uncomfortable for a while. The ultimate hope of Fred's was Dwyer would handle that undertaking. Which is why Fred hadn't told anyone about this meeting. He assumed Donato had no intention of letting Bennett live.

"You're doing the right thing," Donato said. "Be at peace with that knowledge."

"Are you going to kill him?" The cop in Fred had to know, even if it didn't change the outcome or the fact he'd assist in the crime.

"Second thoughts?"

"None at all. Curious, I guess, maybe confirming for my own peace of mind."

Donato rose from the bench, his men instantly at his sides. He stared directly at Fred. "Rest assured. Bennett will not do to another woman what he's gotten away with so far. Some crimes cannot be ignored."

Fred watched Donato and men leave. He gave them a few minutes lead-time, before walking to his own car. If this meeting lost him his place in heaven, Fred wouldn't lose sleep over it. There was a special place for men like Bennett, and Fred knew Donato Giuffrida would send him there with a one-way-ticket.

CLAIRE AND FIVE other women were silent as they walked a smirking Quinn—he mostly stumbling—to a cluttered yet deserted alley a block from one of Eldon Graham's restaurants. She and three of the women were from the neighborhood, had grown up with Fiona and her family. Two of the women, Dorcas and Molly, Claire met through Ian who introduced them as Fiona's friends from the Finn persona.

"This will do," Claire said, once well away from possible prying eyes. Quinn accepted the invitation under a misunderstanding. Claire knew Quinn had the impression they would console him for the loss of his daughter—with sex. The setting sun brought a chill to the air. It seemed fitting, considering the coldness toward this man in the hearts of the women present.

What they planned for him was far more heinous. Claire had learned from Ian how Quinn had not only shared Fiona's true gender with Eldon Graham, but while Jimmy Bennett savagely raped and beat Fiona near to death, Quinn literally sat and watched. Fiona's prognosis for survival was still uncertain. Though she didn't glance to confirm, Claire suspected Margaret watched, since she'd planned to do this deed herself, but Claire wanted this. No, she needed to do this, wanted to do something for Fiona, her friend who held her heart. Claire wasn't a violent person by nature, but she and the others couldn't let Quinn go unpunished. This was justice. Justice in the only way they bring it, with neighborhood justice.

"Yeah, this'll do," Quinn slurred. He placed the bottle of booze on the crate beside him, but bumped into it unsteadily and the bottle fell to ground with a crash of broken glass. Quinn unzipped his pants, letting the garment pool around his ankles. "So, who's first?"

"That would be me," Molly said. She sauntered closer to him, and then slammed a fist into his jaw with surprising strength. Quinn staggered backward with a hiss of disbelief.

The first blow loosed, the rest of the women took turns

punching and kicking him. A couple women picked up nearby objects to use as weapons, with no body part ignored in the punishment. The pummeling only lasted a few minutes. When Quinn lay barely conscious in a bloody heap among the refuse, Claire called a halt.

As the women moved away from him, Claire stepped forward. "All Fiona wanted from you was love. You were supposed to protect her." Claire shook her head. "She kept the roof over your head, worked hard and you squandered her money on drink. Me and mine wash our hands of ya', Quinn." Claire turned to the five women. "We're done here. The trash has been tossed."

MARGARET FELT NO sympathy for Quinn. After what he witnessed, participated in by giving away Fiona's secret, the man deserved every bit of inflicted pain. She paused leaving the safety of her hiding place when the sound of returning footsteps had her pulling back into the shadows. She watched Dorcas as she hurried back to where Quinn lay moaning, trying ineffectually to get to his feet, hindered further by his pants binding his ankles.

Dorcas glared at him with disgust. "Fathers are supposed to defend and protect their daughters. So many of you fail miserably, mostly 'cause you don't really try. How, you putrid worm, can you call yourself a man?"

"Fucking bitch," Quinn grumbled through split lips, blood spraying with the vehemence of his words.

"Glad to see you've learned your lesson." Glancing around her at the litter, Dorcas's gaze settled on the shards of recently broken glass. She picked up the largest piece of glass by the smooth section of the bottles neck, the sharp jagged piece directed at Quinn. "Maybe this lesson will be easier to comprehend." Bending toward him, Dorcas speared the sharp edge into Quinn's genitals. Quinn's pain filled shriek pierce the alley. Tossing the weapon aside, Dorcas wriggled her fingers at him. "Ta-ta now." Skipping away in the direction of Claire and the others, Dorcas whistled.

IAN TIGHTENED THE arm draped over Junior's shoulder, assuring he stayed put. "I'm sure the public defender will do what he can for you, Junior," Ian said loudly. He noticed Fred and two of Jimmy's henchmen exited from the door leading to the cells. "I'm sure glad you gave all the assistance you did."

Junior shot a harassed glance at the two well-dressed men

with Fred. "You know damned well I didn't tell you nothin' at all, Mick."

With a quizzical glance toward Fred, which included an exaggerated eye roll, Ian said, "Oh, yeah, sure, sure kid. You didn't say anything." The three made their way toward Ian's position by the front door. Ian and Fred stayed inside the police station. Jimmy's men left the building immediately. Giving a none-too-gentle push of his hand to Junior's shoulder blades, Ian said, "You're fee, kid. Scram."

A frightened glance skipped from Ian toward the departing men, then back. Junior's voice shook when he said, "I can't go out there now, they'll kill me."

"Too bad," Fred said. "You've been released. Leave on your own, or I'll physically toss you from the station."

"Can't I wait until my mom gets here?" Junior asked, his voice whiny.

Fred crossed his arms over his chest. "Yeah, outside."

"The only way to stay in here is if you're talking to the DA," Ian said.

"I ain't doing that," Junior insisted. "I got the right to remain silent. I'm staying silent."

"Time's up," Ian said, advancing on him. "Stay silent outside."

Junior backed away, hands in the air, the tremor obvious. "Yeah, yeah, I'm going." With the gait of an elderly man, Junior made his way out the station doors.

Fred and Ian followed him, stopping in front of the door. Jimmy's men were near the curb, waving Junior over to them. He hesitated, but complied. Junior reached them just as a black car pulled up beside them. He was forced into the back seat, the two men trailing in his wake.

"Someone has explaining to do," Fred said. "Wouldn't want to be in his shoes right now."

Ian nodded. "Yeah. I should feel bad for him, being young and all, but can't work up enough emotion to fill one of Claire's thimbles." He knew going against the mobsters was fraught with danger on a good day. Ian tried to warn Junior, on too many occasions to count, about what he was getting himself into with Bennett. Worst part for Junior, not only ignoring the advice, he'd picked one of the meanest men to work for on the wrong side of law, someone who made Eldon look like a choirboy.

Fred placed a hand on Ian's shoulder. "You did all you could. Junior made his choices, starting with ignoring sound advice." Fred's lips turned up in a goofy grin. "Speaking of Claire—"

"We weren't," he said. Even vague hints of his sister's name were all it took to refocus Fred's attention. "But, go ahead. What about her?"

"Well, I'd like to court Claire officially, with your blessing." Fred turned serious eyes on Ian. "I know she deserves someone better, but I really care for her. I'll do right by her, Ian."

"I know you will, Fred." Ian opened the door and stepped back into the station. "Because we both understand I'd make your life a living hell if you didn't." He barked a laugh. "And I'll go easier than my mother will." Ian heard an audible gulp from Fred and smiled.

"BACK IT UP, back it up. Good." The night shift supervisor, Derek, gave a thumbs up. The truck stopped, the driver jumping down with clipboard in hand. He leapt onto the train station dock, pulled open the doors of the truck, and held out the clipboard to Derek, who scanned through the invoice and other documents. Derek called three of his workers forwards. "Put this in the storage room. I need to go over these papers. If everything's okay, you can put it on the train."

The employees went about their task. Derek sent the delivery driver off, and waved to the occupants of the car across the street. As the men exited the vehicle, Derek went inside to wait for Donato Giuffrida.

Donato Giuffrida walked with purpose toward Derek, his men following like silent sentinels. Derek gave a slight sigh of relief he wasn't on opposing sides with this man. When Donato and his entourage met him at the door of the storage room, Derek opened it and stepped aside so the group could enter. He followed them inside and closed the door behind him.

"You have everything we asked for?" Donato asked.

"Yes, sir." Derek knew better than to ask questions about the strangeness of the items requested, even if curious. "Everything's on the table behind the crate."

"Good. Let's begin." Donato gave a short nod and his men fanned out around the crate. One picked up a crowbar and pried the lid loose. Once done, two of the men lifted and removed it, laying the crate top to the side. Doing so revealed the coffin inside. Despite the oddity, Derek knew not to question. From experience, Derek understood Donato's methods may be just shy of horrendous, but hadn't meted out punishment not deserved, though maybe excessive. The lid to the coffin was open now.

Derek stood on tiptoe to peer into the coffin from his position by the door. He'd given instructions earlier not to disturb him and his guests, and knew those orders would be followed implicitly. But, he wouldn't step closer, Derek was here to facilitate not participate.

Donato peered down at the thin haired, unattractive man whose eyes blazed with both panic and anger. Cloth was tied around his mouth to prevent too much noise. "Well, Jimmy, seems I caught you at a bad time, all tied up. I won't keep you too long, having a train to catch, and all."

Jimmy squirmed inside his confines. Derek realized Jimmy was securely bound inside the coffin.

"You made egregious threats against me and mine. I can't have that, can I?" Donato paused, as if awaiting a response. None was forthcoming. He continued. "Normally, I wouldn't take such talk, personal as it was, to heart. Then I learned of your heinous acts against women, and of two in particular, one dead and one nearly so. Now, your stupid posturing has taken on new meaning." Another nod. This time, the man at the table stepped forward with a cloth bag and stopped beside Donato. "Augustus doesn't take kindly either. Do you, Gus?"

Gus sneered. "No sir, I don't."

Donato shrugged. "So, we decided to take some preemptive measures. We're going to accomplish what Miss Graham was unable to finish." At the mention of the name, Jimmy's eyes widened, and then gleamed wickedly. With a look and a toss of his head, one of the men removed the binding at Jimmy's mouth.

"You stupid sonofabitch, when I get out of here —"

"So certain are you, Jimmy?"

Jimmy stopped squirming and furrowed his brow. "I heard them talking. I'm to be delivered to Dwyer." Donato nodded confirmation. "You have other plans? You gonna to shoot me?"

"No, no, Jimmy, nothing so final." Donato reached forward and lightly slapped Jimmy on the cheek. "You see, it's like this. You made a deal with Dwyer giving you carte blanche over Graham's enterprises. In return, Dwyer makes sure I wasn't a threat. He lets you... How did you say it? Fuck those bitches senseless before tossing them to the sharks. That's it." Donato shook his head sadly. "Gus was not amused. He's to marry my niece, Amara, and doesn't take kindly to your plans. We know what you're capable of and need to rectify the matter."

"So, what?" Jimmy snarled. "You rough me up, stuff me back in the crate?" He snorted. "I'll come back and make good on my threat. So, go ahead. Shoot me."

"Now, now, don't be so impatient for your punishment." Donato straightened his jacket, adjusted his tie, and inspected the nails on his right hand. "So, you've no intention of learning the error of your ways?"

"Fuck you." Jimmy chortled. "Correction. I'm coming back and fucking every bitch in your household. I'll let you watch when I bang your wife, Donny boy. Bet she pleads me to give it to her good." Derek noted the twitching in Donato's jaw as he clenched his teeth. Jimmy flashed a glare at Gus. "You can watch, too, when I do your girl. Hope she's a looker, they scream the best when they get taken by real men."

"You do realize what position you're in?" Gus asked. "Isn't it rather reckless to piss off your captors?"

"If you aren't going to shoot me, I can survive any beating. Kinda resilient that way. Besides, Dwyer won't let you get away with this."

"Well Jimmy, we are about to find out." Donato took a step away from the coffin.

Gus raised the cloth sack he held.

Was the sack moving? Derek shuddered.

Gus loosened the rope attached to the opening, but didn't remove it. One of Donato's men brought over a metal canister, twisted a valve at the top until a low hiss emitted. He tossed it in toward Jimmy's legs.

"You and your travel companions will take a little nap. When you all wake up, you can get better acquainted."

"What the—" Jimmy eyed the sack suspiciously.

"Since you conducted yourself like a big, fat rat," Donato said. "You should spend some quality time with your kin. Goodbye Jimmy." Donato raised a hand, twirling a finger in a circular motion, and joined Derek at the door. "We're almost done, Derek."

As they watched, Gus stuffed the sack into the bottom of the coffin, shoved the binding into Jimmy's mouth. The men closed the coffin, the crate's lid replaced and hammered to tighten the seal.

"Thank you Derek."

"Don't thank me. We're family. What he threatened included my wife and little daughter, Elsie."

Donato nodded. "Trust me when I say it wouldn't have been something we would have been able to live through, much less our women. This is for the best."

"I trust you." Derek glanced toward the crate.

"Jimmy makes his train. The canister will knock everything out for a while. When it's waky-waky time, the bag of rodents will work themselves free from the loose binding, and a ready-made snack. If Jimmy survives his trip to New York, it may be a while before he can exact his revenge."

Derek nodded and reached out a hand, and Donato returned

the grasp. "Pleasure doing business with you, sir, I'll just get on back to work." He stared after Donato and men until they left the train station dock. Derek called for his employees, ordering them to load the crate to the cargo boxcar. It was just another workday, after all.

Chapter Thirty-four

"CAN I GET you anything from the dining car, honey?" Margaret asked. Fiona noticed Margaret had given up all attempts to touch her, her usual reaction when speaking to her. From the clenched fingers, Fiona realized the task was not an easy one for Margaret. Fiona wanted to reach out to her, but—

"No, I'm fine," Fiona said. On the bench seat across from her, Fiona watched Sunny cross her arms over her chest, her anger radiating in unseen waves. "Sunny? Is there something wrong?" she asked. Fiona wasn't certain why, but realized that in the last day or so of this train ride to Colorado, the tension and silence grew into a tangible thing. Tension so heavy this private room of the boxcar would implode on itself. Fiona, suddenly in a rare mood of humor recently, wondered what that would look like to the outside world. Would there be a large black emptiness in the boxcar? Or, would the boxcar resize itself like in a cartoon strip in the newspapers?

"Fiona?" Margaret whispered her name cautiously.

"Hmm?"

"Are you all right?" Margaret asked.

Dammit. When will this constant hovering and asinine inquiry end? "Yes, why?"

Sunny snickered. "Because for half a second you looked like you might actually smile." She turned away. "Should've known it was too good to be true."

"What's that—" She started to ask, as Margaret snapped, "Sunny, enough."

Of course, Fiona did realize what was wrong with her. Too many emotions were bombarding her at once. So many emotions Fiona couldn't properly single any one out and properly address it. Not that she believed she ever could.

"I'll be back soon," Margaret said, sadness and regret in her tone. Fiona watched Margaret leave, the slump of rejection hunching her shoulders, a reaction growing a little more prominent each time Fiona pushed Margaret away. What was she supposed to do? She had failed them. How could they still want her?

Fiona, body stiff and aching, exhausted from interrupted sleep due to nightmares, couldn't bear living with her own pain and inadequacies. How was she supposed to keep exposing those she loved to her uselessness? Over the course of this journey from Boston, and her healing, Fiona wanted to accept Margaret's touch; wanted Margaret to hold her during and after a nightmare; and, wanted to close the door on the horrid darkness of the reminder of the last couple of months, darkness reminding her of her failures. Fiona hadn't left this train car in three days. There wasn't a need, as anything she required was here. Margaret had outdone herself in that respect when she'd made all the arrangements. The car had bench seats that became sleeper-beds, a washroom, and a wonderful view of the passing scenery. If she required food, Brigid, Margaret, or Sunny would make sure Fiona ate. They also made certain she wasn't alone, in case she needed assistance.

What did they think she was going to do? Although, if Fiona were honest with herself, she had considered the prospect they possibly feared.

Fiona needed fresh air and the car's open window wasn't providing enough. For the first time in her life, Fiona felt claustrophobic. Sunny's drumming fingers and the quick rhythmic pumping of her leg wasn't helping Fiona remain calm. "I need a walk," she announced, grabbing the damned cane—so she could look as useless as she felt—because her body was still weak, although the physical pain receded every day. Sunny rose with her. "You don't have to go with me."

"Yes, I do," Sunny said curtly.

Focused on her own issues, Fiona nearly missed the signals from Sunny. Signals of something, Fiona knew, she should recognize and be addressing. Sunny wasn't simply upset, but scared. "Is there something wrong?" she asked, pausing before she opened the outer door.

Biting her lip, Sunny shook her head. Then, she grunted, "Won't matter for long." Sunny held the elbow of the arm not clutching the cane. "Come on." Sunny slid the door open and waited for Fiona to step through into the aisle.

The swaying of the train as it sped across the tracks made Fiona's balance precarious at best, but it felt good to be up and moving. Sunny's comment swam in her head, nipping like a piranha. It didn't make sense, unless it has something to do with the train ride being nearly over. Yet, the defeated tone is what puzzled Fiona most.

"Please, Sunny, tell me what you mean. Are you leaving me?" she asked. The very thought made Fiona sick. She couldn't lose Sunny or Margaret; and, yet, she felt as if she were losing them both anyway. If you didn't want this, her internal voice asked, why'd you push them away so hard?

They were at the door separating the train cars. Sunny jerked it open and rushed through, pausing near the thin metal rail. When Sunny spun to glare at her, Fiona noticed the fresh trail of tears coursing down Sunny's face. "You lied to me," Sunny accused, pain burning in her eyes.

"No, I never —"

"You did." Even in her anger, Sunny maintained a tone heard above the train noise, but probably not enough for anyone else to overhear.

"How did I lie, honey?" She was truly confused. Fiona hadn't made the travel arrangements as planned, but they'd left anyway, on their way to Colorado and a new life. As promised. Sunny was her new sister. They were a family.

"You said I was still lovable after...after..." Sunny swallowed hard, as if trying to consume something bitter.

Impulsively, unaware of her protesting muscles, Fiona reached forward and pulled Sunny into a tight embrace. "That wasn't a lie. I love you. Margaret and Brigid love you. One day, when you are older, you'll find someone to love you more than us, your new family. You'll find someone who'll hold your heart in their loving hands." Fiona frowned. "Where's this coming from?"

Sunny lightly pushed her away and smirked. "If I were still lovable after...you know, then why are you pushing Margaret away? You're pushing all of us away from you. Dammit, Fiona, we're trying to help you through this, and you move further and further from us." Taking a step back, Sunny glanced toward the railing and back at Fiona, her tears turning in to gasping sob. "I know it takes time to trust. I was there when you helped me. Margaret and Brigid were there for me." She wiped roughly at her eyes. "I started to believe. But I was wrong." Sunny turned to the rail.

Fiona realized Sunny was earnest in her intent. She planned to jump. Panicking, Fiona rushed behind her and pulled Sunny flush to her chest, wrapping her arms around Sunny's waist. She gave a silent prayer Sunny didn't fight her too hard, she didn't know if her strength would hold long enough to stop her from jumping.

"You weren't wrong to believe because I didn't lie. We love you because of you. Eldon did a horrible thing to you, but it doesn't define you or your worth. Men can take our bodies, but they can't take our hearts or souls. We can only give it to them, give our hearts to anyone." Fiona squeezed Sunny tighter, placing a kiss on the back of Sunny's head.

Because Sunny stood in front of her, the wind made it

difficult to catch her next words. "I know you're having nightmares. I hear you screaming yourself awake. So, see. You're letting Jimmy win. He's taking you from us as surely as if you had died that night." Sunny rubbed roughly at her eyes again. "You're lost to us. If someone as strong as you can't move on or accept the love we have for you, the love Margaret has for you, while you heal, what hope do I have?"

Fiona leaned her forehead against Sunny's shoulder. "I'm not strong." She hadn't realized Sunny harbored such pain. How blind had she been to this poor girl's pain, because she'd focused so hard on her own? Granted, she'd been comatose for the seven days, and then lost for nearly three weeks. They'd been traveling since Fiona was able to move about on her own. "Sunny, please, don't do this. Trust in me again. Let me prove to you I didn't lie. Don't leave me."

The thought of Sunny feeling so helpless she'd rather kill herself then go on with life, tore Fiona's heart to shreds. How could she explain to Sunny without proving her own uselessness? Sunny had called her strong. Telling her the truth would only prove that that was the true lie.

IN HER HASTE to get away before she broke down begging and crying, leaving Fiona to her silence, Margaret had forgotten her purse. She'd been surprised—albeit a pleasant one—to see Fiona and Sunny leave their room. From their expressions and posture, Margaret knew something was very wrong. Ignoring her original path, Margaret followed.

Focused on each other, neither Fiona nor Sunny noticed when she slid the outside door slightly ajar to hear their conversation. Margaret knew it wrong to eavesdrop, but felt she was losing them both. She also recognized the true culprit in recent events was herself. If only she'd— But no, she couldn't change the past, only try to fix things now.

The pure anguish in Fiona's plea—*don't leave me*—shot a spasm of pain through Margaret's chest. Opening the door the rest of the way, Margaret enclosed them both in her arms. "Before either of you do anything rash, please let me talk to you, apologize for all the hurt I've caused you."

Fiona pulled away first, and Margaret felt suddenly adrift. Part of her wanted to plead with Fiona to take her back, forgive her for Margaret's mistakes, which had cost Fiona so much. Things she should have said in the hospital, but hadn't because she'd hoped things would work out. Hoped for forgiveness once they all arrived at the house she'd purchased for them in Pueblo,

Colorado, and after Margaret told them of her job as a schoolteacher. It would be the final destination to a new beginning.

"You have nothing to apologize for," Fiona said. Her scowl suggested she meant the words.

Margaret smiled wanly at the confusion on Fiona's face, the matching expression on Sunny's. "Oh, honey, I do. I'm the reason Jimmy—"

"No," Fiona said. "That's not true." Her voice loud and harsh made Sunny flinch.

"It is, Fiona. Can we return to our car, please? Let me explain?"

Fiona didn't give a verbal response, rather shoved at the door and stormed back to their car, her cane thumping on the floor, echoing like a heartbeat. Sunny squeezed ahead and opened the door. Margaret trailed, hoping she wasn't about to make matters worse. She shook her head. Was it possible for Fiona to distance herself and her love more than she already had? Margaret hoped not, but the possibility was formidable.

Brigid, thankfully, chose that moment to return to their car. Once they were all seated, Margaret leaned against the bathroom door. She didn't know how to start.

Fiona did it for her. "How is my—" She gulped as if the words were stuck in her throat.

"Simple. If I'd not asked you to wait, you would never have been with Eldon. We'd have been together that day."

"You don't know that Margaret," Fiona said, shaking her head. She heaved a sigh. "You've done so much for us. I'm the one at fault." Fiona shot a glance to Sunny. "I'm the reason Sunny can't reconcile prior events, willing to jump from the train rather than go on. Die as a Cavanaugh."

Brigid leaned forward, toward Fiona. "How are you the reason?"

Margaret wanted to go to Fiona, pull her into an embrace when she watched the flash of pain twist at Fiona's features, but knew Fiona wouldn't accept her help.

Fiona turned away from them. "I couldn't protect myself. How the hell am I supposed to protect the three of you? I promised to keep you all safe—and failed."

"No, no, no," Margaret wailed. "How can you believe that after all you've done for us?"

Sunny gave a snort, though her features were as twisted in pain as Fiona's. "How could you know Quinn would have told your secret? Otherwise, Jimmy would've only beat you to a pulp."

Brigid gave a bark of laughter. "I see you're the glass half empty sort. We'll need to work on that, cousin."

Sunny blushed.

Hesitantly, Margaret moved closer to Fiona. How could she have believed she failed? There was no way she could have fought off Jimmy. "Honey, none of us fault you for what happened. Had it been one of us, we wouldn't have been strong enough to fight anyone off, much less that horrible brute."

Fiona's hands were shaking and started to reach for Margaret, but dropped to her lap. Cautiously, Margaret moved closer, sat beside Fiona and took Fiona's hands in her own. "We're proud of you, Fiona. Please believe us, trust us with that knowledge."

"What if I let you all down again?" Fiona sniffed.

"We'll dust our backsides as we all get up together," Sunny said. She glanced at Brigid, and then her. "You better take it from here, Margaret. Brigid's gonna buy me supper." Sunny grabbed Brigid's hand and pulled her from their car.

Margaret felt Fiona try to pull her hands free, but held them tighter. Fiona stopped fighting her, and gazed out the window. "How can you touch me, after—"

"Because I love you." Margaret inhaled deeply. "Sunny was right. You love her after Eldon. Why would you believe it would be different for you?" Fiona shrugged. "What happened had nothing to do with your ability to care for us. We—I—don't see you as a failure." She scooted closer to Fiona, hoping she wouldn't pull away. "Please, Fiona, don't doubt yourself, or us. Let me help you through this, through the nightmares. Let me protect you until you're ready to be without us."

"I'll never be ready to be without you, Margaret." Fiona's voice trembled with emotion. She dropped her head onto Margaret's shoulder. "If I lose you, I'll lose my heart."

"I'm not going anywhere," Margaret said. She held Fiona as she cried, as she slept, curled up beside Margaret, her head on top of Margaret's lap. Margaret smiled into the darkness as night fell. Her beloved Fiona had come back to her.

Chapter Thirty-five

THE TRAIN PULLED into the station, the whistle announcing the arrival, and producing a trail of thick grey smoke from front to rear. The train's other passengers had begun disembarking. Margaret didn't seem in a hurry, and Fiona had no intention of rushing her. Sunny already stood on the platform rolling her eyes as if the delay was a personal affront. Fiona shook her head. Next lesson for her sister—she grinned stupidly enjoying the sound of that—would be to learn patience. She waved to Sunny through the window.

"I'm almost ready," Margaret said, stuffing the items from the bathroom into the carpet bag she carried.

"Are you certain you don't need me to help?"

"You'll have plenty to do when we get home."

Fiona smiled at the word. Home. She walked the few steps behind Margaret and wrapped her arms around Margaret's waist. She brushed her lips across Margaret's neck. "Thank you, for not giving up on me."

Margaret leaned into her. "We'll continue this later. Right now, we need to find Mr. Hapcomb and his car, so he can drive us to the house."

"I liked home better than house," Fiona whispered into her ear.

"Me, too. Let's get out of here." Margaret pulled away, clasped the bag in one hand and Fiona's hand in the other. Together, they left the train, Fiona hardly relying on her cane, and buoyed by love.

WHEN MR. HAPCOMB pulled up in front of the large three story home, Fiona was shocked. It was magnificent, sitting on a large expanse of land, a barn out back. How could they afford this? Margaret must have sensed her anxiety because she squeezed Fiona's hand.

"Here you go, ladies," Mr. Hapcomb said, exiting the car and opening the trunk. Sunny began pulling out their luggage, Brigid soon assisting her.

Sore from the train and then car ride, Fiona stiffly slid from the back seat. Margaret was there to lend a hand. "Thank you," she told Margaret. Margaret smiled in return.

Mr. Hapcomb joined Fiona and Margaret. He held out a key, careful to avoid looking directly at Fiona. "I'm sorry for your loss, Mrs. Cavanaugh, Miss Cavanaugh. I sure hope you find some happiness in your new house."

Margaret took the key. "Thank you, I'm sure we will."

As if afraid the helpless ladies might put him to work, Mr. Hapcomb slid behind the steering wheel, shifted into gear, and drove off with a quick wave out the open window. Fiona snorted. "Guess my ugly mug scared him off."

Margaret gave a quick caress to her cheek. "Let's get in the house."

They dropped the bags on the front porch. Margaret turned the key in the lock and pushed the door open. The foyer was open, a room on either side, a staircase in front of them. "Welcome home, ladies."

Sunny and Brigid stepped back from them. "You two first," Brigid said.

"Yeah, you're the newlyweds," Sunny said, then giggled.

Fiona focused on Margaret's beautiful green eyes, brushed a lock of auburn hair off her forehead. "I don't have the strength to carry you over the threshold."

Margaret clasped Fiona's hand in hers, and leaned closer. "Save your strength for tonight." She pulled away slightly. "Together?"

Fiona nodded. "Together."

They crossed the threshold, Sunny and Brigid right behind. As they rushed from room to room on the first floor, Fiona tugged Margaret toward the staircase. "Let's get to our room before they try to take it."

They found the master suite, entered the room, closing and locking the door behind them. Fiona leaned against the door, pulling Margaret into her arms. "How can we afford this?"

Margaret put a finger to her lips. "This is effectively a wedding gift from Eldon." Fiona frowned in confusion. "Before he died, Eldon told me where he'd been hiding money from Jimmy." Margaret placed a hand on Fiona's chest. "There was enough to buy and supply the house, put into savings for us, Sunny, and Brigid." She tugged on Fiona's hand, pulling her toward the bed. When her knees hit the mattress, Fiona gently pushed her backward then, more tentatively lay beside her. Margaret shifted until they were evenly side-by-side. "There should be a truck for you in the barn outside."

"I'll check on that later. Much later." Fiona kissed her, gently at first, but soon the kiss morphed into one of deep passion. She pressed a hand to Margaret's stomach, slowing brushing it upward and stopping at Margaret's right breast. "Right now, I have to properly thank my wife for our new home."

"Our new home," Margaret repeated breathlessly. "What about the girls?"

Fiona raised herself on an elbow. "Do you think they want to join me in thanking you?"

Margaret playfully slapped her upper arm. "You know what I mean."

Chuckling, Fiona said, "Okay, they can thank you later." She released a button in Margaret's dress, then another. "Tonight, you're mine. And it will take all night to properly give thanks."

Margaret put a hand to the back of Fiona's neck, pulling her into another kiss. "At least."

Fiona laughed. "Yes, at least." Schooling her features more seriously, Fiona said, "I still need your patience and time."

"You can have whatever you need."

"I love you, Margaret Cavanaugh."

"And I love you. Now hush up, and start proving it."

"Gladly," Fiona said.

For the rest of the evening, Fiona did her best to prove her love.

The End

More Sharon G. Clark titles:

The Magic Found in Chaos

A disgruntled Gradyln warrior, Belzan, is preparing to destroy the woman who severed his hand and banished him — and all those important to Kareina. Using the fear of the people of Kellshae as a catalyst to building his army, Belzan incites hatred of magic wielders, and the basic need of men to get their women under control.

Gionne needs to bring Kellshae's first oracle to Zheirger Keep, but must traverse the unsettled land filled with angry magicked people, and the common people killing those with magic. Time has Gionne wondering if she may have been rash in her actions to break up with Jahq. Hatred is tearing Kellshae apart. Is it too late to make amends before all hope is lost?

Jahq hasn't spoken to Gionne for nearly three years, has barely left her rooms in the Keep. Now her mothers are asking Jahq to accompany Gionne from Gradyln to Zheirger. She knows this mission is important to Kellshae, and that her absence should make her disappearance afterward easier.

Jahq accepts one former lesson above all: Gionne's rejection was worse for her than any monster Bahalkar spit up from its depths.

ISBN 978-1-61929-312-0
eISBN 978-1-61929-313-7

Chaos Beneath the Moonbeams

The age of magic has been over for nearly three centuries; finalized with the War of Harmony. Even the gods willingly melt into forgetfulness, letting mortal life grow as it would, for good or bad. Not all the gods had agreed unanimously. So, when a mortal man decides to release a banished god for his own purposes, nothing will ever be the same.

Kareina of Clan Gradyln has posed as her twin brother Karr (with the aid of minor forbidden magic) for over a decade, since Karr's disappearance and Kareina's kidnapping and torture. Even Caldier Hassid, her father, forgets her true gender. So, when Hassid agrees to a betrothal between Karr and Mayliandra, it's up to Kareina to figure a way out of it. Meanwhile, someone has brought the old god T'Dar from the depths of Bahalkar to bring back the old ways of chaos.

Mayliandra of Clan Bredwine, about to be given to the fierce Sher Karr, doesn't know if she should be happy for the opportunity to leave her home, where she's nothing but a servant; or, petrified her future husband will learn her secret. Although Mayliandra intends to do her duty to her clan, she can't help wishing Karr were his dead sister, Kareina.

ISBN 978-1-61929-252-9
eISBN 978-1-61929-253-6

A Majestic Affair

A decade ago, Tiara Summers was forced to leave her home with her alcoholic mother, and contact was lost with her father and friends. Tiara built a profitable construction business in Colorado Springs and, if not exactly happy, is comfortable with her life. Then she receives a letter from her father asking for help with a horse, which means returning to Silver Waters, Colorado with all the old memories of kisses and running away...and Jayce.

Jayce Mansfield trains horses for a living. Her focus is specializing the equines for stunts in the movies. Then Tiara returns, though her father is AWOL, and Jayce sees promise in a second chance. Hopes for the happily-ever-after she'd envisioned for them are reanimated, until Jayce realizes the sweet, caring teenager that left ten years ago has turned into a bitter woman.

When a little gangster in a purple limousine comes demanding Tiara give over her father's horse, situations and emotions only become more complicated, compelling Tiara to run again.

Can Jayce get Tiara to realize she belongs in Silver Waters, that they belong together?

ISBN 978-1-61929-178-2
eISBN 978-1-61929-177-5

Into the Mist

Lieutenant Kasey Houston has snuck off the USS Console, to join the Marines in their fight against the Japanese soldiers, in May of 1945. She is a psychiatric nurse, and when the Marines of her unit are all killed, she attempts to take out the enemy. However, a strange gray mist is in the cave, and the enemy soldier releases a grenade that buries her in rubble.

Captain Andrea Knight is locating the occupants of an exploded building. She comes upon a woman without identification and in WWII era uniform. Andrea after learning Kasey is from the past procures documentation to establish Kasey as a Military Advisor to the Militia.

Andrea and Kasey are to meet with the officials and militia, who want them to be a bodyguard for the Ambassador of the United Church. His mission: to explain the severity of the threat of the terrorist gangs and Bad Billy. The United Presidents refuse to believe the threat bad. The Ambassador tries to explain he's capable of stopping Billy by using powers they both possess.

Bad Billy requests a rendezvous and stipulates that Andrea come alone. Kasey pleads with Andrea to ignore the message, and is shocked to learn later that Andrea has gone anyway. Meanwhile, Andrea realizes how much she loves Kasey although she is afraid to admit it. Can she avoid her worst fear that Kasey could be returned to her own time before an opportunity ever presents itself to act on her feelings?

ISBN 978-1-935053-34-7
eISBN 978-1-935053-34-7e

Tears Don't Become Me

GW (Georgia Wilhelmina) Diamond, Private Investigator, dealt in missing children cases—only. It didn't alter her own traumatic childhood experience, but she could try to keep other children from the same horrors. She'd left her past and her name behind her. Or so she thought. This case was putting her in contact with people she had managed to keep a distant and barely civil relationship with for fifteen years. Now the buried past was returning to haunt her. When Sheriff Matthews of Elk Grove, Missouri, asked her to take a case involving a teenaged runaway girl, she believed it would be no different from any other. Until Matthews explained she had to take a cop as partner or no deal. A cop who just happened to be the missing girl's aunt...

Erin Dunbar, received the call concerning her niece from an old partner, Frank Matthews. It should have been from her sister, but their estrangement, compounded by her having moved to Detroit, kept that from happening. Now she would have to work with a PI. One had nearly killed her and Frank years ago; she expected this one would be no different. Matters were only made worse by discovering it was a "she" PI—a Looney-tune one who gave new and literal meaning to: "Hands Off." For the sake of her niece, Erin would put up with just about anything, until...

GW seemed to be strangely affected by this case and Erin, to her chagrin and amazement, was strangely affected by her. If Erin could solve GW's past, give her hope, could they have a hope of finding her niece?

ISBN 978-1-932300-83-3
eISBN 978-1-61929-039-6

About the Author

Sharon lives in beautiful Colorado. She enjoys finding new trails to hike and playing mahjong, although not simultaneously as she's awkward enough under normal circumstances. Sharon has served as a US Marine, data entry operator, and program assistant for Nursing and Forensic Program. She is thankful for electronic readers—otherwise the amount of books she owns would be obvious.

OTHER YELLOW ROSE PUBLICATIONS

Anna Furtado	The Heart's Desire	978-1-935053-81-1
Anna Furtado	The Heart's Strength	978-1-935053-82-8
Anna Furtado	The Heart's Longing	978-1-935053-83-5
Pauline George	Jess	978-1-61929-139-3
Pauline George	199 Steps To Love	978-1-61929-213-0
Pauline George	The Actress and the Scrapyard Girl	978-1-61929-336-6
Melissa Good	Eye of the Storm	1-932300-13-9
Melissa Good	Hurricane Watch	978-1-935053-00-2
Melissa Good	Moving Target	978-1-61929-150-8
Melissa Good	Red Sky At Morning	978-1-932300-80-2
Melissa Good	Storm Surge: Book One	978-1-935053-28-6
Melissa Good	Storm Surge: Book Two	978-1-935053-39-2
Melissa Good	Stormy Waters	978-1-61929-082-2
Melissa Good	Thicker Than Water	1-932300-24-4
Melissa Good	Terrors of the High Seas	1-932300-45-7
Melissa Good	Tropical Storm	978-1-932300-60-4
Melissa Good	Tropical Convergence	978-1-935053-18-7
Melissa Good	Winds of Change Book One	978-1-61929-194-2
Melissa Good	Winds of Change Book Two	978-1-61929-232-1
Regina A. Hanel	Love Another Day	978-1-61929-033-4
Regina A. Hanel	WhiteDragon	978-1-61929-143-0
Regina A. Hanel	A Deeper Blue	978-1-61929-258-1
Jeanine Hoffman	Lights & Sirens	978-1-61929-115-7
Jeanine Hoffman	Strength in Numbers	978-1-61929-109-6
Jeanine Hoffman	Back Swing	978-1-61929-137-9
Jennifer Jackson	It's Elementary	978-1-61929-085-3
Jennifer Jackson	It's Elementary, Too	978-1-61929-217-8
Jennifer Jackson	Memory Hunters	978-1-61929-294-9
K. E. Lane	And, Playing the Role of Herself	978-1-932300-72-7
Kate McLachlan	Christmas Crush	978-1-61929-195-9
Lynne Norris	One Promise	978-1-932300-92-5
Lynne Norris	Sanctuary	978-1-61929-248-2
Lynne Norris	Second Chances (E)	978-1-61929-172-0
Lynne Norris	The Light of Day	978-1-61929-338-0
Paula Offutt	Butch Girls Can Fix Anything	978-1-932300-74-1
Surtees and Dunne	True Colours	978-1-61929-021-1
Surtees and Dunne	Many Roads to Travel	978-1-61929-022-8
Patty Schramm	Finding Gracie's Glory	978-1-61929-238-3

Be sure to check out our other imprints,
Mystic Books, Quest Books, Silver Dragon Books,
Troubadour Books, Young Adult Books, and Blue Beacon Books.

VISIT US ONLINE AT
www.regalcrest.biz

At the Regal Crest Website You'll Find

- The latest news about forthcoming titles and new releases

- Our complete backlist of romance, mystery, thriller and adventure titles

- Information about your favorite authors

- Media tearsheets to print and take with you when you shop

- Which books are also available as eBooks.

CPSIA information can be obtained
at www.ICGtesting.com
Printed in the USA
LVOW10s1526230318
570968LV00011B/616/P